SWEETWATER
gap

**Center Point
Large Print**

**This Large Print Book carries the
Seal of Approval of N.A.V.H.**

SWEETWATER
gap

Denise Hunter

CENTER POINT PUBLISHING
THORNDIKE, MAINE

This Center Point Large Print edition
is published in the year 2009 by arrangement with
Thomas Nelson Publishers.

Scripture taken from the HOLY BIBLE:
NEW INTERNATIONAL VERSION®.
© 1973, 1978, 1984 by International Bible Society.
Used by permission of Zondervan. All rights reserved.

The text of this Large Print edition is unabridged.
In other aspects, this book may vary
from the original edition.
Printed in the United States of America.
Set in 16-point Times New Roman type.

ISBN: 978-1-60285-393-5

Library of Congress Cataloging-in-Publication Data

Hunter, Denise, 1968–
  Sweetwater gap / Denise Hunter.
      p. cm.
  ISBN 978-1-60285-393-5 (lib. bdg. : alk. paper)
  1. Large type books. I. Title.

PS3608.U5925S94 2009
813'.6--dc22

2008047253

one

*J*osephine Mitchell was up to her wrists in dirt when she heard the whistle. She looked past the ornamental iron railing down to street level where Cody Something shut the door of his '79 Mustang.

He approached her veranda, shading his eyes from the sun with his hand. "Hey, Apartment 2B, my friend came through." Cody tugged two tickets from the back pocket of his khaki shorts. "Louisville versus UK."

Josie pulled her hands from under the wisteria's roots and patted the dirt down. "Answer's still no." She smiled to soften the rejection, then poured more of the sandy loam around the vine's woody roots.

"Forty-yard line. Biggest game of the year . . ." A shadow puddled in his dimple.

"Sorry."

He sighed. "When are you going to break down and say yes?"

Josie's cell phone pealed and vibrated simultaneously in her pocket. "Saved by the bell." She wiped her hands on her jeans and checked the screen.

A frown pulled her brows. Her sister hadn't called since she'd gotten the big news four months ago. Josie hoped she was okay.

5

"Sorry, gotta take this," she told Cody, then flipped open the phone. "Hey, Laurel."

There was a pause at the other end. "Josie? It's Nate. Your brother-in-law." As if Josie didn't know his name or voice. He'd only dated her sister four years before finally proposing.

But Nate had never called Josie, and the fact that he was now only reinforced her previous suspicion. "Is everything okay? Laurel and the baby?"

"They're fine."

Thank God. Laurel and Nate had wanted a baby for so long. They'd been ready to start trying, but then Laurel and Josie's dad had the stroke, and the newlyweds had to move in with him and take care of him and the family orchard. Laurel hadn't had the time or energy for a baby.

Josie sat back on her haunches and wiped her hair from her eyes with a semiclean finger.

"I'm calling about the orchard." Nate's tone was short and clipped. "I think it's high time you hauled your city-slicker fanny back here to help your sister."

She almost thought he was joking—Nate was as easygoing as they came, and she'd never heard him sound so adamant or abrupt. But there was no laughter on the other end of the line.

Words stuck in Josie's throat. She swallowed hard. "I don't understand."

"No, you don't. *Responsibility* is a foreign word

to you. I get that. But there comes a time when a person has to step up to the plate and—"

"Wait a minute."

"—help when they're needed. And Laurel needs your help. We can't afford to hire anyone else, you know."

This didn't sound like Nate. True, she hadn't talked to him in ages, but he'd always been the picture of Southern hospitality.

Below the veranda, Cody caught her eye and waved the tickets temptingly. When she shook her head no, his lips turned down in an exaggerated pout, his chin fell dramatically to his chest, and he sulked toward the apartment's main door. But not before he turned and flashed his dimple one more time, just to let her know he wasn't too heartbroken. They both knew he was already mentally sorting through the other candidates in his little black book.

Nate's angry voice pulled her back to the conversation, which, she realized belatedly, had been silent on her end for too long.

"I don't know why I thought you'd care," he muttered. She could barely hear his words over the roar of a passing motorcycle. "You didn't bother coming after the stroke, or for the funeral, why would you care about this?"

"What *this*? Would you please tell me what's going on?"

His breaths were harsh, as if he expected a fight.

"Laurel is having twins. She just found out yesterday at the ultrasound."

Twins. The word brought back a cluster of memories, none of them good.

But Laurel was undoubtedly thrilled. Josie was surprised she hadn't called, but then again, they hadn't spoken much since the funeral almost a year ago. "Well, that's great news."

"The doctor wants her to take it easy. And you know Laurel."

With harvest just around the bend, there wasn't much that was easy about working an apple orchard this time of year. The phone call was making sense now. All except Nate's antagonism. But then he'd always been protective of Laurel.

"When I came home from work today, I found her painting the nursery, and yesterday she spent the afternoon packing apples in cold storage for a new vendor she got. Every time I turn around, she's sneaking off to work somewhere, usually the orchard because she's so worried about it."

Josie stood, stretching her legs, then leaned her elbows on the railing. "She's never been one to be idle."

"She really wants these babies, Josephine. We both do. And after what happened with your mom . . ." His voice wobbled as the sentence trailed off, pinching something inside her.

"Of course, I completely get that." It was all sinking in now. She knew why he'd called. And she knew she wouldn't say no, because, despite the distance between them, she loved her sister.

"She needs help, that's the bottom line. I don't need to tell you how much work is involved this time of year, and she can't do it. We can hardly afford to hire more help."

"No, she can't work the harvest," Josie agreed. His words from a moment ago replayed in her head like a delayed tape. "You said you can't hire someone." Laurel hadn't mentioned financial troubles. She talked about their manager, Grady, as if he were God's gift to apples.

"Not after last year's failure."

"Failure?" Her sister hadn't said anything of the kind. True, they didn't speak often, but when the topic of the orchard did come up, Laurel said everything was fine. At least, Josie thought she had.

"Laurel didn't tell you? There was an Easter frost. We lost the apples."

"Frost?" An orchard could lose a whole crop to frost, though this was the first time it had happened at Blue Ridge. Why hadn't Laurel said something?

Nate sighed. "I'm sorry. I thought she told you."

What else had her sister omitted? Laurel was always trying to protect her. Josie should've inquired more directly. "How bad is it?" The fragrance from her lavender plant wafted by on a breeze, and Josie closed her eyes, inhaled the

9

calming scent, letting it fill her up, soothe her frayed nerves.

"The place is a money pit. We don't have anything else to put into it."

This changes everything, Josie. Do you realize that?

The selfish thought materialized before she could stop it. Her plans . . . How could she follow through now? When Laurel was overburdened with a failing orchard and pregnant with twins?

Nate was speaking again. "Grady insists he can turn the place around, but I'm wondering if we shouldn't sell it."

She and Laurel were the third generation to own the orchard, and as far as Josie knew, not one of the Mitchells had thought those words, much less said them. And she'd thought Laurel would be the last one to do so.

"Laurel's considering that?" Their father's death had left Josie with shares that tied her to the place. Even three hundred and fifty miles away, it dragged behind her wherever she went, weighing her down like an anchor. But if Laurel was considering a sale . . .

Now that she'd slipped the thought on for size, it was starting to feel more comfortable, like her favorite pair of Levi's.

"I haven't exactly broached the topic," Nate said.

That was precisely what needed to happen. It was something her father should've done long ago, before he'd saddled Laurel with his own care and the care of the orchard.

"How does this year's crop look?"

"Promising. She was hoping this year would put us in the black. But a strong crop means extra work and plenty of hands on deck. And I can't afford time off."

Nate ran Shelbyville's one and only insurance agency. Good thing they'd had his income to fall back on.

"So can you come back and help us through the harvest?" he asked.

Josie's eyes flitted over the lacy white alyssum, past the potted strawberry plant toward the haven of her darkened apartment. She closed her eyes and was, in an instant, back at Blue Ridge Orchard. She could almost smell the apples ripening on the trees. Hear the snap of the branch as an apple twisted free. See the ripples of Sweetwater Creek running alongside the property.

And with that thought, the other memories came. The ones that had chased her from Shelbyville six years ago. The ones that still chased her every day. The ones that, at the mention of going home, caused a dread, deep and thick in her belly.

"Josie, you there?"

She opened her eyes, swallowing hard. "I'm here."

"I know you've got your photography job and your plans and your life."

She breathed a wry laugh. Ironically, none of that mattered. The one plan that did matter could still play out. Same tune, different venue.

What mattered most now was seeing that Laurel's life was settled. And Laurel's life wouldn't be settled until she was out from under the orchard. Josie saw that clearly now. And it wouldn't happen, she knew, without a lot of coaxing. She only hoped there was enough time.

"I wouldn't have called if we weren't desperate."

Josie took one last deep breath of the lavender, shoved down the dread, and forced the words.

"I'll come."

two

*J*osie pulled into the long winding drive that led to her childhood home. Gravel popped under her tires, echoing the irregular rhythm of her heart. She passed the shingled storefront where Aunt Lola worked all summer and fall, then accelerated down the hill and into the valley. Out the left window was the dangerously steep slope that led toward Sweetwater Creek where it wound between the high hills like a slithering snake. It was there that everything had changed.

She gripped the sticky leather steering wheel and blinked the memory away. But just as quickly, it was replaced with another: the last time she'd driven this lane, heading the opposite direction, tires spinning, thoughts tumbling, fears pushing her farther from the orchard.

Stop it, Josie. That was a long time ago. None of it mattered now. Not the rippling creek out her window, not the memories that chased her still, not even the family cemetery, high on the hill behind the house.

Think of the orchard. The apples. Getting through harvest. She rounded a bend and started up the hill where she and Laurel had once tried to build a tree house in the gnarly-branched oak beside the drive. It had collapsed before the summer ended, the splintered boards piled in a cockeyed heap at the tree's roots.

Just beyond the highest point of the ridge, she made a sharp turn, and the orchard opened up on both sides. Her breath caught at the rows of leafy trees lining the drive, their branches heavy with red and yellow striped Galas. It was past mid-August, and they would need to be picked soon; should've already begun, but she couldn't find evidence that they'd been touched. It would soon be time to start on the large Jonagold grove. The Ginger Golds, however, seemed to be picked clean, a rusty ladder still leaning against the side of a barren tree.

The drive progressed toward the old farmhouse, through the groves of Jonagold, Red Delicious, and Fuji still ripening on the branches. Nate was right, it was a good crop, and the sight of it made her heart quicken. But a good harvest meant a lot of work and a lot of help needed.

He'd told her they'd already hired the crew of migrant workers, but not enough if they hadn't yet finished the Galas. A part of her itched to hit the fields and start working. It had been so long, and even with her windows up, she could almost smell the tangy fruit and feel the smooth, glossy texture of the apples.

The orchard opened to the lawn, and as she drove under a canopy of oak and maple trees, it seemed evening had fallen instantly. The old tire swing in the back still hung from the branch Josie had once climbed to on a dare. She pulled her Celica up to the side of the house and parked it by an old, beat-up Ford pickup she didn't recognize.

She exited the car, leaving her suitcases for later. The house's white paint was peeling in spots, but otherwise the building looked the same with its green metal roof and wraparound porch. The pines that had once served as family Christmas trees now towered over the roof. Aunt Lola had lined the walk with clusters of orange marigolds and yellow pansies that her sister hadn't managed to kill off yet with her black thumb.

Josie passed the flowers, then took the porch steps, feeling the stretch of her muscles, tight from the long drive. Before she reached the front door, Laurel appeared at the screen.

Her sister stopped, her hand on the knob, her

eyes widening. Laurel was wearing her coffee brown hair longer now, just grazing her shoulders. It suited her.

"Josie!" Laurel burst through the screen door, and it slapped against the frame as Laurel pulled Josie into a hug.

She could feel the rounded bump of Laurel's belly against her stomach. "Look at you," Josie said, feeling a full smile pull at her lips for the first time since she couldn't remember when. "You've got a tummy."

"I should hope so. I'm twenty-seven weeks, you know. And guess what?" She pulled back, her palms still on Josie's shoulders, her hazel eyes sparkling. "It's twins."

I know was on the tip of her tongue, but on instinct she changed her reply. "That's wonderful. I'm so happy for you."

Laurel rubbed Josie's arms as if she couldn't quite believe her sister was standing there. She'd inherited their mother's high cheekbones, and the pregnancy had put a blush in just the right places.

Laurel gave Josie's arm one last squeeze. "This is such a wonderful surprise!"

Surprise?

"Can you stay awhile? Your room's still just as it was, though we almost decided to use it as a nursery. We're using my old room instead since it's closer to ours."

Nate appeared behind the screen door, his image grayed by the wire mesh. "Hello, Josie." His hair was clipped short like he'd just returned from the barber, and he wore his church clothes. He still had a baseball player's build, though he'd filled out a little in the middle.

"Hi, Nate."

"We're just sitting down to supper," Laurel said. "Come in. Aunt Lola will be so tickled."

"I'll get your things," Nate said, giving her a stiff hug.

Inside the door, the smell of home greeted her, taking her back years. Under her Birkenstocks the wood floor creaked where it always had at the base of the stairs. She half expected her dad to lumber around the corner, cradling his coffee mug with both hands, his belly stretching his T-shirt. It didn't seem real that he was gone.

She blinked the image from her mind. "Where's Aunt Lola?"

"In the kitchen finishing supper. I swear, she won't let me do a thing since she found out about the twins. Come on, let's surprise her."

Laurel led her toward the dining room, through the butler's pantry, and into the kitchen where Aunt Lola's backside protruded into the room as she pulled a pan of biscuits from the oven. She slid them into the bread basket and turned, coming up short.

"Guess who's here?" Laurel asked.

"You startled the daylights out of me, missy." Aunt Lola glared at Laurel before settling her eyes on Josie. Her mouth slackened, then her eyes lifted at the corners. "Well, if you aren't a sight for sore eyes. What are you standing there for? Get over here and give an old woman a hug."

Laurel took the bread basket, and Aunt Lola enfolded Josie in one of her sturdy hugs.

"It's about time you came around." Aunt Lola squeezed her shoulders, then released her, looking Josie over.

Her aunt's small, round eyes, set too close, had always reminded Josie of a hawk, and she had the fortitude to match.

She narrowed those eyes now in a critical appraisal. "You're as frail as a starving sparrow," Aunt Lola said. "Don't they feed you up in the big city? Never mind. Go sit down and we'll get some food in you." Aunt Lola poured tea from the old yellow pitcher, her arthritic hand shaking. "I hope you can stay long enough to get some meat on your bones."

"Let me get that, Aunt Lola."

Josie expected a snarl, but her aunt let her finish pouring, then carried the glasses to the table while Josie turned off the oven and put the oven mitt in the drawer.

Laurel and Aunt Lola were already seated when she entered the dining room and Nate breezed in, setting her suitcases by the stairs. It was then she noticed another man in the room, seated in her dad's chair at the head of the table.

The first thing she noticed was his rugged good looks. She couldn't help it.

"Josie, this is Grady, our manager. I told you about him. Grady, this is my sister, Josie."

His chair grated as he stood. The act said Southern Gentleman, but his shadowed eyes and tensed jaw screamed Danger Ahead. She instantly felt like she was invading his turf, and the thought disturbed her. This was her home. Her orchard.

She flipped her hair out of her face and held out her hand. "Nice to meet you."

"Likewise." He shook her hand, his grip firm and confident.

When he released it, Josie took the only empty chair, which was right beside him, as luck would have it. She wondered what bee he had in his bonnet, and she wasn't too thrilled with the fact that he'd assumed her father's old seat like he was the head of the household.

On her other side, Laurel took her hand. "I'm so glad you're here. How long can you stay?"

"Let's say grace before the food gets cold," Nate said.

Hands came up to the table as they joined together. Beside her plate, Grady's large, calloused palm lay open. She placed her hand in it.

She didn't hear a word of Aunt Lola's prayer, only felt the heat of Grady's palm as her thoughts spun like a whirligig twirling down from a maple tree. Why was her arrival a surprise? She'd told Nate she was coming over a week ago. And why was their manager treating her like an intruder? You'd think he'd be grateful for the extra help.

". . . For it's in his precious name we pray, amen."

Josie pulled her hand from Grady's.

"Now, how long can you stay?" Laurel asked.

Josie looked at Nate, who was intent on dishing out a scoop of green beans.

"Well, I—I came to help out for a while." She looked at Nate again, expecting him to speak up.

Finally, he cleared his throat. "I asked her to come and help out through the harvest." He said it like an admission of guilt, and a current of something Josie didn't understand went through the room.

Beside her, she felt Grady go still.

"Are you serious?" Laurel asked. "Can you afford the time away? What about your job, your apartment?"

"Don't look a gift horse in the mouth, Laurel Jane," Aunt Lola said. "Lord knows we need as many hands as we can get to keep you still."

"My lease was about up anyway, so I put my things in storage. And I can find another job easily enough when I go back." If she needed to. She'd worry about that later, after they got the apples in and had the orchard on the market.

"You quit your job?" her sister asked. "Nate, you shouldn't have asked her to up and leave her life, for heaven's sake."

"I wanted to come."

"You should've told me you were coming," Laurel said. "I would've gotten your room ready for you."

"*I* would've gotten the room ready for you," Aunt Lola said.

Josie didn't know why Nate hadn't told them, but his silence on the subject wasn't sitting well with her. "I'm sorry, I thought you knew."

Beside her, Grady dished out a ladle of gravy.

"I didn't want to tell you," Nate said. "Just in case."

Just in case she didn't show. Josie knew the meaning wasn't lost on anyone at the table, probably not even Sunshine over there.

"Well, she's here now's what matters," Aunt Lola said. "Grady says there's plenty of work to be done."

All eyes were on Grady. Josie decided it was his longish dark hair and stubble-lined jaw that made him look all Marlboro Man. Though the brooding expression didn't help much either. His skin was weathered dark from working outdoors, and Josie put him at thirty, maybe thirty-two years old.

Nate spoke up instead. He winked at his wife. "Maybe you can finally relax and settle down. Now that Josie's here, everything's going to be all right."

Josie sneaked a peek at Grady from under her lashes. Seeing his tight grip on his fork and his lips pressed in a straight line, she had the feeling everything wasn't all right. Not by a long shot.

"Can I have a word before I go?" Grady asked Nate after Laurel took her sister upstairs to settle in.

"Sure." Nate scooted out from the table. "Why don't we go out on the porch?"

Grady followed Nate outside and leaned against the porch rail while Nate sank onto the swing. He gathered his thoughts, calming himself. He'd stuffed down his frustration throughout supper, but it would do no good to lose his temper with Nate.

"You're upset about Josie coming," Nate said.

He shoved his hands in his pockets. "Why did you ask her to come? I told you I could handle the orchard."

"We need more help, and you know as well as I do that we can't afford to hire more hands."

"We're doing fine—"

"We're behind schedule and you know it."

"We would've caught up if you would've given me a chance."

"You think Laurel doesn't notice you've only just now finished the Ginger Golds?"

Reality grated sometimes. "I'm working as hard as I can."

Nate held up a hand, palm out. "I'm not blaming

you. You're working all the hours a man can work, but it's not enough. You can't do the impossible, and no one's asking you to."

"We could've made do with another migrant."

"It would've taken three of them to equal one Josie. She's done this most of her life, and she's used to managing things around here."

Could've fooled him. Wasn't she the sister who up and deserted the family right after she graduated? The one who hadn't come home to help Laurel nurse her daddy when he had the stroke, or even be there when he passed? The one who'd left her sister to take on the funeral and the orchard?

The last thing he needed was some scatterbrained woman out there confusing the workers. Not to mention distracting them with her sea green eyes and beguiling smile.

"How do I know she'll be dependable?" After all, Nate hadn't even mentioned she was coming for fear she'd flake out.

Nate crossed his arms. "Look, you need the extra hands and Josie knows what she's doing. She came, didn't she? Laurel will be able to relax now and know the work's getting done."

That was something, he supposed. It seemed he spent half the day assuring Laurel everything was fine, and even still, he was more likely to find her in cold storage than in the house.

"She's got the babies to be concerned about. I don't want her worrying over the orchard too."

Grady had been doing enough worrying for both of them. And now that he had the good crop he'd hoped for, he'd been worried about picking them on schedule so Laurel could get them sold.

"Josie will be good for Laurel. She's missed her sister, and it's important to me that she has what she needs right now."

Much as Grady didn't want the absentee sister around for the next three months, he understood Nate's concern for his wife. Still, he didn't have to like it.

three

*J*osie flopped on her old twin bed, the mattress springs creaking as she settled against the headboard. The ruffles of the frilly, white canopy wiggled and shimmied as if celebrating the room's inhabitance.

Laurel dragged her finger across the top of the white dresser. "It's been awhile, I guess."

"Never mind that. I'll clean it tomorrow." The old mirror, still tilting slightly toward the floor, bore the mascot sticker of the Shelbyville High School Beavers, half scratched off by her best friend, Ashley.

"Aunt Lola will see to it. I would, but heaven knows, she wouldn't let me."

"You have to think of the babies."

"The doctor said take it easy, not fall into a coma."

"You never were good at sitting still."

Laurel's hand went to her belly, a large bump beneath her navy polo. "I never knew it was so difficult."

Josie sat Indian-style and hugged her pillow. "Have you picked names yet?"

"We've tossed some around, but haven't settled on anything."

It was good to see Laurel. Good to see her smiling and content. She'd wanted a baby for so long. "You are going to be a great mom."

"I still can't believe it's happening."

"Well, it is, times two." Josie ran her hand along the quilted bedspread, its fabric soft, nearly threadbare. "Aunt Lola still minding the store?"

Laurel sank onto the desk chair and crossed her bare feet in front of her, lacing her hands over her stomach. "Yes, she's practically had me tethered to the cash register for the past week."

"You can hardly be climbing ladders and picking apples."

"There's so much work to be done. It's hard not being able to help."

"Well, now you don't have to worry about that, do you?"

"Smarty-pants."

Josie was already getting stir-crazy herself from sitting around all evening. As much as she liked catching up with the family, she yearned to get out into the fields. Here in the house, old memories were hovering in the corner of her mind, pressing in and taking hold of her.

"Everyone is going to be glad to see you," Laurel said.

"Any news I should know about? I heard Jackie and Ashley are sharing an apartment in Asheville now." Her best friends from high school had tried to keep in contact, but Josie wasn't very good at that kind of thing.

"You know how Shelbyville is. Nothing ever changes except the hair on Maggie Lou's head. It's red at the moment, just so you know."

"Good to know." Maggie Lou's hair notwithstanding, the town was as stagnant as a pond. It was something Josie used to love. Now, with three long months ahead of her, she wondered if the stagnation wasn't going to smother her.

"Boone still asks about you."

"Good ol' Boone. How's he doing?"

"Still head over heels for you."

She'd known him since they were in diapers. Josie wished she were attracted to him, but love was never that simple, was it? The men she was attracted to weren't just playing hard to get, they actually were. For some reason, she seemed to prefer the dangerous ones, and she'd paid for it many times over.

"What's the scoop on your manager?" *Now where did that come from?*

"Grady?" Her sister smiled coquettishly and fluttered her lashes. "Now why are you asking about him, Josephine Mitchell? Could it be because he's so tall, dark, and handsome?"

Dark, most of all. "Shame, shame, you're a married woman, Laurel Evans."

"Married, not dead, and don't change the subject."

She shrugged. "I'm going to be working with him for the next three months. I figure I should know what I'm up against since he seems to have a chip on his shoulder."

"Don't let his demeanor fool you. He's a big teddy bear."

"Grizzly bear, more like."

"You always did like the dangerous ones."

Josie pressed her lips together and glared.

"All right, all right. What do you want to know?"

She knew her dad had hired him when Hank Leland retired. The thought of the old manager instantly conjured up thoughts of his son, Ian. She could see the boy climbing up a ladder, pressed against the wood, filling his sack with enviable speed.

Not Ian. Don't think about him. She pushed the image away, wishing she could keep it under lock and key.

"Josie?"

She shook her head. "How'd Grady end up here?" Shelbyville, North Carolina, wasn't exactly the go-to capital of the United States. Other than her friend Ashley's family, she couldn't think of a single person in town who wasn't born and raised here.

"I don't know much about his personal history. He was married once, but he's never really elaborated on that subject."

Josie rolled her eyes. "I meant information that actually relates to the orchard."

"How boring. Well, he came from Chicago and has a degree in agriculture. He worked for some kind of urban development company. I think he was tired of city life and wanted to slow down a bit."

"Can't get much slower than Shelbyville."

"Ain't that the truth."

She pictured Grady sitting in her father's old seat as if he were a member of the family. "He always eat here?"

Laurel shrugged. "Just supper. We don't pay the man much, we had to supplement his income somehow. Besides, Aunt Lola always cooks enough for an army, and we couldn't very well pass up a man with so much skill. Daddy was impressed with him from the start. After the stroke, Grady really took the reins around here. He's as dependable as the sunrise, the crew respects him, and he's got great ideas for this place."

If he was so wonderful, why was the orchard in such desperate straits? "Nate told me about the frost last year," Josie said.

Laurel gave a little frown. "I wondered if he had."

"Why didn't you tell me?"

She shrugged. "I didn't want you to worry."

She wondered how they'd afforded to keep going. There were costs involved in maintaining a crop. Bees for pollination, equipment upkeep, not to mention Grady's pay. There was no way they'd had that kind of money set back. "How'd you make it through and manage a bumper crop to boot?"

Her sister shifted, pulling in her legs as far as her stomach would allow. "I was going to talk to you about that."

Josie didn't like the look on her sister's face. She'd had the same look when she had spilled Josie's goldfish onto the floor and it had slid into the crevice between the floor and baseboard and died.

"What did you do?" Josie asked.

"Things were tight financially. We didn't have the money to keep the orchard going for another year—"

"Laurel . . ."

"I sold some of my shares."

Josie dropped her pillow. "You what?"

"I didn't want to take out a loan, you know how I feel about that."

"I can't believe you—" She shook her head and huffed. "Who did you sell them to?"

Her sister ducked her head and raised her eyes, wincing. "Grady?"

Josie sucked in a breath. "Grady!"

"He'd been wanting to buy in. Plus, he has a vested interest now. It made sense."

"Why didn't you offer them to me?"

Laurel cocked her head, smiling gently. "Honey, I knew you wouldn't have that kind of money."

The fact that Laurel was right only irked her more. She'd never been much of a saver. "Still, you could've asked. How much did you sell him?"

"Just fifteen percent. Enough to dig us out of the hole and fund this year's crop. And look how good it turned out."

This new discovery threw a kink in her plans. Josie's thoughts spun. How was she going to convince her sister to sell now? She went over the business arrangement in her mind. Josie owned fifty percent. If she could convince Laurel to sell, Grady wouldn't have a choice but to go along.

Maybe since Laurel had been willing to part with some of her shares, she wouldn't be opposed to selling the whole thing. Because even if this year turned out as well as she hoped, there was always the next year, and the one after that. And with Laurel having twins, how would they make ends meet, especially when she'd just given up fifteen percent of her profits?

four

"Thanks for breakfast, Aunt Lola." Josie wiped her mouth on the napkin and slid from her chair. "I don't suppose Duncan is still around?"

Aunt Lola covered the pancakes with foil to keep them warm for Nate and Laurel. Josie was more than relieved that Grady hadn't made an appearance.

"He's still snorting around in that fence back there."

"I can't believe he hasn't made it to the supper table yet."

"Don't think I haven't thought about it."

Josie slipped on her jacket. "Is Mr. Barrow still bringing him breakfast?"

"Yep. He should be arriving anytime now."

"Good. I think I'll pay him a visit before I head to the orchard."

"Mind that you don't leave the gate open or he'll trample my flowers."

Josie zipped her jacket as she made her way down the porch and around back. Dawn still clung to the horizon, coloring it with brushstrokes of deep purple and pink. The air smelled like marigolds and morning dew. It would be chilly for a couple of hours, then the sun would climb over the mountains and make her wish for the shade of a cloud or two.

Back at the base of the hill, the manager's cabin nestled under the protection of towering white pines. A lone light shone from the window, reminding her there was still life in there, and it wasn't Ian or his father. Her gaze flitted to the top of the hill before she forced herself to look away.

A loud snort caught her attention. Duncan stood at the gate, his fat snout sticking through the mesh of the fence.

"Hey there, big guy." The hinges creaked as she opened the gate. She slid inside, then shut it behind her. Duncan lumbered toward her, and the acrid odor got worse as he neared. "You remember me, Dunky boy?"

Dried dirt caked his snout, and his beady little eyes gazed at her. "You do, don't you?"

He snorted, tossing his huge head backward. "Yes, I know you're hungry." She looked him over. "You've gained weight, mister, you know that? Has Laurel been sneaking you table scraps?"

He'd just been a wee piglet when she'd caught him, all greased up and slick, inside the pen that had been fashioned for the Shelbyville Apple Festival. Her dad had let her keep him only because he'd seen tasty pork chops in his future, but Laurel had talked him out of that eventually.

Josie straightened at the sound of an approaching vehicle. "I think breakfast is here, big guy. Has Mr. Ted been feeding you well?"

She leaned on the gate, watching the car pull to a stop near the big red barn. It wasn't Ted Barrow exiting the vehicle, but his son, Boone.

He waved at her, then pulled three white boxes from his backseat and joined her. His bowlegged walk and the curls peeking from under a green John Deere cap were as familiar as the sunrise.

"Hey, Josephine. Heard you's back."

Josie cocked her head. "Now, where'd you hear that? I just pulled into town last night."

"Nettie Albert passed you on your way in."

"Ah, by now all of Shelbyville knows I'm back." She had no doubt there'd been speculation about her sudden departure, probably everything from an unexpected pregnancy to a secret lover she'd met on the Internet.

Boone handed her the boxes. "You look good, Josephine." He ducked his head, suddenly shy.

Boone's thick hair hung just to his eyelashes, and his ruddy complexion bloomed pink under her gaze. "You do too, Boone. You still making donuts for your dad?"

"I took over the shop for him last July. He started going downhill, and, long story short, we found out he has Alzheimer's."

Josie touched his arm. "I'm sorry. I hadn't heard."

Boone looked down, shuffling his feet. "It's been an adjustment. It's been especially hard on Mom, but we're getting along best we can."

Duncan let out a snort and nudged her jean-clad leg.

"All right, all right, you big pig."

Boone helped her take the lids off the boxes, and they dumped the day-old donuts in the trough. Duncan scarfed down the treat, making quiet snorts in his greediness.

"What brings you back?" Boone settled his weight on the fence.

"The orchard. Laurel needs help with the harvest, what with the babies coming and all," she said.

"That's something else about the twins, huh?"

"Sure is."

"You've got a nice crop this year."

"Looks good so far. But only one thing is sure with an orchard. You can never count your apples until they're picked and sold. How're your mom and Jackie? I heard she moved to Asheville." Josie and Boone's older sister, Jackie, had been tight as the skin on a coon since grade school. Then Ashley had joined their friendship in seventh grade, and the girls had been the closest of friends.

"Mom's in good health. Jackie's the same ol' Jackie. Living it up in the city."

"I hear that tone, Boone Barrow. Jackie's never been a bad seed, she just craves excitement. It's one of the things that makes her fun company."

"Maybe. So, you're staying through harvest, huh? Folks around here thought you'd turned city slicker for good, but I knew it couldn't be true."

Josie let her eyes roam over the landscape, taking in the evergreens and rolling land, the hills, silhouetted against the sunrise. It used to be the place she'd loved most.

"Louisville is my home now. I'll be going back after harvest."

"Shame you can't stay around."

The thought tightened something deep inside her like a knot. If only things were different. If only she could be here without feeling . . . trapped and troubled by the memory of that night.

The truck and trailer were nearly beside the fence before Josie heard it. Grady's elbow poked through the open window of his pickup truck. " 'Morning, Boone. Josie."

" 'Morning," they called.

Grady's eyes swung to Josie. "Need a lift?"

The invitation was reluctant, but she couldn't think of a good reason to turn it down. Maybe on the short drive she could figure out what his problem was.

"Sure."

Boone relieved her of the empty boxes. "I'll get these."

She shut the gate, making sure it latched. "Thanks for the donuts."

"See you tomorrow, Josephine."

She was aware of Boone's eyes on her as she walked around the truck and got in the cab. She gave Boone a wave as Grady pulled onto the drive that led to the crew's dorms.

"How's the crew this year?"

"Good."

"Some years are better than others, don't you think? Repeaters help because they know what's expected."

"True."

True. *Okay, try again, Josie.* "So are we starting on the Galas today?"

"Finishing up the Golds."

Silence settled in the wake of his words. Maybe he wasn't a morning person. A towering thermos lay on the seat between them. Maybe he needed more coffee. Lots more.

The cab smelled of gasoline and man. Grady's nylon jacket swished as he pulled his hand from the stick shift and rested it on the steering wheel.

Outside, she heard a dove calling from the branches of a pine and the answering jeer of a bluebird. Even the birds were having better success at conversation.

When they arrived at the crew's housing, Josie hopped out of the truck and extended her hand to the men as they approached the truck. *"Hola, amigos. Me llamo Josie."*

The men were friendly and greeted her in their native tongue, introducing themselves, then they hopped in the pickup bed.

"You speak fluently," Grady said.

She shrugged. Between three years of high school Spanish and the Hispanic crew every summer, she'd gotten plenty of practice. "Comes in handy around here."

Once they were in the field, it took about two seconds for Josie to orient herself. There were only a couple of rows of Golds left. Laurel had told her she'd gotten an order for Galas that needed to be filled immediately, so she sent two of the crew down to start on those, ignoring the tight-lipped look Grady sent her way.

What, did he think she was going to stand around waiting for orders? While she'd been communicating with the crew, he'd moved the empty bin forward with the forklift.

She climbed a ladder and began picking the Golds alongside the crew. The feel of the apples, smooth and hard against her palm, was as familiar as the sound of the doves calling from nearby trees.

The motion of picking was like second nature. *Grab, twist, pluck.* The smell of the apples, sweet and tangy, mixed with the musty smell of morning dew. This was her element, where she knew who she was and what she was doing. She thought of her plants back home, so carefully cultivated and tended, and hoped Mrs. Rebar from 3B would take good care of them in her absence.

While she worked, she conversed in Spanish with Hernando and Miguel as they picked the other side of the tree. Then when the crew started up a tune, Josie focused on her work. The branch snapped back in place as she plucked an apple. Behind her, Grady fired up the forklift and moved the full bin into the trailer. The smell of fuel and exhaust filled the air.

As the morning wore on, her energy waned, and by the second coffee break, her arms ached. She'd be hurting tomorrow. And her speed had decreased as the hours passed. The crew was picking circles around her.

Josie poured a cup of coffee into her thermos lid, her hand shaking, then boosted herself onto the truck tailgate. The coffee was still hot and strong, and felt good sliding down her dry throat. How was she going to make it through the day? Then all the days after that?

After a few minutes, Grady approached, propping his hip on the tailgate. "Tired?"

Did he have to look so smug? "Not at all." She rested the shaking cup against her thigh. She could keep up with Grady.

Under a nearby tree, Miguel and Hernando conversed in rapid Spanish about their wives. Something about their cooking, though Josie could only hear snatches of the conversation. The silence between her and Grady stretched like a thin, taut wire.

"Where'd you send Juan and Emilio off to?"

He just couldn't stand that she'd come out here

and taken the reins, could he? "Laurel got an order for some Galas and she needs them right away."

"She didn't mention it."

What, did he think she was lying? She wasn't going to dignify that with a response. She took a deep breath. They could get along. They'd have to if they were going to bear each other's company for three months.

Maybe a compliment would soothe his ruffled feathers. "You've got a good crew this year." She could tell they looked up to Grady in the way they responded to him. He spoke Spanish as fluently as she did, and she wondered how he'd come by it.

"They're good men and fast pickers. Can't ask for much more than that." He drained the last of his coffee, then straightened, screwing the lid on his thermos. "I'll get the crew back to work. Take a few extra minutes if you need it," he said, his tone condescending. He tossed his thermos through the open cab window.

Josie dumped the remainder of her coffee and hopped off the tailgate, shooting a glare through the back of Grady's head. Yeah, she'd take a few extra minutes. In his dreams. She would keep up with him and the others as if her life depended on it.

five

$\mathcal{J}$osie let the hot water run over her head until it ran cold, then she stepped out of the shower and toweled off. Deciding on a comfy pair of shorts and a T-shirt, she slipped into them. She was tired, but it was too early to go to bed.

The house was quiet as she made her way downstairs and to the porch. The screen door slapped softly into place and the warm wind ruffled her damp hair. As she sank into the porch swing, it creaked under her. She'd hoped her muscles would loosen under the warm water, but they were already knotting up again. She wasn't sure she could get up from the swing if she tried, and she was too exhausted to try.

Her arms ached and her legs shook with fatigue, but there was no way she was going to quit with Grady standing there while they worked, probably expecting her to bail.

It was more than just being out of shape. The fatigue was getting worse; there was no denying it.

The door swung open, and Laurel appeared under the halo of the porch light, sporting a white gown with tiny pink rosebuds. Her dark hair tumbled around her shoulders.

Josie scooched over, making room on the swing. They swung in silence, listening to the cadence of cicadas and the ripple of the creek just down the valley.

Laurel kicked a leaf aside as she shuffled her feet. "The porch is a mess."

A thin film of dirt coated the concrete, and grass clippings lay scattered around the edges. "It's a big place to keep up. Especially this time of year."

"You look tired, if you don't mind my saying so," Laurel said.

"I guess I'm not used to manual labor anymore. Clicking a camera takes considerably less effort, even when an event runs late into the night or when kids fail to cooperate in group shots. I guess I thought working the orchard would be like it was when I was younger."

"You didn't eat much at supper."

She'd been ravenous when she smelled the roasted chicken, but after a couple of bites, the nausea started. "Too tired to eat. I'll get used to it."

They talked about Laurel's plans for the nursery. Laurel fetched a brochure from a store in Asheville with the baby furniture she wanted. "It's too expensive, but Peggy Tackett has a niece who works there, and she told me they're having a twenty-five percent sale on it in October. That's cutting it close to my due date, but I fell in love with it."

The sleigh-style crib and matching bureau were oak and stained a golden honey finish. They'd look great with the house's woodwork. "It's exquisite."

As Laurel talked about the colors she'd selected for the nursery walls, Josie wondered if it was too soon to mention the idea of selling the orchard. But when a break came in the conversation, she broached the topic.

"Have you thought about how things are going to be after the babies are born?"

Laurel swept the dirt off the swing's arm. "What do you mean?"

"The orchard. Grady's used to having your help, and with you having the twins to care for . . ."

"I guess I haven't thought too much about it. I hope we'll have a good enough year that we can afford full-time help. At least through harvest."

"What about the pruning? It's a lot of orchard for one man." There was no way one person could handle it, no matter how hardworking Grady might be. Unbidden, an image formed of him lifting heavy sacks of apples. He'd had his jacket off by eight o'clock, and in his sleeveless white T-shirt, she saw he was more cut than she'd imagined. Not that she'd imagined.

She shook the thought and looked at Laurel, watching lines form between her brows.

"You're right. I guess I hadn't thought that far ahead what with the pregnancy and just trying to get through this harvest."

Josie fussed with the blue ribbon drawstring on her shorts. "I know this is something we've never talked about. But I can't help but think this place is going to be a strain on you after the babies arrive. Not that it hasn't been a strain already. And you never did care much for working the orchard anyway. You always preferred keeping to the house like Mom."

"We're managing, Josie."

"Barely. Last year's loss about put you under."

"But we turned it around, and look at this year's crop."

"You had to sell shares to make it happen. What are you going to do next time? Sell more shares?"

"There won't be a next time."

"You can't be sure of that. I know you love this place." She nearly said, *I do too* but stopped herself, realizing it was only partly true. "But you know the pressure it put on Mom and Dad, and that was with Dad working the orchard full-time. You won't have that option once the babies are here."

"No one said farming was easy, but it's our way of life. My way of life."

"It doesn't have to be. What about your dreams? You always wanted to sell your crafts, not work the orchard. Maybe Grady would be interested in buying us out."

"Grady doesn't have that kind of money. It took his life savings to buy the fifteen percent."

"How does Nate feel about it? Have you talked to him about the future?"

Laurel ducked her head and pushed the swing

until it swayed gently. "He's concerned about me. He's concerned about our financial stability and doesn't want to keep funding the orchard. But he doesn't understand it's our heritage. We're third-generation owners. That means something to me."

How many times had their father told them the story of their grandfather coming from Germany and working at the mill, buying apple seedlings with every extra penny?

"Don't force yourself into a future you don't want out of obligation to our ancestors. It was our grandfather's dream, not ours."

Laurel sighed hard. "And Daddy's. It's mine now, and I thought it was yours too. Running this place always came as easily to you as breathing. What happened to that?" Her sister sounded more hurt than angry.

The fact was, Josie had thought she'd stay on the orchard all her life, get married, raise her children here. Despite her relationship with her dad, she'd always felt at home here on the orchard. In some ways, the orchard had nurtured her as much as she'd nurtured these trees.

But sometimes plans changed as quickly as the wind's direction.

"I love it here," Laurel continued. "Sure, it's a lot of work, but I want to raise my family here just like our parents did and their parents before that. Are you forgetting all the memories?"

Josie wished she could, at least some of them. But Laurel had always been good at blocking the bad ones, remembering only the good things.

"You've already sold fifteen percent to Grady. And when things get desperate again, you'll have no choice but to sell off a little more. We'll lose the place anyway, slowly."

"Not necessarily."

"Would you at least think about selling? Wouldn't it be better to do it now while the orchard is producing well than wait until things are desperate?"

Laurel's eyes went wide under the porch light. "I know I don't have that natural knack like you and Grady, but two other generations have hung on to Blue Ridge. Surely I can manage too."

"Things are different now," Josie said gently. "Back then men worked the orchard with their wives' help. It took Dad and Hank working full-time to run the place, not to mention us kids when we were old enough." She thought of Ian but couldn't bring herself to say his name aloud. "Nate has his own business to worry about. He doesn't have time to run the orchard too."

"I don't expect him to." Silence settled around them like an itchy wool blanket.

The swing swayed back and forth under their weight, the chains squawking with each pass, their bare feet shuffling quietly on the dirty cement floor.

• • •

Grady was watching *Farmer's Forecast* when he remembered an issue that had come up about Miguel's paycheck. He'd meant to discuss it with Laurel over supper, but somehow it had slipped his mind. Josie's image hovered in his mind like a pesky fly, and he swatted it away.

The clock read half past eight, and he hated to bother Laurel, but he wouldn't see her in the morning since he was in the orchard by dawn, and it needed to be resolved before she cut the checks.

He dialed the house and waited for the ring. A busy signal blared across the line. Probably Aunt Lola talking to Mr. Murphy. Within twelve minutes of their conversation in the cereal aisle at Ingles two weeks earlier, the Shelbyville grapevine had picked up that the two were a new item.

He slipped on his shoes and left the cabin. His eyes adjusted to the darkness as he made his way down the dirt path. The sky was clear, and a million stars twinkled back at him, giving the landscape a faint glow. Somewhere an owl hooted, its call sad and lonely, echoing through the valley.

All was quiet in Duncan's pen. He was a large, lumpy shadow in the corner by the barn. Grady thought of Josie and how he'd seen her that morning feeding the pig with Boone Barrow. The kid could hardly take his eyes off her. He had a lot to learn about women. Grady had pegged her for a spoiled city slicker before he met her, and working with her had only confirmed his opinion.

For all the hype about her work ethic, he'd been frustrated by her performance in the orchard. She'd started strong, but by midmorning, his migrants were working circles around her. Although he had to admit, she knew her way around the orchard. And she knew how to connect with the crew. He'd thought they might have trouble taking orders from a woman, but one pretty smile and they were putty in her hands.

That's not fair. She did go out of her way to build a relationship with them and she knew what she was doing, he'd give her that much. He'd wondered when Laurel bragged about her. From what he knew of Josie, he'd surmised that she was flaky and unreliable, but he was unsure what to think of her now.

He heard voices as he approached the side of the house. Maybe Laurel was on the porch and he wouldn't have to disturb the family.

He heard his name and slowed his footsteps, coming to a halt at the corner of the house. He probably shouldn't interrupt the private conversation. Grady turned to go, figuring he'd have to leave a note for Laurel in the morning.

". . . things get desperate again, you'll have no choice but to sell off a little more. We'll lose the place anyway, slowly."

It was Josie's voice. He stopped, torn between going and staying.

"Would you at least think about selling?"

Sell the orchard? Is that what Josie was trying to convince Laurel to do? His jaw tightened.

She had some nerve. He and Laurel had been here working their tail ends off, trying to get this place back on its feet, and she wanted to sell the place out from under them.

Maybe that was the only reason she'd come to begin with. She probably wanted the money so she could go out and waste it on fancy clothes or refurnishing her house. She was more like Danielle than he'd ever expected.

The women had gone quiet on the porch. Would her sister's suggestion persuade Laurel?

The squawk of the porch swing faltered, and he heard Josie bid Laurel good night and enter the house. Just as well. He needed to talk with Laurel, and he was too angry to face Josie.

He didn't have to read his contract to know how this worked. With only fifteen percent of the place, he'd have no say at all if Laurel agreed to sell. He'd lose it—all his hard work down the drain. He'd already lost one orchard, and he wouldn't lose another—not if he had any say in the matter.

six

*T*he bad thing about manual labor was it left too much time to think. Josie's hands went through the mechanical motions. *Grab, twist, pluck, bag. Grab, twist, pluck, bag.* The crew worked on ladders around her, and she picked the Galas from ground level, grateful she didn't have to worry about losing her balance in her fatigue. Still, her neck and back ached from reaching up.

On the other side of the tree, Miguel stepped down from the ladder and emptied his canvas bag into the bin, filling it to the brim. He exchanged a few words with Grady, who answered in Spanish.

The crew worked hard and carefully for Grady. Josie had learned that most of their wives washed and packed the apples after Grady moved them to cold storage.

Miguel climbed the ladder again, and Josie continued working. *Grab, twist, pluck, bag.* When her right arm tired, she switched to her left until that one fatigued.

The lift tractor roared to life as Grady moved the bin to the trailer. She was glad it was full now and he would be taking the load to cold storage. She was in dire need of a break, but with Grady around, she'd felt compelled to push herself. He already thought she was a slacker. She could tell by the way he spoke to her, treating her like one of the crew instead of the majority owner.

Today he'd hardly spoken to her at all.

One of the crew started a Mexican song and several others joined in. The sun beat down hot and harsh, making her wish she were picking on the shady side of the tree. Sweat trickled down her back.

She was picking as fast as she could, but on the other side of the tree, she could hear the apples dropping into Miguel's bag twice as fast. She tried not to think about it. Miguel was used to this work, and her body wasn't up to speed.

The image of Ian floated into her mind, an unwelcome intrusion. How many hours had she spent picking with him and her dad?

"Step it up, Jo," her dad had said from the ground, waiting for another sackful that would finish off the bin.

"Here you go, Mr. Mitchell." Ian had descended the ladder and was emptying his canvas bag into the bin, turning his boyish face up to her father as if he lit the moon.

"Good work, son."

Josie grabbed for the next apple, trying to match Hank's pace on the next tree. The apple slipped from her small hand and thunked to the ground.

Her dad gave her a look that said more than words. Her face heated. She could pick just as fast, just as well, as Ian. Her dad made her nervous, was all. She tried so hard to be what he wanted, but it seemed she always was falling short.

Ian interrupted her thoughts. "Your dad said the trout are biting. Wanna go fishing after supper? I got some new gang hooks, and I can't wait to try them out."

Still smarting from her dad's look, she was disinclined to do anything with Ian. "Not today."

Ian peered around the tree, smiling as he twisted off an apple lickety-split. His freckles were popping up faster than air bubbles in a can of 7UP.

"I already have the worms. I'll bait your hook . . ."

She didn't want to be reminded that she was still a girl under the scruffy jeans and baggy T-shirt. "I said no, Ian." Her tone came out sharper than she intended.

His smile slipped and she felt a little guilty. She tried to remind herself it wasn't his fault her dad liked him so much, but it didn't work. It never did.

"Well, I'll be down by the sunken log if you change your mind."

Why was he always so nice to her? Couldn't he see she didn't like him? He was always tagging along behind her as if he were her little brother or something.

Behind her, the truck started up, choking out a blue cloud of smoke that smelled of fuel. "Ian," her dad called from the open window. "Ride with me. I need your help unloading."

Ian scurried down from the ladder and set his

canvas bag beside an empty bin, then hopped into the passenger side of the truck.

Josie let her arm fall to her side, a knot tightening in her throat as she watched them ride between the rows of trees, the trailer bumping along behind them.

Now, Grady's truck roared to life, startling her from her thoughts. The bad memory lingered as she watched Grady guide the trailer between the rows of trees, just as she'd watched her dad and Ian that afternoon so long ago. She wasn't good enough then, and it seemed she wasn't good enough now. Because long after Ian was gone, the memory of him clung to her like a heavy morning mist.

seven

Josie was walking up the porch steps when she heard Aunt Lola call that supper was ready. The concrete all but sparkled beneath her feet and a few potted plants had been set along the perimeter.

When they were seated at the supper table, Aunt Lola led a prayer, then they all dug into the ham and fried okra.

Josie sliced into her ham with the side of her fork. "Aunt Lola, the porch looks terrific. I can actually see some paint from when Dad painted it green." They'd all hated it, though no one had the nerve to tell him that. "Remember that, Laurel?"

"It wasn't me." Aunt Lola aimed a glare at Laurel, who shifted.

"It needed to be swept," Laurel said, then promptly stuffed her mouth with okra.

"Laurel, you didn't." The porch had been more than just swept. Someone had gotten down on her hands and knees with a scrub brush.

"You have got to relax, hon." The endearment softened Nate's firm tone. He shot Josie a look as if it was her fault.

What? her eyes tried to communicate.

"I'm sorry. I'll do better." Laurel squeezed Nate's hand, but he didn't look mollified.

"The ham is delicious, Aunt Lola," Laurel said, changing the subject.

"You just like how salty it is. Mind you don't eat too much of it or your feet'll swell up like helium balloons."

"Too late." Laurel gave a dry smile.

"That cleaning frenzy probably didn't help," Aunt Lola said. "But your mama was in house slippers her last three months with the both of you. And she swore her feet never did go back to normal."

Josie's mom had passed away when she was nine, and she remembered very little about her. She did recall sitting on her lap every Sunday while her mom read the comics. And she remembered her mom's obsession with root beer floats.

Her dad had seemed different then. More content. Or maybe Josie had been too young to notice.

"Remember that, Josie?" Laurel was asking.

Josie chewed a bite of ham. "What?"

"I was telling Grady about the time we caught Mr. Murphy's bushes on fire. Gracious, Mom about had a conniption."

"I should think so," Nate teased.

"I have trouble imagining you as a mischievous child," Grady said to Laurel.

Josie noted he had no such compunctions about her.

"We were only setting off firecrackers, weren't we, Josie? And Mr. Murphy's grandson was the instigator. Well, I guess Josie was too."

"Sure, blame it on me."

"Well, you were the one who wanted to see what would happen when we lit a whole package. Who threw them in the bushes?"

"They were going to catch me on fire otherwise. Besides, I was only a little kid."

"It was your idea to run. That's what really honked Mom off."

"Not to mention Mr. Murphy," Josie said. Poor Logan had to face his grandfather alone, but he'd squealed quick enough.

"I'll have to remind Mr. Murphy about that next time I talk to him," Aunt Lola said.

"Which will probably be tonight," Laurel teased.

"You two tie up the phone lines like a couple of teenagers."

"I'm sure Mr. Murphy didn't forget our little mishap," Josie said. "We weren't allowed to play with Logan for three summers."

"But Dad hired Hank the next summer, so we had Ian to corrupt," Laurel said.

"That was Hank's son?" Grady asked. He took a deep sip of iced tea, his big hands shrinking the glass.

"Right," Laurel said. "He was a sweet kid, a few years behind Josie, though he was always very mature for his age."

Discomfort filled Josie at the mention of Ian. It was as if he were still here, haunting her. She couldn't get away from him in the orchard or the house. He'd made things hard while he was living, and had made them even more difficult in his death.

"Remember when we played hooky from our work and went creek stomping that time?" Laurel turned to Nate. "That was the hottest summer ever—it was above one hundred degrees for days. We were supposed to be picking apples, but soon as Dad left for the farmer's market, we sneaked off to the creek."

"He was so mad when he came back." Josie remembered that day as if it were yesterday. She'd thought he was cruel for making them work in the orchard when it was so hot. She'd talked Laurel and Ian into taking a dip with her. Their dad had forgotten something, and when he returned home, he caught them.

"I can still see the look on Ian's face," Laurel said. "He was all flushed and nearly in tears when Daddy showed up."

Josie remembered too. Ian had apologized sincerely, and her dad had nodded and told him he could ride into town with him. Laurel had been sent inside to help their mom with the apple pies for the store. Only Josie had been sent back to the field to pick apples.

Somehow she'd been blamed for everything that went wrong, and even when she'd managed to do something right, her dad didn't notice. But Ian, her dad noticed every little thing he did. It was almost like Ian was more his child than Josie was.

The memories stirred up the past the way tires stirred up dust. She could hardly breathe in this house, on this property, without choking on them. The thought of three months here made her throat swell and her insides hollow out. There was so much she hadn't faced, and she feared if she opened the past now, it would swallow her whole.

The ham she'd eaten churned uneasily in her stomach, and the rest of the food on her plate mocked her.

She set her fork down and took a sip of water. "Supper was great, Aunt Lola." She put her napkin on her plate and stood.

"I made Apple Delight for dessert," Laurel said.

"And left flour all over the counter," Aunt Lola added.

"Whoops. I'll clean it up."

"Already done."

"I'll have some later." Josie took her plate to the sink and took the back stairs to her room. The walls felt too tight, confining and suffocating.

Ian.

She shook her head as if to dislodge his name.

She had to get out of here, if only for one night, one day. Tomorrow was Sunday and she didn't have to work. She could just as easily spend those hours someplace else.

She thought of her friends in Asheville and knew they wouldn't mind a last-minute guest.

Once in her room, she pulled her address book from her purse and looked up the number she hadn't called in months, her hands shaking.

They probably had plans—it was a Saturday night after all—but it was early, only six thirty.

Jackie answered on the second ring. "Josie! It's great to hear from you. Boone said you were back in Shelbyville. When can you come see us?"

After feeling like an unwanted intruder in the orchard all week, Jackie's enthusiasm was a relief. "Uh, tonight?"

Jackie laughed. "Hey, Ash, Josie's coming over tonight." She addressed Josie. "When can you get here?"

She had to pack a few things and her car needed gas. "An hour and a half?"

The line clicked and Ashley was there. "Are you serious? Tonight? It'll be just like old times."

"You don't have plans?"

"Of course we do," Ashley said. "But we'll wait for you. One of my friends has a show at an art gallery, then we're going out after that."

Josie smiled, feeling better already. "That doesn't sound like your cup of tea." Ashley had been a jock in high school, leading the girls' basketball team in rebounds and setting school records.

"The gallery will be a drag for me, but you might enjoy it. Plus, we'll party afterward."

"There won't be time for any of it if you don't let her off the phone," Jackie said in the background.

"I need your address."

She wrote down the address and directions to her friends' apartment, then threw a change of clothing into her duffel bag. She needed to change too.

She put on a pair of black pants, heels, and a trendy red top that flattered her skin tone. There wasn't much time, so she made do with a coat of mascara and a little blush, then threw her cosmetics in the bag. She needed to find Laurel and Aunt Lola and tell them she was taking a quick trip.

Finding them was easy since they were still gathered around the supper table, finishing the apple dessert.

Laurel's fork stopped in midair when Josie entered the room with her overnight bag.

"Going somewhere?"

Her sudden trip would seem strange, no matter how she worded it. "I was just talking to Jackie on the phone. She and Ashley invited me down for the night."

"Oh, that's nice," Laurel said.

"I haven't seen them in several years." They'd visited her twice since she'd left Shelbyville, but the last visit was a long time ago.

"I was hoping you'd go to church with us tomorrow," Aunt Lola said. "Pastor Keeley was asking after you the other day."

"Pastor Keeley's still preaching? Maybe I'll go next week." Josie moved toward the door. The clock was ticking, and now that she'd made plans, she couldn't wait to follow through.

"Well, have fun and drive safely," Laurel called as the screen door slammed.

Grady heard the door shut behind Josie and breathed a sigh of relief at her departure. He didn't know why the woman made him so tense. It disturbed him that she had any effect on him at all.

"Well, that was sudden," Nate said.

"She can't seem to sit still these days," Laurel said, frowning.

"Wonder where she gets that." Aunt Lola rubbed

her hands, probably aching with arthritis again. "She ought to go to church while she's here."

"Don't push her, Aunt Lola. Josie's always had a mind of her own."

Grady had seen that already. The other day he'd asked her to take part of the crew down by the creek to pick some Arlets for an order. Before he knew what hit him, she'd turned everything around, and he was the one filling bins down by the creek.

And after one week in the country, she was already taking off for the city like a bat out of hell. He watched Laurel smile gently at her husband and wondered how two sisters could be so different.

"Well, I think I'll head home." Grady said good night and made his way back to the cabin. The moon lit the trees and the rooftop of his cabin. He passed the smelly pigpen and continued up the stone walk to his door.

Warm, stuffy air greeted him, and he turned on the air conditioner before grabbing a coke and settling in his recliner. He'd already read the thin copy of the *Shelbyville Gazette* that lay on the end table. What would he do with the rest of the night? Normally he looked forward to the peace and quiet of his cabin, but tonight it just felt . . . lonely. He was thirty-one, with nothing but the company of a TV on a Saturday night.

Maybe it was time to start dating again. The image of Josie's pixie face and solemn green eyes filled his mind, startling him. He set his coke down hard on the table.

What is wrong with you? Can't you see she's just like Danielle? Trouble with a capital T.

He was just bored, needed something to do. He flipped on the radio where WFJT was hosting *House Call with Dr. Shay.* A caller was explaining her problem with bunions, and even if Grady hadn't recognized her voice, he would've known it was Peggy Tackett. Everyone in Shelbyville knew the history of her bunions.

He turned to WXKC, and a country ballad filled the room. The music broke the silence, but the house felt no less empty.

There had been things he'd liked about marriage, things he'd liked a lot. In the beginning, he'd thought he was the luckiest man alive, but how quickly that had changed.

Danielle seemed content at first in their suburban Chicago home. Her trips to the city became more and more frequent though, and when he talked of moving to the country and starting his own orchard, she looked at him as if he were crazy. As if he hadn't gone to school with that dream in mind, as if he hadn't spent hours talking about it when they'd dated. He should've seen the signs.

But he hadn't—not until it was too late. Until he'd already been made a fool of ten times over.

It had been the first Saturday evening after Thanksgiving, and Danielle had gone into the city to shop for Christmas. She thrived on the holiday, an excuse to spend more money than they earned. A light snow fell and began to coat their small, square lawn.

Notre Dame was playing at Stanford that night, and he intended to watch them finish their season. The thought of watching the game alone held no appeal though.

Mike, his best friend since college, was an even bigger Notre Dame fan than he. Grady decided to run over to his house, only several miles away in a new subdivision, and watch the game there. He dialed Mike's number and got a busy signal. His cell phone was off, so Grady grabbed his keys and left. The game would start in fifteen minutes. They'd have enough time to grab a coke and a snack before kickoff.

The streets looked like they'd been dusted with powdered sugar as he pulled onto the main road. When had he last gotten together with Mike? A couple of months ago at least. Mike's new position at Citibank came with too many hours. Whenever Grady had called, he'd been working overtime. But he had no wife, and his money was probably piling up in the bank because he had no time to spend it.

He turned on the heat, and a blast of cold air hit his face. He wondered if something was wrong with Danielle. She'd seemed distracted lately, and she hardly sat still long enough to talk. He supposed her mind was on her job. They'd recently hired another interior designer, and maybe Danielle felt threatened. She'd been putting in more hours, but with their credit card debt, he wasn't complaining.

The tires of his Jeep slid as he made the turn into Mike's driveway. Faint tire tracks, leading into the two-car garage, were barely visible through the fresh layer of snow. Hopefully those tracks were from him coming, not going. Seven minutes 'til game time.

He slid from the Jeep, pocketed his keys, and left his hands there for warmth. The wind was brutal tonight, whipping snow into his face, biting his skin. Danielle was probably freezing on her trek from store to store. She'd worn one of her trendy coats that was built more for fashion than warmth.

He stepped up on the stoop and pulled open the door, eager to escape the bitter cold. "Mike, it's me," he called. A lone lamp shone in the living room, and the noise that filled the house wasn't a TV but music blaring from a radio or CD. The TV wasn't even on yet.

He wiped the snow from his shoes and went into the kitchen, following the light. But when he got there, it was empty. On the counter, a half-empty bottle of wine and one empty wine glass sat on the counter.

Above the chorus, he heard Mike laugh in the next room—the bedroom.

Grady winced. He hadn't known Mike was dating anyone, much less dating someone seriously enough to have her in there. He suddenly felt foolish for stopping over as if his friend didn't have a life. But Grady was going to have a man-to-man with him about this. Mike had never been promiscuous, and Grady was disappointed in him.

For now, though, a quiet exit was in order.

He padded across the kitchen, eager to escape unnoticed, and nearly ran into someone coming around the corner.

He stopped short as the woman let out a squeal.

His eyes focused on her tousled blonde hair, her flushed face, her doe-brown eyes.

Danielle.

Confusion swirled his mind the way the wind swirled the snow outside. *Danielle?* He noticed her clothes. Or rather, lack of. She stood barefoot, a man's shirt skimming her slender thighs.

"Grady!" She clutched at the stiff collar. The music swelled in the background.

Danielle was here. Not in the city. She was here. With Mike.

In the bedroom with Mike, wearing this . . . this little scrap of nothing.

Mike came around the corner, oblivious, wearing a smile. He stopped in the hall, behind Danielle. His eyes collided with Grady's, the smile sliding from his face. He swore.

"Grady," Danielle was saying.

63

But Grady heard no more. A thick fog of black welled up inside of him and he charged Mike, knocking him flat against the wall. A picture slid to the wood floor and cracked.

His fists pummeled blindly, a rage he'd never felt overpowering him. A moment later, Mike regained his composure and rallied, calling out his name.

Somewhere behind him Danielle was calling his name too. "Stop it, Grady!"

But her words meant nothing to him. Nothing, like all her words of affection. How long had this been going on? This affair between his wife and the person who'd been the best man at his wedding.

They fought until they were staggering to stand, both of them with bloody cuts. Mike had a trickle of blood streaming from his nose. His right eye had already begun to swell, and his lip bulged at the corner.

Grady felt no pain other than the deep ache in his heart.

"I'm sorry," Mike grated out when they were both breathless. "I didn't mean for it to happen." He dragged his hand across his mouth, smearing the blood.

Grady glared. Then his eyes swept back to his wife. Danielle stared back from the corner, her scrawny arms hugging her chest, her eyes wide in her pale face. He wanted to yell at her. Curse her out.

He turned and left, slamming the door behind him. Left his wife, standing in his best friend's house, in his best friend's shirt. He drove until his tank was nearly empty, and when he got home, Danielle was there. They fought loud and hard that night.

Later he found out Mike was the second affair in their fifteen-month marriage. If he'd hoped to salvage the relationship, that fact had changed everything.

Now, the jingle from JD's Used Cars rang from the radio, snagging his attention. He hated divorce, still did, but it had been the best thing under the circumstances. Maybe he was a little lonely now and then, but that was better than living with an unfaithful wife.

He looked forward to sharing his life someday with a good woman, a Christian woman, whom he could trust and take care of.

One thing he was sure of—that woman was not Josie Mitchell.

eight

*J*osie followed Ashley and Jackie to a table in the darkened corner of The Bistro and took a seat. On the ceiling, someone had painted a Michelangelo-like painting that was filled with chubby cherubs and fluffy clouds.

"You'll like this place, Josie," Ashley said.

"Especially the dessert. They have a cobbler that's to die for."

Josie wasn't hungry, but she was so glad to be out on the town, she didn't care. The Bistro was noisy with boisterous chatter and silverware scraping plates. In the background, jazz music played. After the quiet of Blue Ridge, the atmosphere was energizing.

Josie ordered a bowl of soup to sip while the other two ate supper. When the server left, Ashley leaned forward, planting her elbows on the table, her broad shoulders looking awkward in the spaghetti-strapped dress. "So what did you think of the show?"

The gallery had featured photographs of city life. "Your friend is good. She has a way with capturing light."

"You're just as good as her," Jackie said.

"I should rediscover my passion for artistic photography while I'm here. When I'm shooting events, my mind is always on pleasing the customer. I left my digital camera in Louisville, but I'm sure my old camera's still buried in my closet somewhere."

"You should dig it out," Ashley said.

There had been a stirring inside her to do just that as she'd browsed the exhibit's photographs. Josie had spent hours photographing the orchard and mountains when she was in high school. Then when she'd been chosen as the photographer for the school yearbook, she'd traipsed all over the school shooting pictures of her classmates. She'd attended more athletic events her senior year than in all the rest of her life combined.

"Remember that shot you took of me spiking the ball on Haley Hannigan? I still have that photo framed on my dresser."

"Right—that's one of my favorites." The look of intent concentration on Ashley's face and the play of her arm muscles as she slammed the ball, all of it frozen for eternity.

"I *should* dig out my camera," Josie mused aloud. She felt in control when she was snapping pictures. An observer, not a participant. There was something safe in that.

"Okay, enough small talk," Ashley said. "We've been dying to know what you think of him."

The server set their drinks down, then went to take the next table's order. "Did I miss something?" Josie asked.

"She means a certain Mr. Grady Mackenzie." Jackie made the most of her Southern drawl.

"Otherwise known as tall, dark, and dreamy." Ashley winked.

"He is a hunk," Jackie said. "Too bad he's such a stick-in-the-mud."

Ashley grinned. "You're just sore he didn't ask you for a second date."

"You went out with Grady?" Josie had trouble imagining dark, brooding Grady with her vibrant friend. She couldn't image two people less suited.

"I think he must've asked me on a dare," Jackie joked.

"He did not," Ashley said. "It was her mom's doing."

Jackie took it from there. "Grady walked into the donut shop one day, and Mom was certain he was just the right Christian man to turn me from my wild ways."

"And Jackie took one look at him and agreed."

"Can you blame me?"

"Where'd you go?" Josie asked.

Jackie shrugged. "We went up the Blue Ridge Parkway, had a picnic, and stopped at Grandfather Mountain. That long drive, and he never even made a move."

For some reason that set off a flare of relief in Josie. The fact that it did sent off an entirely different kind of flare.

"But enough of Jackie's sad tale. What do *you* think of Grady?" Ashley wiggled her blonde brows.

Josie took a sip of her tea and set it back on the Navajo-print cloth. "He's a reliable manager. He's produced a good harvest this year, and he manages the crew particularly—"

Jackie's head fell sideways as her eyes closed and she pretended to snore.

"What?" Josie asked, all innocence.

"Come on. Aren't you working with him in the hot, sweaty orchard all day?" Ashley asked. "Give us the dirt."

"There is no dirt. He took one look at me and decided he didn't want me there."

"Ooh, sexual chemistry!" Jackie said.

"Details . . . ," Ashley chimed in.

"Oh, for heaven's sake. There is no sexual chemistry. He doesn't even like me."

"That's the way it always starts in romance novels," Jackie said. "They meet, they don't like one another, they zing barbs back and forth, and next thing you know, they're locked in a passionate embrace."

"That's true," Ashley said.

Josie shook her head at the absurdity of it, the image of them together filling her mind. *Stop it, Josie.* Good grief, she was as bad as her friends were.

"Look, she's blushing," Jackie said.

"I am not. You guys are barking up the wrong tree."

"I thinketh the lady doth protest too much," Jackie said.

"Didn't you flunk senior lit?" Josie sipped her iced tea, cooling her hand on the glass.

Jackie wagged her head. "I paid attention when it counted."

Josie was relieved when the server brought the food, setting their plates in front of them. The steaming soup tempted her. "Y'all need anything else?" the server asked.

The girls said no and dug into their meals.

"So," Josie said after blowing on a spoonful of the creamy soup. "How are your jobs going?"

Ashley filled her in on her promotion at the bank, and Jackie told her about plans to expand her jewelry-making business. Several boutiques were already carrying her jewelry line, and one of the local jewelry stores wanted to stock a case and see how it sold.

After they finished their meal, Josie felt nauseated again and skipped the wildberry cobbler the girls were crazy about. As they returned to the apartment, dread swelled inside Josie. As much fun as tonight had been, and as much fun as tomorrow would be, she would soon have to turn her car toward Shelbyville, toward the place that deluged her with memories faster than a sudden summer storm.

nine

*T*he girls talked Josie into staying Sunday night and leaving early Monday morning. It had seemed like a good plan the night before, but now, as she pulled into the drive, she knew it had been a mistake. It already felt like she'd been up half the day; she was groggy from staying up late two nights in a row, and she was going to be two hours late getting to the field. A fact that was sure to go over well with Grady.

Josie tried not to let it bother her. *What do you care what he thinks? Who's the majority owner here anyway?*

Still, as she walked out to the field where the crew was picking, she felt like a schoolgirl on her way to the principal's office. Grady turned just then, and his arms stuttered as he dumped a sack of apples into the wooden bin.

He probably wouldn't say a word. She should walk over, grab a sack, and get started. She didn't owe him an explanation. Laurel would have told him she was coming home this morning.

She grabbed a sack from the truck and slung it over her shoulder.

"Nice of you to join us," Grady called out.

She let the comment go and chose a tree far away from Grady, greeting the crew as she went.

She worked hard all day, breaking only when the crew did. Instead of focusing on her aching body, she breathed in the fresh air and listened to sounds distinct to the orchard: branches snapping, apples thunking to the ground, blue jays' jeers.

Grady ignored her, not even making eye contact when she dumped her sack into the bin.

Supper was much the same, and through it all, Josie felt indignation rising from deep inside her. What had she done to him? Who did he think he was, treating her like a fungus that had invaded his precious grove? Did she need to remind him it wasn't even his orchard? A measly fifteen percent didn't make him the king of the apples.

Josie shifted on the sofa. Beside her, Laurel snuggled up in a quilt, then flipped the TV channel to a news program. The *Shelbyville Gazette* crinkled as Nate flipped a page.

Josie stared at the TV, letting it go blurry as she reviewed the day. The crew members, who hardly even spoke English, were beginning to sense the tension between her and Grady. When she'd asked Antonio and Juan to pick some Arlets, they'd looked to Grady, waiting for his approval. Finally, he'd given a silent nod.

The more she thought about it, the more it annoyed her. He was undermining her authority with his attitude. It was affecting the crew and her work in the orchard, and she wasn't putting up with it.

She stood abruptly and Laurel looked at her.

"I'm going out to—I need to talk to Grady for a minute."

Laurel raised her eyebrows, the corners of her mouth tilting.

Let her sister think what she would. It seemed everyone wanted to think something was going on between her and Grady. They couldn't be further from the truth.

She slid on her Birkenstocks and took the porch steps quickly. The air was still warm and even the slight breeze felt like a hot breath on the back of her neck. The sky was clear and the moon cast a silvery glow, glazing the treetops with shimmering light.

She tried to collect her thoughts. What was she going to say? She needed to know what his problem was. Maybe if they got it out in the open, there would be no need for his passive-aggressive behavior.

She approached his porch with quick strides and stopped short when she saw him sitting there, his ankle propped on his knee. He'd been watching her advance in the dark. A light filtered through the front window, shedding a golden glow on his skin. It was then she noticed that more of his skin was showing than she'd seen before. The light streamed over his bare torso, shadows carving valleys between his stomach muscles.

Don't just stand here staring, for heaven's sake. She met his gaze.

He cocked a brow, waiting.

He wasn't going to offer her a seat or say good evening. She crossed her arms, glad she was standing in the dark, grateful it would hide the flush that was undoubtedly climbing her face.

Get on with it, Josie. "I think we need to talk."

Silence stared her in the face, and she shifted awkwardly. Finally, he gestured toward the wooden chair catty-corner from him.

She took the one porch step and sat. He had yet

to speak. He was intentionally making this as uncomfortable as possible. It was what he'd done since she'd arrived a week ago.

Just get to the point and get it over with. "Since I've been here, I can't help but notice that you don't seem to like me. Have I done something wrong?"

She sounded needy. "Not that you have to like me, but you obviously resent my presence—I think it's important that the crew respects my authority, and right now, I'm not sure that's the case."

She hated when she rambled, but he was sitting there so stinking quiet. *You do not need to fill the silence.* She snapped her mouth closed.

He set something aside, a folded copy of the newspaper. He stretched his arm across the wide seat and shifted. "The crew will respect your authority when you prove you're a responsible member of the team."

Little prickles of heat bit at the skin under her arms, then spread to the base of her neck. "I called Laurel last night and asked her to tell you I'd be late."

He raised his chin a notch and stared at her. "Show up on time and work as hard as the crew, and you'll have their respect."

A fire burned in her gut. She was working as hard as she could under the circumstances. He was trying to change this all around to be about her, but it was really about him and his attitude.

"That's not the point," she said. "You've been rude to me since I arrived—"

"Rude?"

"Yes, rude." If not in what he said, then in what he didn't say. He had a chip on his shoulder, and she'd knock it off if she had to.

He looked away then, his jaw working.

"Just say it. Have I said something, done something? I came here to help, for heaven's sake."

"I don't need your help."

She gave a wry laugh. "Well, Nate felt otherwise. And apparently so did Laurel, because he could hardly keep her from working before I arrived."

It had to be more than that. Why should he care if Josie was here? He couldn't be that stubbornly independent.

His gaze fixed on her, his eyes hard, unyielding. "I might be a minority owner, but this orchard means a lot to me. I won't lose it."

She shifted under his gaze, an uneasy feeling swelling inside her. He knew she wanted to sell the orchard. Despite the dim light, she could see it written clearly on his face. She couldn't believe Laurel told him.

He must've read her thoughts. "I overheard you on the porch."

She was relieved Laurel hadn't told him. Still . . . "You were eavesdropping?"

"I came over to talk business with Laurel. It's not my fault you were spilling your guts in public."

"You could have said something."

"I'm saying it now."

Saying what? That he was going to fight her tooth and nail? She wondered why it meant so much to Grady. It was only fifteen percent. Sure, he'd worked hard on the orchard, but nothing like Josie's family. They had three generations invested.

On the other hand, Laurel listened to and trusted Grady. If he was bent on keeping the orchard, his opinion would carry a lot of weight with her sister.

Maybe if she knew why it meant so much to him, she could find a way to convince him selling it was for the best.

She did nothing but breathe for a moment. Getting angry wouldn't accomplish anything. It was unfortunate he knew she wanted to sell the orchard. It had certainly done nothing to help his opinion of her, which, she reminded herself, had been poor even before he'd set eyes on her. But she'd explore that another time.

She took a deep breath and swallowed her pride, feeling it go down in a tasteless lump. "I'm sorry I went off on you. I didn't get much sleep over the weekend, and I guess I'm a little irritable."

He studied her as if weighing her sincerity. Was he always so skeptical? Even when she was trying her darndest to be nice, he still treated her with all the warmth of an ice pack.

• • •

Grady listened to Josie's reluctant apology and tried to think beyond the fact that she'd had a wild weekend away with her friends. She'd probably been drinking at some bar in the city, picking up guys. Maybe she'd stayed the night because she was too drunk to drive home and was hungover this morning.

That would explain the dark circles under her eyes and her testiness, though, to her credit, she'd managed to hold her tongue all day.

Her thumbnail clicked as she picked at it with her middle finger. She seemed to be waiting for a reply.

Fine. Whatever. "Apology accepted," he muttered.

Her hair, still damp from her shower, hung in waves around her freshly washed face. The lamplight was complimentary to her skin tone, and with those long eyelashes and full lips, he thought she looked better without any makeup.

He looked away, disturbed by his thoughts. A cricket chirped from somewhere just off the porch.

"Why don't we start over?" she was saying. "Tell me about yourself. You've probably heard plenty about me."

She was trying, he'd give her that. The least he could do was meet her halfway. He shrugged. "I grew up on an orchard in Indiana near a little town called Middlebury. We lost the orchard to hard times when I was fourteen, and my parents divorced shortly after that. My mom and I moved to Chicago then."

"That must've been a big change." Her voice was soft now, and he noticed a lilt, the remnants of a Southern accent.

"I adjusted—made friends and all that. Never lost my love of the country though."

"And apple orchards in particular?"

Chicago had always felt like a place he was visiting. Even after he married and settled there, it was never home. "Mom always said I have apple juice flowing through my veins."

"Is that why you studied agriculture?"

"I dreamed of having my own orchard someday. There's just, I don't know, a sense of belonging when I'm working an orchard, a calling, you might say." He wondered if he'd said too much. It wasn't as if he was trying to take over Blue Ridge. But Josie had settled in her chair and didn't seem alarmed by his words.

"Did you accept the position here right out of college?"

If only he had. If only he'd skipped the whole ordeal with Danielle. "No, I—I lived in Chicago for a while. I was married." He didn't know why he added that last bit.

Josie didn't seem surprised. Maybe her sister had mentioned it.

"After the divorce I saw an ad online for the foreman position. Your dad posted it, I guess."

"Right." She stared into the darkened yard. "After Hank retired."

"In Chicago I worked at a company that transformed urban lots into agricultural centers. It was rewarding work, but I was eager to escape the city and try my hand at an orchard. This was only going to be a step toward getting back to my roots, so to speak. Being a family operation, I didn't hold out any hopes for ownership."

"Then the frost came."

It wasn't like he'd planned it. The loss had hit hard after all the work he'd done to prepare the trees.

"It was a difficult time for your sister. I had money set back and she offered to sell me some shares." He hoped he wasn't stepping on a minefield by bringing up the subject, but Josie needed to see how much this place meant to him. Surely she knew how much it meant to her sister.

He wanted to ask why she wanted to sell the place. Didn't three generations of family ownership mean anything? What he'd give for that kind of history. All he had was an absentee alcoholic father and a newly married mom who lived too far away.

"Enough about me. What do you do in Louisville? I don't think Laurel's ever said."

She shrugged. "I'm a photographer. I work—or worked, I should say—at Special Occasion Photography."

"They fired you?"

"Not exactly. I might have a job when I get back, just depends how busy they are."

He hadn't given too much thought to what she'd left behind.

"I can get another job if I have to."

"How did you get into photography?"

"I've always been snapping photos. When I left here, I moved to Pittsburgh and got a job at a restaurant, but I took some courses in photography. It eventually turned into an associate's degree." Her eyelids dropped, a shutter over her eyes, as she studied her feet. She laid her head against the back of the chair and sighed. She looked tired, ready for bed, but suddenly he didn't want her to go.

You really are lonely, pal.

He'd finished the newspaper, and there was nothing on TV tonight. At least she was someone to talk to. She was being amiable at least, and their conversation was easing some of the tension that had flowed between them.

"Ever married?" *Now, why'd you go and bring that up?* She didn't seem surprised by his tactless question.

"Nope." Her lips tilted, just at the corner, under-lining her world-weary sigh. "Never found the right person."

She sounded like it was over, like she was seventy and it was too late. She couldn't be older than twenty-five, twenty-six.

"I heard you went out with my friend Jackie." The other side of her mouth rose until she was almost grinning.

"Does that amuse you?"

"Little bit." A full-fledged smile, the kind that could take a man's breath away.

"We didn't have much in common."

"No kidding."

She'd been talking about him with her friends over the weekend. He'd give his best ladder to know what they'd said.

"I can set you up with some of my old friends," she offered.

"I'm doing fine on my own, thanks just the same."

"That's not what Laurel seems to think." She was teasing him.

How long had it been since he'd been teased by a woman? "You seem to be spending an inordinate amount of time talking about me."

He was sure if the porch weren't so dim, he would've seen a blush bloom on her cheeks. Finally, she lifted her little chin and crossed her arms as if she were chilly.

"Don't flatter yourself," she said. "It was nothing good."

He felt a smile work its way to his own lips. Sassy thing.

"So, who'd you set me up with?" he asked, not even sure he wanted to hear the answer.

She squinted, biting the corner of her lips. "Emaline Jacobs maybe?"

Their town clerk, Emaline Jacobs, talked in long run-on sentences and had hips so narrow, she could squeeze through a crack without turning sideways. "Not my type."

Her face brightened. "Oh, I know. Anna Tackett."

She was a server at the café. Cute, but loud and bossy. She was known for deliberately changing orders she felt were less than nutritious. She would've been fired by now if it wasn't for the fact that her mother owned the place.

"Nuh-uh," he said.

Josie laughed. "She'd keep you in line."

"I can do that on my own."

"That so?" She was flirting.

And he liked it. Too much. *What are you doing, Mackenzie? Making friends with the enemy? She wants to sell the place from under you.*

They did say keep your friends close and your enemies closer. Still, in this case, he didn't think it was wise. He was enjoying her attention, her company, but she was the last kind of woman he needed. Too much like Danielle, a danger to his heart.

Maybe he did need someone to keep him in line. He sure wasn't doing a good job of it. He picked up the newspaper and shifted forward on the chair, leaning his elbows on his knees. "Getting late. I think I'll turn in now."

Josie's eyes flickered. "Oh. Okay." She stood

slowly, as if puzzled, maybe even hurt, by his sudden announcement.

For one awkward moment he felt frozen to his chair, frozen by her vulnerability. She'd been enjoying herself too. Maybe she was just as surprised by that as he was.

"Well," she said. "Good night."

"'Night." He watched her walk into the darkness, fading like a ghost as she distanced herself from the halo of light. He wished she would fade so easily from his own thoughts.

ten

Josie's cell phone rang as she pulled up to the front of the house. She took it out and looked at the screen, hoping for reception. Two bars, hopefully that was enough.

"Hi, Josephine, this is Allen Linkletter from Dunbarger and Associates."

Josie turned off the car and greeted the attorney.

"I sent those papers we finalized a couple weeks ago, but they were returned in the mail. I was wondering if you had a new address."

She'd forgotten to have her mail forwarded. She'd have to handle that.

She gave Allen the new address and hung up, relieved that was taken care of. If she could only convince Laurel to sell the orchard, everything would be in place.

The house smelled like lemons when she entered. Laurel stopped midswipe, a dusting rag in hand.

"What are you doing?" Josie snatched the rag from her sister.

"You're home early."

"Is this what you do when no one is around to keep an eye on you?"

"I feel fine." Laurel tried to grab the dust cloth, but Josie pulled it from her reach.

"Go sit down. I'll bring you a nice glass of tea."

"Why don't you just hook me up to an IV and be done with it?"

Josie pointed at her. "Don't tempt me."

When Josie returned from the kitchen, Laurel was sitting in the recliner, her feet propped on the ottoman.

"If I have to sit, so do you," Laurel said. "You're looking pretty tired yourself."

Josie didn't want to admit she'd been relieved when Grady asked her to take a bushel of Galas to the store for Aunt Lola. By the time she was done, it would've been a waste of time to return to the field.

Josie sank onto the sofa, glad for the reprieve.

"Are you feeling okay?" Laurel asked.

Her eyes popped open. "I'm fine." Had Laurel seen her symptoms? She'd tried so hard to hide them.

"You haven't seemed yourself since you've been home. And you haven't been eating much."

"Maybe I'm getting sympathy morning sickness," she joked.

"So you have been feeling sick."

"Can't a girl watch her weight without everyone getting paranoid?"

Laurel narrowed her eyes. "Don't even talk about weight." Laurel looked at her own belly, burgeoning beneath her maternity top.

"What do you expect? You're carrying two people in there."

"Am I carrying them in my thighs too?"

"You look great, Laurel. Besides, Nate doesn't seem to mind your new figure." Laurel's husband always seemed to have an arm around her sister, as if he couldn't keep from touching her. Their closeness sometimes made the hollow spot inside Josie stretch open. Not that she wasn't happy for Laurel.

The back door shut and sounds emerged from the kitchen—the refrigerator door sucking open, a pot being pulled from its cupboard.

"Aunt Lola's fixing her famous spaghetti tonight."

"Sounds good." Josie's empty stomach complained, whether from hunger or in revolt, she wasn't sure.

"Who's been in my kitchen?" Aunt Lola called from the kitchen.

"Sorry!" Cringing, Laurel addressed Josie. "I baked cookies," she said. "Hey, did I tell you I have an ultrasound this week?"

Josie had seen the ultrasound she'd had weeks ago, but the fuzzy black-and-white photo looked more like bad TV reception than two babies. She imagined that would be different now. "How exciting. Is Nate going?"

Laurel sipped her tea. "He wouldn't miss it. I'll bring home a picture for you."

"Will they know if you're having boys or girls yet?"

"Yeah, but Nate doesn't want to know. I do, but we've agreed to wait until they're born."

Josie imagined she would too. Not that she was ever going to have the chance. Sadness curled around her like a vine, but she wouldn't let it grab hold.

"I sure wish he'd change his mind," Laurel said.

It took Josie a moment to realize Laurel was talking about the sex of the babies. "Do you have a preference? You always wanted a little girl."

"Honey, at this point, I'm just happy to have a baby. Well, two babies."

"I hope they're identical." An old memory sprang into Josie's mind. "Remember when Jeff and Jordan Seavers switched identities for those classes my freshman year?"

Jeff had been an algebra whiz and Jordan loved English, so they took each other's place one semester.

"Oh, man." Laurel laughed. "I'd forgotten. They 'bout got away with it too."

Except Jeff's ex-girlfriend had discovered the truth and ratted them out. "They got suspended for two weeks, remember?"

Laurel grimaced. "I've decided I don't want identical twins."

"I'm sure yours would be little angels." It wouldn't be long, and they'd be here, tiny bundles of wiggling joy. It would do this house good to see some little ones again. The thought pressed hard on her heart. Would she even be here to greet them?

"I've been giving some thought to what we talked about on the porch." The change of subject was abrupt.

She was surprised Laurel was bringing it up, but maybe she'd seen the light. Maybe she'd been thinking about life after the babies' arrival.

"I don't know how I thought I was going to manage the orchard and the babies. Would've been hard enough with just one baby, but two'll keep me busy for sure."

"Some parents of twins hire extra help. Of course, Aunt Lola will be here, and it'll be winter when the babies come, so she'll be free to help out."

"Yeah, I'm thankful for that."

Josie realized she wasn't helping her own cause. "But Grady won't be able to prune all the trees himself."

"And once fall comes again, Aunt Lola will have

to mind the store, and Grady will still be short-handed."

"Exactly." A rush of relief flowed through Josie.

"And you're right," Laurel said. "The orchard has never been to me what it was to you and Daddy. I mean, I love the place, and I love the history, but the work of the orchard was never really my thing. I've only done it all these years because I've felt responsible for it."

A prick of guilt stabbed Josie. She'd abandoned her sister here, forcing the load of the orchard on her.

Dad was here when you left. You couldn't have known he'd have a stroke.

But since then, the responsibility had fallen on Laurel. It would do her good to be out from the strain of it, to have the opportunity to pursue her own dreams. She probably didn't even realize the weight of the stress she carried. And once the babies were here, she wouldn't need the extra worries.

". . . So I was wondering if you'd consider coming back."

Josie had missed something important; it was what she got for letting her mind wander. In the kitchen, Aunt Lola dropped something that clanked to the floor.

"What?"

"I know you have a life in Louisville, and I don't want you to think I'm discounting that. But really, the orchard has always been your passion. I always thought you'd stay here and take over when the time came."

Josie didn't like where this was headed. She stared at Laurel, hoping she was wrong, but her sister was studying her stubby fingernails, the pink polish half chipped away.

Josie gathered her courage around her like armor. "What are you saying?"

Laurel wrung her swollen hands and took a deep breath, her chest expanding and deflating in the space of two seconds. "I want you to consider coming back home to stay."

Josie felt her face freeze. This wasn't supposed to be happening. This wasn't why she'd come home. Laurel was supposed to be thinking about selling the orchard, not restructuring Josie's life.

"I've caught you by surprise," Laurel said.

That didn't begin to describe her emotions. How did she explain to Laurel why she couldn't come back? She couldn't tell her everything. It brought her shame just knowing it herself. Shame and guilt.

The feelings welled up inside her, but she pushed them down firmly. No, this wasn't what she wanted. This would spoil everything. Somehow she had to make Laurel see the impossibility of her request so she'd consider the only real solution to their problem: selling the orchard.

"You don't have to answer right away," Laurel was saying.

Unbidden, the image of her and Grady working the fields came to mind. She imagined the spring with the trees in full bloom; the air filled with the fragrance of their white, velvety blossoms; honeybees buzzing through the fields and pollinating the flowers. Spring brought a fresh sense of hope, an expectation for nature's bounty. She could almost feel the excitement building inside her now.

No, no, this was all wrong. What was she doing?

She shook her head. "I don't have to think about it." Josie tucked her hands under her legs, pinning them to the sofa cushion. "My life is in Louisville now. I'm not staying."

"But why?"

"I'm just not, Laurel." Frustration rose like a thermometer under the hot sun. Laurel had always tried to tell her what to do, but Josie was an adult now and her sister wouldn't have her way this time.

"Is this about Daddy? I know the two of you—"

"No. This isn't about that. But now that you mention it, he should've sold this place a long time ago. It would've saved you a lot of trouble."

"What are you talking about?"

"Come on, Laurel. Don't you think it was selfish of him to ask you to drop your life and come nurse him for months on end? To put your family on hold, to run the orchard, give up your house in town—"

"He's our dad. It was my duty—"

"It was his responsibility to look out for your needs. If he'd sold this place, he could've afforded health care and not expected his daughter to drop her whole life to be his nurse. I would never be a burden on my family like that."

"He wasn't a burden. I didn't know you felt that way."

Josie had bitten her tongue through too many phone conversations. She hadn't meant it to come out now—it was too late to change things.

"Well, Daddy's gone now, and the orchard is my responsibility. If you came back, you'd be in charge. You could run the orchard any way you wanted."

Josie imagined Grady overhearing that sentence, imagined her becoming his boss. A wry laugh slipped out. Yeah, that would be the day.

"It's not a ridiculous thought, Josie."

She recognized the tone of Laurel's voice. Her sister was getting frustrated right back at her.

"You always planned to stay here anyway, and it's not like you have anyone waiting for you in Louisville."

The truth hurt, dug down deep into the private places where a Do Not Disturb sign hung on the door.

"You probably don't even have a job anymore, so what is there to return to?"

Josie shook her head.

"You have family here. That used to mean something to you. You have me and nieces or nephews on the way." She lowered her voice. "And Aunt Lola won't be around forever, you know."

Josie needed to take a hard line. She wasn't staying here, couldn't stay here, and she needed to make Laurel understand that whether her sister got her reasons or not.

"I won't do it, Laurel. I *like*"—she forced out the word—"my life in Louisville. It's not much, but it's mine, and I'm going back after harvest." She stood, needing to retreat to her room, needing space.

She left her sister staring after her, her hands laid protectively over her belly. Josie's legs trembled as she took the stairs. In all her thoughts of coming to Shelbyville and convincing her sister to sell, she'd forgotten one major detail that could ruin everything: her sister was capable of digging in like a tick on a rottweiler.

eleven

Josie closed her bedroom door behind her, shutting out the garlicky smell of spaghetti sauce. Nausea worked its way into her throat and lodged there, an acidic lump. She rooted through her purse for the roll of antacids, bumping aside her wallet, checkbook, and a packet of tissues.

A bottle dislodged from the corner of her purse, the pills clacking against its plastic shell. She stilled, her eyes settling on the amber-colored bottle, on her name typed across the label.

She could open the bottle and swallow a pill and be done with it. Her stomach turned, as if in agreement. Her legs shook, the fatigue settling over her like a lead blanket.

Her fingers closed around the bottle. Should she? Was it worth it?

The phone call she'd received from the attorney flitted through her mind. All her planning, all her reasons.

It was that—the reasons—that made her release her death grip. Let the plastic bottle fall with a quiet clack to the bottom of her purse.

She grabbed the antacids and chewed two tablets, then curled up on the bed, wishing it were bedtime so she wouldn't have to face Laurel again.

The sound of a mourning dove beckoned outside her window, calling back all the mornings she'd awakened to that very sound. If only she could go back and change things . . .

But there were no do-overs in life. Not really. Not when death stole them away.

She tried to smother the thought before it had a chance to ignite, but her sister's proposition fueled the flame. The memory came quickly, incinerating everything in its path.

They'd had a particularly cold January her senior year in high school, with more snow than usual and winds that stained her cheeks red.

On that day, they'd had a snowfall, and Josie had talked Laurel into digging their old sled from the barn in an effort to recapture their youth. After supper, they had headed to the best hill at the peak of their driveway. It was almost a mile away, but well worth the walk.

Josie was first, starting from the top. The sled was smaller than she remembered, and her legs were scrunched up, the rubber soles of her boots flat against the steering board. She gripped the rope tightly in her mittened hands and shoved off. The runners coughed up snow that hit her face, burning her skin. She passed Laurel at the turn, pushing hard with her left foot to make the sharp curve and avoid veering off the drive and down the dangerously steep slope toward the creek. Once around the corner, she flew down the second incline, closing her eyes against the snow shower.

Her sled slid to a stop at the bottom and she jumped off, exhilarated by the fast ride. By the time she reached Laurel at the halfway point, she was huffing from the climb.

"You almost didn't make the turn," her sister scolded.

"I always make the turn, and you always say that."

Laurel straddled the sled and sat, choosing to start halfway down for safety's sake.

"Besides," Josie said, "the creek is probably frozen."

"No matter, that hill's too steep even for you."

Laurel pushed off and down she went, screaming all the way. On Laurel's third run, Ian appeared wearing an impossibly thin parka and his old beat-up Nikes that made his feet slide with every step.

He and Laurel shared the sled, making the runs from the middle of the hill. Josie started her runs from the top.

Laurel was first to quit, complaining of frozen fingers and an icy-cold nose. After Laurel left, Josie wished Ian would go home too. Now that he was fifteen, she had to look up at him. He'd had a few growth spurts the past two years, and he towered over her by ten inches. She hated that.

"Why don't you just start from here?" Ian handed her the rope. Snowflakes clung to the long lashes framing his brown eyes, and his freckles stood out on his pasty winter skin.

"Same reason I didn't last time." Josie took the sled and started the steep trek up the hill. Her boots crunched through the packed snow. Ian was such a wuss. He was too cautious, and the way he looked at her dad, like he'd set the moon and stars in orbit, made her sick. Wasn't one father enough for him? He had to claim hers too?

After school her dad had taken Ian to the hardware store. When she'd offered to go, he'd reminded her of her English homework. It rankled to see Ian and her dad leaving together while she was stuck at the table with a number-two pencil and a blank sheet of paper.

It wasn't fair. She didn't have a mom anymore and she may as well not have a dad. He didn't care about her. He was too busy doting on crummy old Ian. She hated the way it made her feel inside, like something black and ugly was swelling up.

Josie reached the top of the hill and turned. It was getting dark. This would have to be her last turn.

Ian stood at the inside of the curve, well out of harm's way, waiting. The thing that swelled up inside her felt like it was going to bust. Why didn't he just go home and leave her alone? Why did he always have to hang around?

"The corner's getting kind of slick," Ian called.

The runners had packed it down good, but she could make the turn. She sat on the sled. A thought buzzed in her mind, begging escape.

"I think I might go down toward the creek this time," she called, just to get under his skin.

"You know that's too dangerous." The edge to his voice fed her mean streak.

"The creek's got to be frozen. It'll be fun." She wasn't going down the slope anyway. Even if she made the bump off the drive and the steep ride down into the gap, there was always a chance the creek wasn't frozen enough to withstand the impact of the sled or the slice of the runners.

She pulled her feet up and set them in place.

"No, Josie!" His words were as firm as she'd ever heard from him, like a parent to a naughty two-year-old.

Who did he think he was, bossing her around? He might have her dad wrapped around his long, skinny fingers, but he didn't have her.

Somewhere between the top of the hill and the curve, she made the decision. Entering the turn, Josie pushed on the right side of the board, and the sled veered toward the hill.

"Josie!"

She barely heard her name through the tornado of snow that whirled around her. She hit the bump at the edge of the drive at an angle and went airborne. The sled tilted crazily, then she landed.

She sped down the impossibly sloped hill. She was falling through a wet, white world. Her breath choked on the cold, her eyes blinked blindly. Where was the bottom?

The runners cut through the snow. She braced her feet against the board, grasped the rope in her gloved hands, leaned back. Gravity pulled her forward, downward. She remembered the big rock that jutted out into the creek. What if she hit it? She looked for it, but the spray of snow blinded her.

Abruptly, the slope leveled, then a bump. She held her breath, pulled hard on the rope. The ground leveled as the sled skated across the ice. The runners sliced through the snow, and the sled came to a gradual stop.

Her heart pumped blood in thumping bursts. Her vision cleared. She was in the middle of the frozen creek. She'd made it!

The scariness of the ride drained away, leaving an aftertaste of exhilaration. She scooted off the sled, onto her knees, screaming, "Woohoo!"

No one had gone down that hill before. No one. And she'd made it. It was better than a roller-coaster ride at Six Flags.

Ian stood at the top of the slope, his gloved hands on top of his head. "That was the dumbest thing you ever did!"

She'd never seen him mad before. That just made the trip even more worthwhile. Josie stood to her feet and reached for the rope. "Oh, just shut up." She was so tired of him. Why couldn't he just—

There was a sickening sound. A sharp crack.

Josie froze, her hands in midair, reaching. A longer sound followed, like a chunk of Styrofoam snapping in half. The sound of ice cracking under her weight.

She stopped breathing, afraid the weight of filled lungs would be all it took to make the ground split beneath her.

"Come on, Josie, stop goofing around. It's time to go home."

Should she lie down flat? Tiptoe off the ice?

She bent her knees slowly, easing down, reaching with her hands.

A loud crack split the night. Then she was falling.

"Josie!"

The water swallowed her, the edge of the ice cut through her mitten and into her fingers. Coldness enveloped her. Her lungs sucked in a mouthful of water.

She kicked hard, and the water opened to air. She coughed, sputtering, reaching for the edge of the ice. The wet cold permeated her clothing. The weight of it dragged her down.

Her hand found the edge of the ice and she braced her body on it.

"I'm coming, Josie!"

The ice in her hand snapped, and she went under a second time. When she came up, her head hit ice. The current had carried her from the hole.

She panicked, sucking in a breath. Her eyes opened wide under the murky water, searched frantically.

There! She was so close. She grabbed for the ice and pulled herself up. The cold air hit her face. Her lungs coughed up the water, stinging her throat.

Her body shivered, her hands moved mechanically across the ice, shaking.

"Josie!"

The shore seemed so far away. Ian stepped toward her, out onto the frozen creek.

Josie grabbed the edge of ice and tried to pull herself up. She grunted with the effort. Her sodden clothes weighed her down. If she could only get a little leverage with her feet. But the bottom was too far down.

She strained, pushing with her arms, trying to get high enough to lay her body across the ice. She groaned and screamed with the effort.

"I'm coming, Josie!" Ian was lying belly-down, slowly moving toward her.

Her arms collapsed under the strain and she sank down until her chin touched the water's surface. Her teeth knocked together. Shivers shook her whole body. How long could she last like this? The water was frigid, and she'd already been cold. Her arms and legs felt numb.

"Help me!"

"Hang on, Josie!"

She tried to pull herself up again, but her arms were weak. *What if I don't make it? What if I die here in the creek?*

Tears tracked down her face, freezing halfway down. Her skin stung. She was helpless. But Ian was coming. He was getting close.

"Hurry!" Her voice betrayed her panic.

Ian scooted to the rim of ice, hand reaching out.

She grasped it, then the other. Ian pulled, grunting. But instead of drawing her from the water, he slid forward, pulled by her weight.

"Wait. Let go," he said.

But he was her lifeline, and she couldn't make her fingers loosen.

"Let go, Josie! I'm not going anywhere."

She straightened her stiff fingers and clutched the ice. She couldn't feel her fingers anymore. Her legs hung limply. They didn't feel cold anymore. She tried to remember what she'd seen about hypothermia on TV last winter when some kid had gone skating on a pond he'd thought was frozen.

"Grab my hands." Ian was sitting now, bracing his feet in front of him. What if the ice cracked under him? Then they would both die.

"Maybe you should get help!" But even as she said the words, Josie wondered if there was time for that.

"Grab on!"

She took his hands and he pulled. Her chest scraped against the edge of the ice. Ian grunted.

Josie strained. "Help me, God!" She kicked as hard as she could. *Don't let me die!*

Then the ice cracked under her torso and she slid back into the water.

Ian scooted back and they tried again.

"Kick your legs! Kick hard!" Ian pulled.

Josie tried to kick, but her legs responded in slow motion as if they were drugged. Her arms felt like they were being ripped from their sockets.

The ice under her gave way again, and she grabbed for the new ledge, a fresh batch of tears clogging her throat.

Ian backed up, gasping. "It's no use."

"Go . . . for . . . help!" The words escaped

between chatters. Why was he just sitting there? "Hurry!" Her feet felt funny, all tingly. Her hands weren't doing what she asked of them.

And still, Ian sat.

"Go . . . Ian . . . *please!*" She wouldn't last much longer. Maybe she could hold on long enough for help to arrive. *Please, God! I don't want to die.*

"I have an idea." Ian scooted toward her.

What was he doing? She didn't have the strength to ask. Until he scooted close enough that the ice cracked under him too. And he was falling into the water in front of her.

"Ian!" *No, God!* What hope did they have now? What was he doing?

Then he was beside her, shivering. His eyes had a look she'd never seen. A confidence, almost a resignation. And a strength of will she didn't expect from Ian.

"I'm going under," he said, his teeth knocking together. "Put your feet in my hands and I'll push you up."

"But . . . what about—"

Ian was under the water. She felt movement around her. Somehow he found her feet, and then she was being pushed upward. She used her hands. They pushed against the ice. *Please don't crack. Please don't crack.*

Then she was out of the water. On her belly. Everything hurt, tingling painfully. She scooted like a snake away from the hole, slowly, her muscles not cooperating.

She had to help him! But how? She wasn't strong enough to pull him out, even if the ice didn't give way. She had to go for help, and quick. She crawled, afraid to stand, her knees scraping the ice.

When she reached the shore, she turned, breathing hard. "Ian!" She had to help him, but she could barely move.

"I'm here," he called.

"I'm going for help!"

The slope she'd slid so quickly down was now a formidable enemy. Even on a good day it would be a difficult climb with its slippery covering.

It was slow going. She didn't know how long it took her to climb the hill. It was dark when she reached the top. She called Ian's name and he didn't answer. She fell several times on the long trek home, stumbling clumsily.

When she got home, Aunt Lola called for help and her dad called Hank. They left Josie at the house, warming up. They were gone a long time. Long enough that feeling had crept back into her limbs and warmth had seeped into her flesh. What was taking so long?

They heard sirens, and Josie told herself that was good. Ian was getting help and he would be okay too. How long had it been? It seemed like hours.

She was wrapped in a blanket on the couch,

snuggled between Aunt Lola and Laurel when her dad returned. He didn't even look their way as he removed his coat.

"Is he okay?" Josie asked.

When he turned, she saw the answer on his face. Long lines etched his forehead, but it was his eyes that told her what she didn't want to hear.

Beside her, Laurel began to cry.

"We were just . . . too late." Her dad stood there as if he didn't know what to do next.

There were two full minutes of shocked silence, then Aunt Lola slid off the sofa. "You need something warm in you. Where's Hank?"

Her dad gestured toward the door. "He went to the hospital with—Ian."

Everything in Josie froze up all over again. A different kind of freezing. This one started on the inside and worked its way out.

It was all her fault. All her stupid fault. She just had to go down that dumb hill.

And Ian had saved her life.

If only she hadn't let her temper take over. If only she'd gone the other way. But she hadn't. And now Ian was gone. Gone forever. He'd saved her life.

No, he had sacrificed himself for her.

It should be her body being driven to the hospital. A hollow spot opened up inside her, wide and gaping. Why was she alive and Ian dead?

It was supposed to have been her.

"He should've known better," her dad mumbled.

He never should have jumped in the water. What had he been thinking?

He'd been thinking about saving you.

He should've gone for help.

Now he's dead and it's your fault.

She looked at her father, standing by the door, snow-covered boots dripping all over Aunt Lola's clean floor. He was going to hate her when he found out what her foolishness had done. Hank was going to hate her. They all were.

Laurel was sobbing now, and her dad seemed suddenly aware of it. He turned toward them.

Then his eyes found Josie. "You did the right thing, coming for help."

They didn't know. They didn't know what had happened out there on the frozen creek. They'd seen the sled. They'd assumed Ian hadn't made the turn, that Josie had tried to help him out of the water.

She tried to find it in her to speak. *Tell them the truth, Josie. Just say it.*

Her tongue stuck to the roof of her mouth.

Ian saved me. She had to tell them the truth.

But she couldn't make herself say the words. Not that night, not the day of the funeral, and not any day afterward. No one had pressed her for details. Seeing the sled, the hole, they assumed they knew what had happened.

The truth had stayed buried inside, a tiny seed

that had eaten her alive every day since. Not a day had gone by that she hadn't questioned why Ian was dead while she remained alive. Not a day that she hadn't questioned why he gave himself for her. She was unworthy of such a sacrifice and no one knew it better than she.

twelve

*L*aurel was taking a bath and Mr. Murphy was on the front porch with Aunt Lola. He'd brought his mandolin and Josie could hear the sweet strains of a hymn as he practiced for his solo performance at the Shelbyville Apple Festival. Her mind filled in the familiar words of "Redeemed" as he played.

> *Redeemed and so happy in Jesus,*
> *No language my rapture can tell.*
> *I know that the light of his presence*
> *With me doth continually dwell.*

The music halted as Josie walked toward the back door. With everyone else occupied, Josie could finally have a private word with Nate. She found him in the backyard, raking the grass cuttings. "Need help?" Josie hoped he'd say no. She was already shaking with fatigue.

"I'm almost done." He raked the clippings into the burn pile with broad sweeps. Behind him, the laundry waved on the line like horizontal flags.

Josie tested the strength of the tire swing with a hefty tug on the frayed rope. Satisfied, she put her legs through the opening and pushed off.

"Laurel said you two used to spin each other until you were dizzy."

How many hours had they spent under these shade trees, playing and swinging, the pine-scented air rushing through their hair?

"I can't believe it's still here."

He gave the rake one last sweep and leaned against the handle. "I was going to take it down a couple summers ago. But you know Laurel, she's so sentimental."

"Now your kids will swing on it when they're old enough and—"

"Spin each other until they're dizzy. I know, that's what Laurel said." Nate ran his hand through his short clipped hair. He seemed to be taking in the property, probably calculating how many days until he had to mow again.

Now was as good a time as any to ask. "Did Laurel tell you what she asked me?"

"I guess not."

Josie was surprised. Nate and Laurel seemed close. Maybe she figured there was no point unless Josie decided to move back. "She asked if I'd come back for good."

He leaned the rake against a tree and stuffed his hands in his pockets. "What did you say?"

Josie dragged her feet until she came to a stop. She shook her head.

He nodded, not seeming to need further explanation, which was good because she wasn't going to offer one.

"When did she ask you?"

"Yesterday."

He nodded again slowly.

"She has a lot on her mind. Besides, she's probably hoping I'll change my mind."

"That still wouldn't solve much. She'd still fret over every frost, every season. Worry we'll lose another crop."

"It's unending, part of the job." Josie ran her hands across the rough treads of the tire.

"Grady thinks he can turn things around, given time. He has ideas for using a different type of tree, bringing in tours, stuff like that."

"Which would require more workers."

"I know."

Other orchards did it, but ultimately the responsibility would fall on Laurel. She'd always feel a duty toward it, just as she'd felt a duty toward their dad after his stroke. She would always need help, and Laurel had never enjoyed the work the way Josie and her dad had.

"I think she might change her mind after the babies are born. Her focus will shift to them, and she might see she needs to let loose of the place."

Might. After the babies are born. It was all so

iffy, all too far away. Josie might not have that much time, and she wanted this albatross off her sister's neck before she was gone. She couldn't leave her sister knowing she'd dumped the entire weight of the orchard on her.

"I think it would be better if we put it up for sale soon. We can't guarantee a good harvest next year or the year after, and no one will pay a premium price for a failing orchard."

Nate nodded, chewed his lip. "I see your point. I'm just worried about Laurel. It's a stressful time for her with the pregnancy. I don't want her upset."

Did he think Josie did? She had a ticking clock motivating her, but there was no way to tell him that. "Selling the orchard will lessen her stress."

"Eventually, yes. Initially, she'll feel guilty though. You know how she is."

"She'll still have the house and acreage around it. It's not as though she'll lose all our history."

"I know. I know. I just think we need to bide our time a bit."

That was where they parted ways then. Because time was one thing Josie didn't have much of.

thirteen

Josie's old Nikon whirred as she pressed the button. After all these years and a change of batteries, it felt like an old friend again, fitting into her palms as if it were made for her.

It was the perfect time of day for photos, when the sky gave off a golden glow leaving no shadows, no harsh highlights on the subject—in this case, the covered bridge on Old Fork Road that spanned the gap over Sweetwater Creek. It was even better light for portraits, but she'd left the orchard to be alone.

She shifted the camera, capturing a leafy twig at the edge to frame the photo, and snapped the shot. The week had dragged so slowly Josie wondered if it would ever end. She would've given her best pair of jeans for a trip to Asheville, but money was tight. She couldn't afford to leave every weekend. Still, that didn't mean she had to stay cooped up at the orchard. Just leaving the property, escaping the ghosts of the past, renewed her.

Especially today, after the tension of the week. She'd avoided the subject of the orchard with Laurel after their argument. Instead, they'd focused on the ultrasound pictures Laurel had brought home the day before. The photos had shifted her sister's attention from their argument.

If Laurel hadn't told her husband about her hopes of Josie running the orchard, Josie was sure she hadn't told Grady. As much as he wanted to keep the orchard, she was sure he didn't want to be under Josie's supervision.

Why are you dwelling on this? You didn't walk all this way for nothing. She drew in a deep breath, relishing the fresh piney smell. The creek trickled

110

under the bridge, punctuated by a dove's occasional call.

She'd snapped two rolls of film when a distant peal of thunder reached her ears. Dark clouds had gathered, capping the hills around her in a smoke-colored haze. She'd best start home. The light was fading anyway.

Josie capped the camera and knelt beside the one-lane road to stow it in its bag. She'd just zipped the case and stood when her eye caught a gray-haired man walking toward her. Worn jeans hung on his thin frame, and a plaid shirt, buttoned crookedly, flapped in the sudden breeze.

He'd aged more years than could be accounted for, but she knew it was Jackie and Boone's dad. As he neared, she saw a layer of gray stubble coating his jaw and neck. His eyes widened, he looked this way and that.

"Mr. Barrow?" She remembered Boone telling her about his Alzheimer's.

He stopped a car's length from her, his house slippers scraping the asphalt.

"It's Josie Mitchell. Remember me?"

There was no flicker of recognition in his eyes. He scanned the hills and road as if looking for an escape.

Another peal of thunder sounded and he jumped. "I can't—I don't know—" He scratched his jaw.

She approached Mr. Barrow slowly, not wanting to frighten him further. "Let's go home, okay, Mr.

Barrow?" She took his arm in hers and turned him toward his home. "This way."

They started a slow shuffle up the incline of the winding road, their shoes grinding the loose pebbles into the old pavement. Mr. Barrow moved in slow, stiff movements, his bony arm jerking with each step. He must've wandered off from home. Mrs. Barrow was probably worried sick.

If only she'd brought her cell phone, she could've called and set the woman's mind at ease. But then, reception was spotty around here anyway.

"I don't—" Mr. Barrow worked his jaw but couldn't seem to finish the sentence.

"I know, I know." Josie patted his arm. "It's okay. We're going home."

Thunder roared loudly, closer this time. Gray clouds seemed to have dipped down into the valley. The Barrows lived a good mile away in the opposite direction of the orchard. Josie realized with a start that, at this pace, they'd never beat the storm.

Grady pulled out of the driveway and turned toward town. Darkness was beginning to fall, enough so he'd put on his headlights. The smell of rain was heavy in the air that streamed through his window. He liked the earthy smell, liked to hear the patter of the rain on the truck's metal roof.

Lightning lit the sky south of town. He hoped

Peggy didn't close the diner early as sometimes happened when bad weather cleared town. He was hungry, and the only things in his fridge were butter, coke, and a few slices of crusty-edged bologna. He really needed to get to the grocery store.

The first drops of rain came in slow, heavy splashes on his windshield. They were followed by quick pelts of water. He rolled up the window and turned on his wipers. A roll of thunder echoed loudly through the canyon.

At least it had come after work hours. The orchard would dry out tomorrow and the apples would be ready to pick again come Monday.

Rounding a corner, he caught sight of two figures walking on the opposite side of the road. He recognized the bright blue shirt and slowed beside Josie and Mr. Barrow. Josie's head was ducked against the rain, a futile position. Her hair hung in wet strings around her face.

He put the window down. "Get in," he shouted over the rain.

She wasted no time, ushering Mr. Barrow into the middle before climbing in beside him. She pulled the door shut, set her camera bag on the floor, and wiped her wet hands on her jeans.

" 'Evening, Mr. Barrow." Grady put the truck in gear.

The man seemed oblivious to his drenched condition. Grady grabbed his hoodie from behind the seat and handed it to Josie. She used it to dry off Mr. Barrow's arms.

"I found him walking along the road. I guess he's lost." She dried the man's face, speaking to him now. "But we're going home, aren't we? Everything's going to be okay now."

Grady accelerated up the gradual incline. He thought of calling Mrs. Barrow on his cell, but there was no reception on this stretch of the road.

Josie was rebuttoning Mr. Barrow's shirt in the dim light of the cab and talking to him softly. The soothing sound of her voice discomforted Grady almost as much as her ministrations did. This wasn't a side of her he'd seen before.

He pulled into the short gravel drive and stopped beside the farmhouse. The rain pummeled him as he made his way around the truck. Josie had already helped Mr. Barrow from the vehicle.

As they walked the man up the porch, Mrs. Barrow burst through the door. "Ted! Where have you been?" Fright ignited an angry tone.

"I'm home," Mr. Barrow said as if it was any ordinary day and he was arriving home from work, sopping slippers and all.

"He was walking along Old Fork Road," Josie said. They ushered him inside.

"You're soaking wet," Mrs. Barrow said to Ted, then addressed Josie and Grady. "Thank you so much. He slipped out while I was fixing supper. Boone went looking for him, but I wanted to stay here in case he came home on his own. I'd better call Boone and let him know he's home."

Grady hadn't known how bad Mr. Barrow had gotten. Or maybe the symptoms came and went. He'd seen the man in the hardware store a couple of months ago and he'd seemed lucid.

"Are y'all hungry?" Mrs. Barrow asked after she made the phone call. "I can heat up some supper for you."

Grady met Josie's eyes, but she must've been thinking the same thing. The Barrows had enough on their minds without having company tonight.

"No, thanks, Mrs. Barrow," Josie said. "We'll be off now. We just wanted to make sure he got home okay."

The woman thanked them profusely as they left, then they darted through the rain into the dry comfort of the truck. Grady started the engine and backed down the drive, his thoughts heavy on the Barrow family and their difficult journey. It was a good thing Mrs. Barrow had Boone's help.

"I'm glad you came along when you did," Josie said.

Her hair was flattened to her head, one wet string strung across her neck like a rope necklace. Inside the house he'd noticed her lashes were wet and spiked. "It's not like you could've gotten any wetter."

She almost smiled. "True. But Mr. Barrow was getting anxious about the thunder. He kept wanting to duck into the woods, to hide or something I guess."

He turned toward town. "They have their hands full."

"I didn't realize it was that bad." Josie looked out the window into the fading daylight.

It was only then he realized he'd turned toward the diner without thought to the fact that he had Josie along now. "I was on my way to get supper at the diner." He checked his watch and saw he had twenty-five minutes until they closed—if they hadn't closed early on account of the storm. "I can take you home first if you want."

"Actually, I'm starving."

Aunt Lola didn't cook on Saturday nights, so they were on their own. Laurel and Nate often went out for a date night in Burnsville, but tonight they'd stayed home, just the two of them.

A part of him was relieved he'd get a decent meal, but another part realized it meant spending the evening with Josie. For some reason, that made him shift uncomfortably on the seat. He told himself it was on account of his rain-soaked jeans.

Josie grabbed the hoodie and ruffled her hair with the cotton material. "I must look like a wet dog."

"I can't look much better." His own hair was dripping after their slow trek up to the porch with Mr. Barrow. The rain had slowed now, and he turned his wipers to low.

Josie pulled at her shirt and it made a sucking sound as it left her skin. He should've taken her home for a change of clothing. Too late now.

He eased the truck into town, the headlights slicing through the fog. The rain-slicked roads reflected their glow as he pulled up to the diner. The windows were darkened, the neon Open sign off.

"They're closed," Josie said.

Grady's empty stomach let out a growl. "Bummer."

Up ahead, Maggie Lou was closing the Curl Up and Dye salon, the red of her dyed hair almost fluorescent under the streetlamp. She waved as she slipped into her retro Volkswagen Beetle.

Grady turned his attention to the problem at hand. The nearest restaurant was in Burnsville, but that was a good twenty minutes away.

"What do you think?" he asked.

"I think they roll up the sidewalks way too early around here."

He glanced at his watch. "It's eight forty-two. Respectable citizens are home in bed by now."

"And hungry ones are out of luck."

"There's always Burnsville."

"Either that or we could grab some snacks at Joe's."

He wasn't taking her to some smoky tavern. "By the time we get to Burnsville everything will be closed. And I need something more than pretzels and peanuts."

"I'd fix something at the house, but I hate to do that. Aunt Lola went over to Mr. Murphy's, and, well, Laurel and Nate don't get much time to themselves."

"You don't even want to see what's in my fridge."

"I'll take your word for it."

In the distance, the shimmering lights of Ingles mocked him. *It's what you get for going three weeks between trips to the grocery.*

Josie's eyes had gone in the same direction. "Are you thinking what I'm thinking?"

"That bachelors don't shop often enough?"

"That the only food in town is over there."

He pulled his eyes from her face and stared at the lit store. They did have a deli. And a few booths tucked away in the corner. If his mom ever found out he'd taken a woman to a grocery store for dinner, she'd have his head.

Saturday night at the grocery deli. "How sad are we?" Grady gave a wry grin.

Josie shrugged. "Look at it as an adventure."

Grady put the truck in gear. "Like I said, how sad are we?"

Josie reached for her fork, then paused when Grady bowed his head in prayer. She quietly set her fork down and tapped her foot under the table.

When he was finished, she popped a bite of grilled chicken into her mouth, then washed it down with a sip of coke. "This isn't bad."

She was warmer and drier after trading her shirt for Grady's hoodie, though her hair was a lost cause.

Grady grunted, slicing into his mashed potatoes with a plastic fork. His hair was just as wet, but somehow it only made him look more Marlboro Man. Life was so unfair.

"It's not Aunt Lola's, but at least it's warm," Grady said.

Their conversation turned to orchard business, then ventured off into new growing techniques and tree varieties.

After a while, Josie's stomach began its quiet churning, and she decided to call it quits. She set the fork on her plate and waited for Grady to finish. There was only a handful of shoppers in the store, and they were the only ones in the eating area.

Josie wiped her mouth with the paper napkin. "Thank you for supper. It was a unique dining experience." He'd insisted on paying since he'd kind of dragged her along.

"You're a cheap date," Grady said, then seemed to realize what he'd said. "Not that this was a date. I mean—you know what I mean." He pressed his lips together, probably figuring they'd gotten him in enough trouble already.

She watched Grady squirm in his seat, amused by his discomfort. Sometimes she wondered if he was as confident as he appeared.

Finally, he put his napkin on his plate. "Are you finished?"

"Yep."

They dropped their trash in the receptacle, but when Grady started for the exit, she grabbed his arm. "Where're you going?"

He looked down at her, his brows tilted. "Home . . ."

"Well, for heaven's sake, you said you needed groceries." Her hands waved, encompassing the store.

He slumped as if all his energy had left his body, leaving him wilted. "Aw, I don't want to shop."

"Men. You can be such babies. We're here, let's just get it over with. We could have it done in half an hour. Besides, with our quick supper, we've hardly given Laurel and Nate time enough for a quiet meal."

"Josie . . ."

She tugged his arm, enjoying the way her name sounded on his lips, the way his thick arm felt in her hand. "Come on, stop being such a man."

"I am a man, in case you haven't noticed."

She felt her lips twitch. "I've noticed."

Fifty-five minutes later, Josie understood Grady's dread. She watched him compare the prices on three packages of popcorn. Cost, price per unit, coupons from the flyer they found in the cart.

"At this rate, Laurel's babies will have graduated

from high school before we get back." There was a reason women did the shopping. "Can you just get the generic and be done with it?"

He looked up from his task as if suddenly aware of her presence.

"I'm all for a bargain, but, uh, my clothes are actually dry now."

"Aren't you the one who insisted I shop?"

"That was before I knew you were Mr. Thrifty."

She sighed, leaning on the cart handle. Her feet ached from being on them the past two weeks.

He set the generic brand in the cart. "There's no crime in being careful with your hard-earned money."

"There's careful and then there's—" She stopped at his glare, feeling her lips twitch again. This was almost fun. She couldn't believe she was enjoying Grady's company.

"Okay, I guess I'm done."

"Already?"

He tossed a frown over his shoulder, and she pushed the full cart forward to the register.

"Howdy, Grady," the cashier, Harmony Schneider, purred. She would've been pretty if not for the thick black liner rimming her brown eyes. She was barely into her twenties with a smattering of cute freckles on her nose.

"Evening, Harmony." Grady helped set the groceries on the conveyor belt.

She seemed to notice Josie's presence as she

scanned a can of chili beans. "Hey, Josephine."

Josie greeted her, suddenly realizing her mistake. When a man and woman shopped together, it indicated a certain intimacy. Not that Harmony had a big mouth, but a thing like this didn't go unnoticed in Shelbyville. By tomorrow the town would be placing bets on their wedding date.

Grady was loading groceries into plastic bags at warp speed, probably thinking the same thing. Harmony finished scanning the items, gave a total, then took the cash from Grady.

"Y'all have a nice night now," Harmony said, her eyes for Grady only.

He nodded good-bye, and they exited the store in silence. The rain had stopped, thankfully, but they set the groceries in the cab just to be safe.

Darkness swallowed the truck as they turned out of town and up the hill toward home.

"I guess that'll be all over town by daybreak tomorrow," Grady said.

"If not sooner." Oh well, she'd never let what people said stop her from doing what she wanted. She was half sorry she hadn't laid a big wet one on Grady right there at the Ingles checkout counter. Might as well give them something to talk about.

Heat flowed up her neck and settled into her cheeks at the thought. How long had it been since she'd been kissed, much less swept off her feet by passion? Too long.

She'd bet her favorite Birkenstocks Grady was a good kisser. Her eyes traveled to the left where his work-calloused hands gripped the wheel. She imagined what it would feel like to have those hands cup her chin, brush her hair back from her face. What it would feel like to have his lips close over hers.

"Some people and their crazy ideas." Grady was shaking his head at the notion of the two of them as a couple.

Josie closed her eyes, wincing. *Yeah. Some people and their crazy ideas.*

fourteen

Something was torturing her. Josie moved away, but it followed her, writhing, twisting. She jerked her legs, but they tangled in a knot. She kicked, trying to free them.

Something was ticking. She listened, zoning in on the sound. The alarm clock ticked beside her, bringing her more fully aware. She worked her feet from the sheet and rolled onto her side, pulling her knees toward her stomach.

The clock read twelve seventeen. She'd only been in bed an hour, and she was already regretting that slice of apple pie. She hadn't wanted it, but Aunt Lola was fine-tuning her recipe for the Shelbyville Apple Festival bake-off.

She smothered a moan as the nausea worked into

her throat. She tried to swallow it down, but it hung there stubbornly.

Her heart pounded, and she knew she was going to see that apple pie again. She bolted from bed and ran to the connecting bathroom, barely making it in time.

Sweat dotted her upper lip and cooled the back of her neck. She hung there, waiting, wondering if it was over.

She'd felt more nausea the last month, but this was the first time she'd vomited. It was getting worse. There was no denying it.

Josie flushed the toilet, hoping it wouldn't awaken Laurel or Aunt Lola, then sank down on the linoleum, leaning her head against the hard oak cabinets. Was this going to become a regular occurrence? How would she hide it from her sister? From Grady? She was going to be skin and bones by the end of harvest. Already, her jeans hung on her frame. She remembered trying so hard to keep her weight down in high school. She would've given anything for loose jeans then, but this was no way to lose weight.

She grabbed a towel from its hook and wiped her face, then closed her eyes, waiting for her stomach to settle. It had only been three months. She hadn't expected it to progress so quickly. But then, the doctor hadn't expected it to worsen at all.

Her thoughts rewound to that day. How many tests had she had leading up to it? She'd felt like a human guinea pig. And paying the insurance deductible from those tests had wiped out what little savings she'd managed to accrue.

"Have a seat, Josephine," the doctor had said. She was fiftyish with Carol Brady hair and a warm smile that was currently absent.

Josie sank into the chair across from the desk, feeling like she'd had a four-shot Americano, but in fact she'd skipped coffee altogether today. It was bad news. They never called you in unless it was.

"As the nurse told you on the phone, the results of the ACTH stimulation test are in. The test showed that your output of cortisol in response to synthetic ACTH is blunted."

The words made no sense. Josie swallowed. "What does that mean exactly?"

"It means that your adrenal glands are damaged. They're not producing sufficient amounts of certain hormones. That's why you've been feeling fatigued and having dizzy spells."

Josie tried to recall anything she could about the adrenal glands from her high school physiology class. She was drawing a blank.

Dr. Nichols continued. "Your adrenal glands are located above your kidneys. They're part of your endocrine system, and they produce cortisol, which gives instructions to practically every tissue and organ. Your body hasn't been making sufficient amounts of this hormone."

Josie's mouth was dry. "That sounds bad."

Dr. Nichols folded her hands atop the manila folder. "Your tests show you have Addison's disease."

Addison's disease? A tremor passed through her. She'd never heard of it. "Is there a cure?" But even as Josie said the words, she knew the answer.

"Not a cure per se, but a treatment. Most people who have Addison's function quite well as long as they follow the treatment. I'll be writing a prescription for a corticosteroid to replace the deficiency. It will mimic the amount of hormone your body would normally be making, thereby minimizing your symptoms."

The doctor's words jumbled into an auditory blur. Oddly though, the news settled into Josie as if it'd always been there.

Dr. Nichols was still talking, and Josie forced herself to listen. "It's especially important to monitor your health when you're facing a stressful situation or a major illness. We may need to increase your dosage during those times."

"What else?" There was more, Josie was certain, though how she knew it, she wasn't sure.

"As I said, it's very important to take your medication, and we'll work closely together to make sure we have you on the optimum dose, which will likely fluctuate from time to time."

She paused and seemed to be gauging Josie's response. "Although the disease can be managed, there is potential for something called an

Addisonian Crisis, or acute adrenal insufficiency. This can happen when the symptoms of Addison's suddenly become worse. The condition can result in death if left untreated."

Death.

She tried the word on, draping it over her shoulder, glancing in the three-way mirror to check the fit. She'd always thought of death as being black, but today the color of death didn't seem so dark or ominous. It wasn't white or bright red either, but a subtle hue that suited her.

Maybe she was just numb. Or in denial.

"I'll be writing a prescription for injectable cortisol that you'll need to have with you at all times." Dr. Nichols tilted her head. "I know this is a lot to take in all at once."

That was it. She was numb. It wasn't every day someone told you that you could die—that your body was malfunctioning.

"Here's a pamphlet with more information about the disease, including the symptoms of an Addisonian Crisis. One thing I highly recommend is getting a medical ID bracelet. And we'll need to set up another appointment in two weeks. Do you have any questions?"

She should have dozens of them, but right now, she was swimming in some kind of warm, fuzzy place. "No, I don't think so."

"Well, I'm sure you'll have more questions when you have time to digest this a bit."

Josie walked out of the office with two prescriptions. Mechanically, she drove to the nearest Walgreens and waited in the molded plastic chair while the prescriptions were being filled.

She watched people coming and going, browsing products, loading carts. People going places, buying things, while she waited for medications to treat her disease. It seemed odd this disease had been going on inside her body and she hadn't known.

Disease.

The word sounded foreign in her mind. *I have a disease.*

I have a disease.

This isn't what she thought she'd feel upon hearing such a diagnosis. She did feel stunned, maybe even numb, but there was something else. Something she was sure wasn't normal. As all the information settled in layers inside her, something rose from the midst like a spring of water.

She wasn't unsettled or panic-stricken the way she thought people felt upon such a diagnosis.

She felt something else. She struggled to put a word to the feeling.

It was a sense of inevitability. As if her life had been heading toward this point, none of it making sense until now. A puzzle that had no recognizable image until that one last piece had slid into place.

The disease was that last piece.

For the first time since Ian died, she felt things were . . . *right*. In the years since that night, she'd felt like a person who'd gotten away with a crime. The guilt of surviving had been a heavy load that weighed her down like an anchor.

Now, with the discovery of her illness, she felt like she'd finally been caught. There was relief. Great relief. The penance was easier to bear than the weight of guilt.

"Josephine Mitchell." A voice through the store intercom interrupted her thoughts. "Your prescriptions are ready for pickup."

Mechanically, she went to the window. A man with gray hair and ruddy cheeks took her money, then handed her the crinkly bag with the drug information stapled to it.

"Have a nice day," he said.

As Josie exited the store, she opened her purse and dumped the prescriptions inside, wondering why she'd bothered to fill them at all.

fifteen

*J*osie set the last plate on the table as the family entered through the front door.

"I knew they'd been watered," Aunt Lola was saying. Her matronly black dress swayed with each step.

Laurel ducked her head, laying her hand on her stomach. Josie thought she looked adorable in the white maternity dress that sported an empire waist-line and wide collar.

Nate followed his wife, a protective hand on Laurel's back.

"What's going on?" Josie asked as she finished setting the table.

"Little Miss Busy has been at it again," Aunt Lola said. "She weeded the beds and watered my flowers." She shot Laurel a look as she helped get the food on the table. "You keep your black thumb away from my flowers, missy."

"Not to mention, she should be *resting*," Nate added.

Josie had a feeling they were all wasting their breath.

Grady entered the dining room, a surprise. Having been gone the weekend before, she didn't know he ate with the family on Sundays. Josie grabbed another plate from the cupboard, flummoxed by the way her heart betrayed her at the sight of him in beige jeans and a black suit coat.

You'd better watch yourself, girl. It won't do any good to lose your heart to a man you're going to leave behind.

She placed the plate at his spot as he slid into his seat, and he offered her a half grin. Her heart was not cooperating.

"Missed a good service, Josephine," Aunt Lola said, carrying the plate of sliced ham into the dining room.

They'd invited her to church, but after her rough night, she'd slept in. "What was the sermon on?"

"Hellfire and brimstone," Nate said.

Laurel swatted him on the arm as he helped her into her seat. "Was not. Pastor Keeley taught on the Israelites and their grumbling and complaining."

"And the Smiths' new baby let out a wail at just the right time," Grady said.

Josie took her seat as Aunt Lola set the last dish on the table. She'd skipped breakfast, and the smell of baked ham stirred her appetite.

The family joined hands, and Aunt Lola began a prayer. "Heavenly Father, we thank thee for this wonderful Lord's day . . ."

Feeling Grady's hand around hers, Josie's insides fluttered like oak leaves in a summer storm. His hand was warm and strong. It wasn't the first time they'd joined hands, but something had changed. Their time together had shifted something inside her.

Grady had let his guard down, and Josie liked what was beneath it. Her thoughts returned to the night before when he'd dropped her off. After he'd parked and leaned over to open her door, there'd been an awkward pause.

" 'Night," he said. He was so close, his breath tickling her drying hair. She hadn't noticed how deep his voice was. In the darkness of the cab, all her other senses came alive. The touch of his breath, the sound of his voice, the musky scent of his cologne.

She found her voice. "Good night." Her legs trembled as she took the porch steps. She tried to tell herself it was fatigue, but her heart didn't quite buy it.

Now she startled as Grady pulled his hand from hers. The prayer had ended and she hadn't heard a word. She raised her head belatedly and grabbed her fork, hoping no one had noticed her day-dreaming.

"Mary Beth Keeley said she saw you two at Ingles last night." Aunt Lola regarded Josie, one eyebrow disappearing under her choppy gray bangs.

Josie's gaze skimmed Grady's face. He was busy cutting his ham, but she saw the faintest twitch at the corner of his lips. The rumor mill was oper-ating at full speed. Well, she didn't care what anyone said about her and Grady, or her absence from church. It was none of their business.

"Are you feeling okay?" Laurel asked. "You were up in the middle of the night."

Josie hoped she hadn't heard everything. "I didn't sleep well. It felt good to sleep in this morning." She hated that she felt compelled to make excuses for missing church. She respected her family's desire to attend. Why couldn't they accept her as she was?

"Maybe you can go next week," Aunt Lola said.

"I was thinking about going to Asheville next weekend." Actually, she hadn't thought that far ahead, but now that she'd said it, the idea jelled. She should call Jackie and Ashley and make plans. Her thoughts filled with shopping and fun and gabbing late into the night.

In Asheville there were no reminders of her past, no reminders that she wasn't good enough, no reminders of the guilt that chased her around the orchard like a swarm of angry bees.

Grady watched Josie mentally retreat. He wished Aunt Lola wouldn't press her about church. He didn't know her well, but he had a feeling pushing Josie was about as effective as trying to push a seven-hundred-pound hog into a bathtub.

He watched her slide a bite of potatoes into her mouth, her eyes fixed on her plate. He couldn't get the previous night out of his mind. Pictures of her guiding the cart through Ingles, flopping around in those wet sandals, sending him exasperated looks . . . he'd reviewed it a dozen times in bed, then a dozen more times during church.

They'd talked about the orchard while they'd eaten at Ingles. The woman knew her stuff, and he'd enjoyed talking shop with her. He could see her passion for the business in the way her eyes lit when she talked about new methods versus old, and semidwarfs versus dwarfs. He felt understood in a way he hadn't felt before, certainly not by

Danielle, who hadn't even liked the outdoors. It was refreshing and energizing to talk agriculture with someone who shared his zeal.

What is with you, Mackenzie? It wasn't good, this connection with Josie. He had to stop this nonsense. He ticked off all the reasons why.

Josie was leaving in a few months, and even though she seemed to fit in here, she was determined to go back to Louisville. Josie didn't appear to share his faith either, and that was nonnegotiable. On top of that, she wanted to sell the orchard and she was too much like his ex-wife. There was every reason in the world he shouldn't give her a second glance, yet here he was, tripping over thoughts of her.

But was she really like Danielle? She was so at home in the orchard, connected to it in the same way he was. And he remembered the way she'd dealt with Mr. Barrow. The way she'd been content to have a grocery-store supper. Danielle wouldn't have done either of those things, not without complaint.

"The ham was delicious, Aunt Lola." Josie suddenly stood and removed her plate from the table, but not before Grady saw she'd left half her food.

"How are we going to fatten you up if you eat like a bird?" Aunt Lola frowned.

"I'm not interested in being fattened up." A smile softened her words.

Josie carried her plate into the kitchen and he

could hear her footsteps as she took the back stairway. The woman didn't eat much.

"She was sick last night," Laurel was saying quietly. "I heard her when I got up to use the bathroom for the hundredth time."

"You mean throwing up?" Nate asked.

"Must've been that food at Ingles last night." Aunt Lola's gaze flittered by Grady.

Prickles of heat climbed the back of his neck. He hoped she didn't have food poisoning from their cheap night out.

"She's been getting tired easily, too, I've noticed," Laurel said a little too casually just before she and Aunt Lola exchanged a look.

Aunt Lola pressed her lips together in a firm line.

Laurel stirred her potatoes, her fork tines screeching against the plate, before she took another bite.

What was that about? The question had no sooner entered his mind than the dots began connecting. Vomiting . . . fatigue . . . Laurel had those symptoms at the beginning of her pregnancy.

Could Josie be pregnant? The thought weighted him like a brick tied to a balloon. Is that why Josie had been working so slowly in the field? Why she took so many breaks? He'd once seen her sway on the ladder and grab the rail, blinking. He'd thought she'd lost her balance, but maybe she'd gotten dizzy the way Laurel did sometimes.

Suddenly he wasn't feeling too well, the food

135

congealing into a solid lump in his stomach. If there was another man in Josie's life, that was just one more thing to add to his list of reasons to get the woman out of his head.

"Can we talk?" Laurel poked her head into Josie's room as she was about to turn off the light.

"Sure." Josie wore the hoodie Grady had loaned her the night before, telling herself it wasn't the smell of the jacket but the warmth that she craved.

Josie pulled the sheet to her chin, covering the sweatshirt. "What's up?"

Laurel perched on the edge of the bed, twisting her wedding band around a finger that looked like a little swollen sausage.

"I'm worried about you," Laurel said. "You don't quite seem yourself."

Josie had thought she'd been covering so well. She shook her head. "I'm fine." If all else fails, change the subject. "Hey, guess what? I found my old camera and took it out for a test run yesterday."

"That's great. You always did have a way with that thing. But don't think you can change the subject." Laurel nailed her with her hazel eyes, and Josie knew this was going to be a direct conversation. She was right.

"I heard you throw up last night."

She'd been afraid of that. Josie cleared her throat. "I guess that deli food from Ingles didn't settle too well. I'm fine now." What was she going to say next time and the time after that? Maybe she could get something for the nausea.

"You haven't been eating much. And you're tired all the time."

Josie pulled her knees to her chest, the pink sheet draped like a tent around them. "I'm not used to working in the heat, and I'm not a teenager anymore, in case you haven't noticed."

"Are you pregnant?" The bold question vibrated the air between them.

"What?"

"I'm intimately acquainted with the symptoms, you know."

She couldn't believe what Laurel was thinking. Josie's laugh was brittle. "Not unless it's an immaculate conception."

Laurel studied her face. "You'd tell me if you were . . ."

"I haven't had a date in months, Laurel, much less . . . anything else."

Her sister's shoulders slumped a fraction of an inch, her back hunched in an arc that left the mound of her stomach resting on her thighs. "Okay. I had to ask."

"One pregnant woman in the house is more than enough, don't you think?"

sixteen

*T*he weather was an accurate reflection of Josie's emotions. The sky, a gray abyss, promised a full day of rain. She could smell the rain in the air already. She'd been relieved when Grady had given the ladders to the others. With her balance problems, she didn't need any help from a wet ladder.

The Red Delicious apples were big and colorful, perfectly ripened and ready for picking. There were many Red and Golden Delicious trees, mostly on the outskirts of the area she'd avoided since her arrival. The creek.

Even now, she kept her eyes on her job, not wanting to see it. *Grab, twist, pull, bag. Grab, twist, pull, bag.*

But the nearness of the creek, the ripple of the current, was a constant reminder of its presence. The rain leaked down her face like misplaced tears.

Focus on your work, Josie. She shook her head as if to jar the memories free, then hitched the rough canvas bag higher on her shoulder. *Only one more day and you get away from here. Focus on that.*

She'd called Jackie early in the week and they were set for the weekend. The girls had even offered to split the gas cost with her. They were going to have friends over to the apartment Saturday night, a casual party that would no doubt result in Jackie trying to set her up with every single man present.

Josie wasn't interested, but that didn't matter. What mattered was getting away from here where the memories smothered her. At least when she was someplace else, there was some relief.

Asheville was her reward for making it another week. Something to look forward to. It was what kept her hands reaching up for the next apple and the one after that.

The migrants sang a jaunty Spanish tune, passing the time. Behind her, Grady pulled the truck and trailer forward, bringing it closer to the next empty bin. The tires bumped over the ground, the chains on the trailer rattling against the hitch as he pulled to a stop.

She wanted to broach the topic of selling the orchard again now that she and Grady were on better terms. Ever since their night out together, he'd softened toward her. She wasn't sure why, but what did it matter?

It matters, and you know it. Okay, so maybe she was crushing on Grady. What harm was there? It felt good to have a man looking out for her, being nice to her. He'd brought her a bottle of water earlier and suggested a break.

Grady walked toward her now, hooking a bag over his shoulder, then began picking the other side of the tree. They picked in silence awhile, though Josie was sure she felt Grady's eyes on her a few times. She was glad for the distraction from her darker thoughts, no matter where it came from.

"These look great," she said, bagging a deep red apple, smooth and supple in her palm.

A limb snapped back in place as he plucked an apple from its branch. "We had plenty of sun this summer. Turned out some nice color."

They bagged in silence, and when she'd filled her bag, she emptied it into the bin and returned.

"I've been thinking about what you said about selling," Grady said.

Josie couldn't believe he'd introduced the subject. "Yeah?"

"I'd like you to consider selling to me." He lowered his hands, peeking around a leafy branch at her.

To him? But Laurel had said he didn't have that kind of money. Why hadn't he said so before?

"It makes sense," he continued. "No outsider knows this place like I do. I'm sure I can keep it going and turn it around. I could make this place into an orchard your father and grandfather would be proud of."

"I'm sure you could. I didn't realize you were in a position to buy us out." Relief breezed through her, whistling a happy song. She never dreamed there was such an easy solution. She smiled at Grady, but he shifted his eyes to an apple as he grabbed it.

"Well," he said, "I'm not exactly, at the moment." He hurried on. "But we could work something out. You want to be rid of the property and I want to buy it. It might take awhile, but I could return the fifteen percent profit to you and Laurel each year."

Her relief deflated like an inner tube with a gaping hole. Fifteen percent of the profits? How many years would it take at that rate? And that wasn't counting the years when there was no profit. Or, like the year before, when there was a loss.

"Plus, I'd give you whatever I manage to save besides. I could get a part-time job during the slow season."

She addressed the most obvious flaw in his plan. "You won't be able to get all the pruning done alone as it is."

"You're not seeing the big picture. As this place grows, we'll be able to afford more help. We could have a self-pick area. I can see school field trips in the autumn, hayrides, campfires. We could have a cider press and sell our cider to local markets—"

"All that costs money."

"A lot of other orchards make it work. It's good extra income for minimal start-up costs."

She could see Grady's passion, had felt it in their conversation at Ingles. She hated to burst his bubble, but this wouldn't work.

Grady's cell phone rang, sparing her a reply,

giving her time to think about how to word her rejection.

He took his phone from his pocket and answered, leaving the tree and heading for high ground and better reception. She'd stopped bringing her cell phone to the orchard since she wasn't able to get reception out here anyway.

Maybe he could do everything he said. Shoot, he probably could with his knowledge and determination, but it would take years. Way too long to give her peace of mind. And even if he were buying Laurel out, it would still be her sister's responsibility for years. It would still keep Laurel from pursuing her own dreams. The twins might be in high school before the deal was complete, and that was if Grady managed to make the orchard profitable. Half her sister's life would be gone before the load would be lifted.

She couldn't live with that. She gave a wry laugh. She couldn't die with it either.

She heard Grady's words as he approached. "We'll be right over," he said into the phone.

Something was wrong. She could see it in his eyes.

He closed the phone. "That was Aunt Lola. She's been trying to reach you. Your sister's having contractions and the doctor wants her to go to the hospital."

"Contractions? It's too early."

He shrugged off his bag. "Come on, I'll drive you to the house."

She followed him to the truck and got in. *No, please. Don't let anything happen to the babies.* She didn't know who she was pleading with. God had never listened to her before.

Grady started the truck and pulled away, towing the trailer behind them. The orchard whizzed by as they bumped through the field. What if Laurel lost them? She was almost thirty weeks; were they big enough to survive on their own? The pictures from the sonogram flashed through her mind. Laurel had been so proud, so thrilled when she'd showed them off.

She couldn't shake the bad thoughts, couldn't shake the memory of her mother's difficult pregnancy and the devastating result.

"Aunt Lola thought you should meet Nate at the hospital in Burnsville."

They would save a little time that way. Could the doctors stop labor if it had begun? She knew nothing about this kind of thing.

"I'm sure she's going to be okay," Grady said.

"You can't know that." What if Laurel was doing too much? Heaven knew they'd had an impossible time keeping her off her feet. Maybe Josie should've stayed at the house instead of working the fields. Nothing was more important than Laurel and her babies, certainly not a bunch of apples. Let them fall off the trees and rot on the ground.

But that wouldn't do anything for Laurel's peace of mind.

They pulled onto the gravel drive that led to the house. "Are you going to be okay? Do you want me to drive?"

"I'll be fine. Is Aunt Lola with Laurel?"

"Yeah. Laurel called her at the store." But Aunt Lola didn't have a driver's license.

"Is she in much pain?"

"She didn't say."

A few minutes later, Grady pulled up to the house. They both jumped from the truck and ran inside.

Laurel was sitting on the couch, leaning back, her hands plastered to her belly. "Thanks for coming so quick."

Aunt Lola entered the room with their purses and Josie's keys. "You're all set. I'll be praying hard for you, Laurel. God will see you through this."

Josie and Grady helped her off the couch.

"Is it bad?" Josie asked.

"Not so much. But they're coming every ten minutes." She looked into Josie's eyes. "I'm afraid."

"You listen to me. You're going to be just fine." She was making the same promise Grady had made only moments ago, but the words seemed to strengthen her sister.

Two hours later Josie wished there were words to calm her own nerves. What was taking so long? She twisted the straps of her purse until they were too tight to twist any further. Nate had come out over an hour ago and told her they'd put Laurel on a fluid IV to see if that would stop the contractions, but she hadn't heard anything since.

Was this what her mom and dad had gone through? Or had it been a normal pregnancy up until the tragic birth?

That was a long time ago. Medicine has come a long way since then. This is Laurel and everything's going to be fine.

Meanwhile, Josie watched patient after patient being admitted and taken back through the double doors while she waited, wondering what was happening. The evening news was coming on a TV in the corner, put there, no doubt, to distract relatives from the fact that they were in the ER.

The entrance doors beside her whooshed open and Aunt Lola entered, her purse hanging from the crook of her elbow.

"I couldn't sit around the house all evening. I've been praying up a storm. Any word?"

"No, nothing since we last spoke. I tried to call Nate, but he has to keep his cell off back there."

Aunt Lola sank down in the chair beside her.

"How did you get here?" Josie set down this week's copy of the *Shelbyville Gazette*.

"Grady. He's parking the truck."

Warmth flowed through her, and she told herself she was just grateful for the company. Still, it was nice of him to bring Aunt Lola. He'd practically become a member of the family.

Josie and her aunt stared at the TV in silence until Grady appeared and took a seat on Josie's other side.

His denim-clad leg rested against hers, giving her a feeling of stability and strength. "Any word?"

Josie shook her head. "Nothing for over an hour. I guess it takes awhile to see if the fluids are doing their job."

Grady propped his elbow on the armrest between them and leaned back.

"Thanks for coming." She'd meant to say, "Thanks for bringing Aunt Lola."

His eyes met hers. Golden flecks shone under the bright fluorescent lights. "Sure."

The double doors opened, revealing a tired-looking Nate. He walked toward them. Josie couldn't read his expression.

She and Grady stood as he approached. "How's she doing?" Josie asked.

"Sorry it took so long. I didn't have anything to report until just now. The fluids didn't stop the contractions and her labor was progressing, so they gave her an injection of something that's supposed to stop them. So far it seems to be working."

Relief slumped Josie's shoulders. "That's great news."

"Thank the good Lord," Aunt Lola said.

Nate looked like he'd aged five years since this morning. "Well, keep the prayers coming."

Nate went back to be with Laurel, and she and Grady took their seats again. The medicine might be working, but Josie couldn't help but wonder how Laurel was going to get through the rest of the pregnancy. Would she have to be on bed rest? And if she did, how were they going to manage both Laurel's care and the orchard?

seventeen

*B*ed rest!" Laurel said. "I can't believe this is happening."

Josie pulled the worn quilt over her sister, then propped her hips on the side of the firm mattress. Laurel was washed out, her makeup long gone, her nose red from crying.

"Everything's going to be fine. You have to take care of those babies."

Laurel closed her eyes. "I know, I know. And I'm so grateful the contractions stopped. I was so afraid—"

"Well, you don't have to be afraid anymore. Your only job is to lie around and do nothing."

"I stink at that."

"No kidding. I'll go to the library and get some books tomorrow." Her weekend trip to Asheville would have to be canceled. Nate had called a family meeting to discuss how they were going to manage. They were waiting for her downstairs.

"I guess I could start cross-stitching and knitting again," Laurel said, a pout outlining her words.

"That's a great idea. I'll run over to Burnsville tomorrow and find some things for you to work on. Hey, you could do bibs or blankets for the babies."

"I guess so." Laurel sank deeper into the feather pillow.

"I'm going to let you get some sleep." Behind the fretting over the bed rest, Josie knew her sister was concerned that the contractions would start again. "No worries, now, all right?"

Laurel sighed deeply. "All right."

Josie flipped out the lamp and left the room. Downstairs, Nate, Aunt Lola, and Grady sat in the living room waiting for her. The clock ticking on the mantel was the only sound breaking the silence. Josie took a seat beside Aunt Lola on the couch. She guessed Grady really had become part of the family.

Nate seemed to read her thoughts. "I asked Grady to come since this is going to affect the orchard."

Josie nodded. "What are we going to do?"

"Someone needs to be here round the clock," Nate said. "The doctor doesn't want Laurel walking around."

Laurel's voice barreled down the stairwell. "I do not need a babysitter!"

Nate rolled his eyes and Grady grinned.

"Go to sleep, darlin'," Nate called, then lowered

his voice. "She means well, but I don't trust her to stay down like the doctor told her to do."

"I agree," Aunt Lola said. "Someone needs to keep an eye on her."

"I can't quit my job, obviously," Nate said. "And you can't do it, Aunt Lola. We need the income from the store, so we can't shut that down."

"And I need Josie in the orchard," Grady said.

His statement made Josie feel good. It felt good to be needed, even if it was only for picking apples and helping to manage the crew.

"Right," Nate said. "None of us can drop what we're doing, so that presents a problem."

"Can we pay a high schooler to come stay with her?" Aunt Lola asked.

Laurel would love that. Her own personal babysitter.

"I'd rather not if we can work around it, both for financial reasons and for Laurel's mental health." Nate gave a wry grin.

"How about shifts?" Grady suggested.

If they each gave a little less time to their jobs, they might be able to juggle it all. "That might work," Josie said.

"I could cut back my hours at the shop," Aunt Lola offered. "We're not busy in the mornings. I could open up at noon instead of nine."

"I could cut my day short, not take appointments after two for a while," Nate said. "I could be home around three."

"And I could take the noon-to-three shift." Josie looked to Grady for his approval.

He nodded. "That should work."

"I'm here all weekend," Nate said, "so that won't be an issue. And I can take over payroll, too, if she wants me to."

"What about sales?" Josie asked. Finding markets for their apples was imperative, otherwise they'd go to waste. "Should I take that over?"

"She'll probably want to keep doing those things. It'll give her something productive to do and keep her out of the kitchen," Aunt Lola said.

Josie nodded. "Sounds like a plan." Laurel wasn't going to be happy about it, but that didn't matter. Nothing mattered now but giving those babies a chance at life.

eighteen

*G*rady watched the family fall into a pattern over the next two weeks. Their shifts became as regular as clockwork. Laurel had taken up residence on the living room couch during the day where she could feel like an active part of the family. Josie had gathered up a basketful of things to keep her occupied.

Laurel had completed a bib for each baby and read enough books to start her own library, or so she said. Her mood had gotten progressively worse and tonight at supper she'd been downright snippy.

Not that he could blame her. He wouldn't want to vegetate on the couch for days either.

Josie worked in the orchard from sunup until eleven forty-five when she drove back to the house. At three fifteen, she reappeared, her old car spitting out blue exhaust. She did it all without complaint, even when he could tell she was exhausted.

Sometimes he found himself glancing at her stomach, wondering if Laurel's suspicions were true. She was a little thing, and he couldn't see anything that resembled a lump under her T-shirts. But women didn't show for a while, did they? As the days passed and the symptoms persisted, he became convinced Laurel was right.

The timer on the microwave dinged, and Grady opened the door and removed the swollen, steamy bag of popcorn. Somewhere outside a cricket chirped. With the microwave silent, the house was too quiet.

With the tension of Laurel's mood, he'd been eager to leave the main house after supper, but now the night stretched ahead of him.

He wished he had something to do.

And someone to do it with.

It was Friday night and his big plans involved the couch, a movie, and a bag of popcorn.

Pathetic, Mackenzie. It wasn't even that he minded a night at home. Shoot, he preferred it. But being alone all the time was getting to him.

He needed some single friends. But all the men his age in Shelbyville were settled down with two kids, three cats, and six chickens.

It was what he missed most about marriage— sharing life with someone. The Mitchells were great and all. They treated him like family, but there was something about that special bond between a husband and wife.

The bond Danielle broke when she cheated on you with your best friend?

Yeah, there was that. Grady filled a glass with ice water and sank into his favorite recliner, the worn leather creaking under him. He wondered what Danielle was doing these days. Last he'd heard she was dating some hotshot Chicago lawyer. He pitied the poor fool who fell for her. Of course, there was always the chance that she'd changed. Life had a way of doing that to you.

He grabbed the remote from the end table and flipped on the TV. "Looks like it's you and me again." He opened the popcorn bag and steam rolled out.

Maybe he needed a dog. He hadn't had one since he was a boy on the orchard. Barney had been a brown and white mutt they'd found alongside the road after school one day. He'd had him for several years until he disappeared. They never did find out what happened to him.

A knock sounded on the door, pulling him from his thoughts. He set the bag down and padded barefoot across the wood floor, bits of dirt sticking to the bottoms of his feet. He really needed to sweep.

He opened the door and Josie stood on the other side.

"Hey," she said.

"Hey there."

She held out a packet of papers bound by a paper clip. "Laurel forgot to give you these."

Printouts of the hours each employee had worked. "Oh, thanks."

Josie shuffled her feet, then put her hands behind her back. She looked adorable there on the stoop with the golden porch light pouring over her face.

She tucked her hair behind her ears. "Everything going okay with the crew? I feel out of the loop since I'm spending less time in the field."

"Everything's fine." They'd caught up on the schedule since Josie had arrived. The season looked to be the best he'd seen at the orchard.

With the door open, he could hear faint sounds of music coming from the migrant housing. They liked their parties on the weekend.

"Sounds like they're having a good time," she said.

"Not so much in the morning." He gave a wry grin.

She matched it with one of her own. "No, not so much."

An awkward silence ensued. The cricket chirped again. Once. Twice.

Maybe he should invite her in. Was she trying to say something and couldn't find the words?

Her gaze bounced off him. Finally, her shoulders fell and her tongue loosened. "Laurel's in a rotten mood. I know she's my sister, but man, I can't offer her a magazine without getting snapped at. And poor Nate. I think he's at his wits' end. I guess I just needed to get out of the house . . ." Her hands came up in a little shrug.

His own tongue seemed to be inoperable. *Invite her in, stupid. You were wanting company.*

Yeah, but Josie Mitchell? Is that a good idea? She was already pulling on his heartstrings, and time alone with her wouldn't diminish that. *You do not need another Danielle in your life.* He was surprised she hadn't run off to the city to shop or party or whatever she did while she was there.

Not to mention, she was quite probably pregnant.

She stepped back, looking sheepish and vulnerable. "This was stupid. I'm sorry." She turned.

"Wait." That was all he had—he hadn't thought any further. He crossed his arms. "Uh, you're welcome to hang out here awhile if you want. I was just getting ready to put a movie in."

Her face slowly brightened like the sky at dawn, and just as pretty. "You don't mind?"

"I even have an extra bag of popcorn." *What are you doing, Mackenzie?* He told his inner voice to shut up and opened the door wide enough for her to pass.

"Have a seat." He entered the kitchen and put the last packet of popcorn in the microwave.

"Can I get you a drink?" he called over the noise of the microwave, then opened the refrigerator. "I have—" He surveyed the empty fridge. Shoot. "Well . . . water or water." Why was he always in need of groceries?

"Water's fine," she called.

Grady fixed her a glass of ice water, and when the popcorn finished, he poured it into a big bowl and joined her in the living room.

"You haven't gone to the grocery since that night, have you?" she asked.

"So?"

She shook her head, then held up the DVD case. "*Jaws*?" Her eyebrows disappeared under her bangs.

"It was a busy night at the Pick-a-Flick."

She handed him the DVD and he put it in.

"I don't care what it is," she said. "By the time it's over, Laurel will be asleep, and that's all that matters."

He offered her a consoling grin.

She winced. "I'm awful. Being immobile is hard on her. I should just suck it up."

"Go easy on yourself. You have all weekend to suck it up."

She laughed. "Oh, thanks."

Grady flipped off the lamp, then settled in the recliner as Josie grabbed her bowl of popcorn from the coffee table. The faint glow of the TV lit her face. *I'd rather watch her than the movie.*

He snapped his head toward the screen. *I cannot believe you just thought that.* What was it about her?

She's just here to kill time. She wants to sell the orchard, remember? She is not your friend, much less anything more.

But curled on the sofa, her bare feet tucked under her, her mouth working on a handful of popcorn, she didn't exactly conjure up the picture of an enemy. A few moments later, she set the popcorn on the table and leaned back, resting her hand on her stomach the way he'd seen Laurel do in recent weeks.

He wanted to forget, just for tonight, that she might be pregnant. That she wanted to sell the orchard, that she was a little too much like his ex-wife. It was just a movie, after all.

Josie set down the bowl of popcorn. It had managed to upset her stomach even though it had been the blandest popcorn she'd ever had. She remembered watching Grady select this particular box. He'd vacillated between the store brand and a name brand for several minutes. He'd picked the wrong one.

The screen options came on the TV and Grady selected Play.

He looked at her, meeting her eyes, swallowing a

bite of popcorn. "It's kinda bland." His tone was apologetic.

"I wasn't going to say anything."

He fetched the saltshaker and shook it over his bowl, then offered some to her.

"No, thanks."

"I guess taste has to factor in there somewhere."

She shrugged. "Live and learn."

Grady forwarded through the previews as Josie glanced around the dim room. She was suddenly aware that before Grady lived here, it was Ian's house. She never came inside when he and Hank lived here. Their old manager liked his space, fixed his meals here in the house, and didn't come around her family unless he was working.

Ian, on the other hand, was a household fixture, butting in, usurping her father's attention. Every time she turned around, there he was. And her father with him. No wonder she could never please him.

Josie turned back to the screen. *Forget about Ian. Forget about everything else. Just relax and watch the movie.*

But it was impossible to forget Grady, stretched out on the recliner, his body claiming the entire chair. In the light of the TV screen, shadows flickered across his face.

"Have you seen this before?" he asked.

She shook her head. "I'm probably the only person on the planet who hasn't."

"It was a little before your time. Wait until you see the special effects."

The movie started, and Josie soon became wrapped up in the plot. She forgot everything but what was happening on the small screen. The movie was tense, and when the first shark attack came, she shrank back in her seat and closed her eyes. She hadn't expected the blood. And those teeth . . .

From beside her, she heard Grady's chuckle. "Can you believe how fake that—"

Screams screeched from the TV. And that terrible music.

"Are your eyes closed?" Grady asked.

"It's an old seventies movie and it said PG. I didn't think it would be this scary."

"Want me to turn it off?"

She wanted to know what happened next. She just didn't want to watch the scary parts. "No."

A few minutes later, he said, "You can open your eyes now."

She shifted, feeling a little silly under Grady's scrutiny.

"You know Spielberg directed this, right? I saw a documentary on him once. He was only twenty-something at the time, and it was the second film he directed. He wrote most of the—"

"Shhhhh." Now that the scary part was over, she wanted to hear what was going on.

"Yes, ma'am," Grady drawled.

They finished the film in silence, and Josie found several more scenes through which she closed her eyes. She'd never liked scary movies, but she thought an old movie wouldn't have enough realism to terrify her. Wrong.

When the credits rolled, Grady kicked in his footrest and shut off the DVD player.

"I am never going in the ocean again. Actually, the thought of dipping my feet into any body of water is now out of the question."

"I didn't know you were such a chicken."

"Even Laurel on bed rest isn't that scary."

His smile took her breath away. "You can pick next time."

His gaze darted away and his grin slid from his face as if he suddenly realized he'd just invited her over again.

"Deal," she said before he could rescind his offer. Laurel still had weeks to go on her pregnancy. "Maybe a romantic comedy . . ."

He groaned.

"You can close your eyes through the scary parts," she offered.

"Chick flicks are scary all the way through."

"Wimp," she muttered as she stood and stretched. After putting her bowl and glass in the sink, she walked to the door and slipped into her Birkenstocks.

When she turned to say good-bye, Grady was right there, opening the door. The scent of musk and pine overtook her. His face was inches from hers, the door frame at her back. Man, he was good-looking. His bangs hung roguelike over his deep-set eyes. Her breath caught at his closeness, trapping the smell of him in her lungs.

His gaze swept downward to her lips and her heart stuttered. Time suspended, her body froze. *Is he going to kiss me?* He had that look. She'd seen it before.

Do I want him to?

Before she answered the question, he stepped away. An awkward silence fell between them like a heavy curtain.

"Well," she said, then waited for a thought to form. Nothing came. *Say something.*

"Well," he echoed.

Why hadn't he kissed her? She was sure he'd wanted to. *You can reflect on that later, Josie. For now, say something.*

"Good night." "At least—" They spoke at the same time, then laughed nervously.

"What were you going to say?" Josie asked.

"At least Laurel will be in bed when you get back."

She shifted toward the open door. "True. Thanks for letting me hang out." Josie walked outside and crossed her arms against the breeze. It blew across her skin, raising chill bumps and erasing the awkwardness of the moment.

A long path of darkness lay between his house

and hers. Not even the moon and stars were out tonight to light her way. Outside the circle of the porch light lay a darkness so inky black it made her wonder what secrets it held.

The movie's music echoed in her head and the tension of the scenes clung to her like yesterday's nightmare.

He leaned against the door frame. "Good night."

"'Night." She started down the porch steps and exited the glow of the porch light. Her feet tapped along the flagstones, then swished through the damp grass. Darkness enveloped her, and she could hear her own heartbeat. An owl hooted nearby, startling her.

This is why you don't watch scary movies. You know better.

Behind her, Grady mimicked the music from the movie that warned of an impending attack. Brat.

She kept walking, not bothering to turn around.

The staccato music continued, cutting through the darkness.

"Shut up!" she called even as she quickened her pace.

Her only answer was a distant chuckle.

nineteen

*A*unt Lola's making your favorite cake for your birthday," Laurel said.

Josie handed her sister a glass of tea, then sank into the recliner. Her birthday was tomorrow, but she was leaving for Asheville after work for the weekend.

"I smell it baking." She hadn't tasted Mississippi mud cake since her last birthday here, her eighteenth.

"I wish you weren't going into the city tomorrow. We could order pizza and watch movies until late like we used to."

She felt bad for deserting Laurel, but she needed to get away. Especially on her birthday.

"I think I'll head to bed. Do you need help up the stairs?"

She shook her head. "Nate will be in soon. He's at a town council meeting. Peggy Tackett is stirring up the whole parallel parking quandary again."

"It never ends."

Josie went upstairs, shutting her bedroom door behind her. It was early, barely nine o'clock, but the disease had stolen her energy. All she wanted was to crawl under the covers and pull them over her head. At least she'd be working all day, staying busy. Then after supper and the cake, she could leave.

But when she awakened, it would be her birthday. She wished she could sleep through it. When she was away from here, it passed uneventfully.

She changed into her pajamas, washed her face, and flipped off the lamp. The sheets felt cool against her heated skin. Outside her window, an owl's lonely call sounded.

Even with the door closed, she could smell Aunt Lola's cake baking. The rich, chocolaty smell made her stomach turn. She hoped she could hold it down.

Jackie and Ashley wouldn't remember her birthday. She'd always let her birthday pass without a fuss. Especially after her tenth birthday when Aunt Lola had told her about the other baby.

It had been her first birthday without her mom. Aunt Lola had come to live with them, tried to fill the gaping hole her mom had left.

"Happy birthday, Josephine!" Aunt Lola appeared in the dining room doorway with Laurel, carrying a cake ablaze with ten flickering candles.

Josie's taste buds watered at the sight. She only got Mississippi mud cake on her birthday.

She was *ten*. Almost a preteen. Practically a young woman. The scent of chocolate and smoky candles and melted wax filled her nostrils as Aunt Lola set the cake in front of her.

"Make a wish!" Laurel said. At thirteen, Laurel had become a mother figure to Josie as well. When she wasn't bossy, they got along just fine.

She closed her eyes, her thoughts already spinning with wishes, when the scrape of her father's chair snagged her attention. Her eyes popped open.

He was out of the chair and walking away before Josie could say a word. His jaw was set, his shoulders a broad, hard line. She felt the rejection down to her dirty toes. It stirred like a hornet's nest deep in her belly.

Josie looked at Aunt Lola for some explanation. Was he sick? Angry? He'd always been in the background on days like this, her mom leading the celebrations.

But he'd never done this. Just walked away. She watched him now as he reached the top of the stairs, leaving her line of vision. She heard the door to his bedroom shut.

"Hurry up, now," Aunt Lola said. "Make a wish. The wax is melting all over my pretty cake."

With one last glance up the stairs, Josie closed her eyes. *I wish . . . I wish Daddy would . . .*

Josie bit her lip, thinking hard. She couldn't quite finish the sentence. Didn't know how to word what she wanted. *Want me? Accept me? Love me?*

Oh well. Wishes don't come true anyway.

She drew a lungful of air, then released it in a huff, blowing out all the candles.

Afterward, Aunt Lola cut the cake, and Josie ate the gigantic piece that was put on her plate, though she'd forced it down. It didn't taste so good this time.

Aunt Lola gave her a small box wrapped in glossy pink paper. The tag on the card read "From Daddy and Aunt Lola." But it was Aunt Lola's messy scrawl, and Josie had a feeling her dad didn't know what was inside the box any more than she did.

She pulled off the wrapper and opened the lid. Inside, nestled on a velvet pillow, was a silver necklace with a delicate heart pendant.

"Open it," Laurel said, leaning forward until her face was peeking over Josie's shoulder.

Josie pried the heart open with her blunt thumbnails. Inside, a tiny photo of her mom stared back. She gazed at the image. Her dad had removed all the pictures of her mom from the house. Aunt Lola said it was too hard for him to see them. Lately, she'd had trouble remembering what her mom had looked like. Her eyes began to sting.

"Thank you." It was all she could scrape out past her swollen throat.

She clenched the locket tightly in her cold fist. Now, when she had trouble remembering, she could just open the locket.

Aunt Lola blinked fast and began gathering the plates.

"Wait, I have something too." Laurel reached under the table and pulled up a limp package wrapped in the same pink paper.

Josie unwrapped a lavender crocheted hat. "Thanks, Laurel." She wondered how her sister had made it without her knowing.

"It's too hot for it now, but come winter, you'll need it."

"I love the color." She ran her fingers along the soft, fuzzy surface.

"You wanna watch a tape?" Laurel asked. "I got your favorites at Pick-a-Flick today."

"Sure."

Laurel scurried off to the living room to start the movie, and Josie gathered the candles from the table and carried them to the kitchen where Aunt Lola was running water in the sink of dirty dishes.

Her dad hadn't come back. Every now and then she could hear his footsteps overhead, could hear things banging around like he was angry.

"Aunt Lola?"

Her aunt turned off the faucet and picked up a plate. "What is it?"

She wasn't sure how to ask or even what it was she wanted to know. "Why did Daddy leave?"

Aunt Lola scrubbed hard, then ran clean water over the plate and set it in the strainer. "He's just having a bad day, child."

"He always has a bad day on my birthday." Josie hadn't realized it was true until she said it. But hadn't her father always seemed distracted on her special day? Wasn't he always like a ghost in the corner?

She thought back to Laurel's birthday, only two months ago. He'd taken them all out to Crusty's Pizza and he'd let her have Anna Tackett stay all night. The two had yakked half the night, keeping her awake, the sounds tunneling through their connecting bathroom.

Now Josie looked to her aunt for answers. Aunt Lola's mouth was tight, pressed into a flat line.

"Tell me." Had Josie done something wrong? Is that why her dad didn't like her? The thought drove a sharp peg into her heart. She'd never had that thought, though she realized it sounded true.

"Did I do something wrong?" The ache that had begun behind her eyes when she'd seen the locket formed tears that welled up, blurring her vision. She clutched the locket at her chest.

Aunt Lola turned. "No," she said firmly, then sighed hard. She looked out the window into the darkened yard. "I don't know why they kept it from you," she muttered.

A bad feeling started, swelling slowly, until Josie wasn't sure she wanted to know what Aunt Lola was talking about. She didn't like secrets. Not even good ones.

"It's not your fault. You ain't done a thing wrong, you understand?" Aunt Lola placed a finger under Josie's chin.

"Then what is it?"

Laurel called from the other room, "The movie's ready!"

Josie wanted to go in the living room with Laurel, wanted to go far away from Aunt Lola's answer, but her feet wouldn't move.

Aunt Lola answered Laurel, but her eyes never left Josie's. "She'll be right there." She turned and dried her hands on the towel hanging on the oven door, then scraped her hair off her face.

"All right, I suppose it's time you know. I sure didn't want to tell you on your special day, but now that your mom's gone and—" She shook her head like she needed a do-over.

Josie held the locket tightly, like it might protect her from her aunt's words. And somehow she knew she needed protection from them.

"When your mama was pregnant with you," Aunt Lola said, "there was another baby. Twins."

Twins? *When she was pregnant with me? How can that be?*

"What I mean is, you had a twin. A little boy. Your mama was pregnant with both of you at the same time."

She'd had a twin? Her breath caught. "What happened to him?"

Aunt Lola flinched. "He didn't make it, child. Sometimes these things happen. God knows what he's doing and we just have to trust in his plan. Your mama was almost to term when she went into labor and she lost him. Nearly lost you too."

How had she not known about this? Why had she lived and the other baby died? It didn't seem fair.

"Your daddy's just sad for the baby they lost."
Aunt Lola turned and picked up another plate. "I
suppose every man wants a son, and your daddy's
no different. Especially with the orchard to pass
down and all, he always had his heart fixed on a
boy. Your daddy—well, it's nothing you did. You
see that now."

Josie did see now. Her dad was sadder at the loss
of the baby boy than he was happy to have her.
And every birthday reminded him of what he'd
lost. Kind of the way the pictures of her mom
reminded him.

"When your mama got ill and passed away, he
lost all hope of having a boy, I suppose. You might
have noticed a headstone up at the family cemetery, next to your mom's. That's where your
brother's buried."

Josie had only been up there once, for her mom's
burial. And she hadn't seen anything that day but
the blurry shape of her mom's casket against the
frozen grass.

There was a new feeling where her stomach was,
like someone had turned it into a heavy, wobbly
water balloon.

"Your daddy's just sad today, is all. We need to
pray for him." Aunt Lola scrubbed the cake from
the plate.

Laurel called out then and Josie somehow found
her way to the living room. The movie played, but
Josie didn't see it. She wanted to go to bed, wanted

her birthday to be over. She didn't want another birthday ever again. Aunt Lola had said it was sadness that drove her dad from the table, but even at ten, Josie knew it was more than that. She knew her dad blamed her for her brother's death.

twenty

*J*osie escaped the house while it was still quiet and not quite light out. The ground was damp from last night's drizzle and the horizon hinted there might be more coming. Maybe the sky would open up and pour down on them, and she could leave early for Asheville.

As if to mock her, the clouds parted and the sun peeked over the hill. *Happy birthday, Josie.*

She zipped her jacket against the cool air and walked toward Duncan's pen. She'd bought a sack of oats to round out his diet. He'd turned up his nose at the grains at first, but then she'd started putting it out in the evening when he was hungrier.

Now he lumbered toward the trough, bringing his pungent odor with him, as she poured the oats in. "There you go, Duncan." He'd scarf down the donuts, too, but at least he had some grains in him. She'd try wheat after the oats were gone.

Boone's car pulled over the hill, spitting pebbles.

"Looks like your donuts have arrived," she said. Duncan didn't even look up from his meal.

"'Morning," she said when the car pulled to a

stop. She opened the back door and withdrew the boxes.

"'Morning, Josie."

Duncan snorted as she dumped the donuts into what was left of the oats. The smell of yeast and chocolate filled her nostrils. "Eat up, Dunky."

When she turned, Boone had joined her. He held out a colorful bouquet of flowers. "Happy birthday."

She couldn't believe he'd remembered—wished he hadn't—but it was awfully sweet of him. "Thanks, Boone."

Josie took the flowers, a spray of yellow daisies, chrysanthemums, purple asters, and miniature hot pink carnations. The wrapper sported a sticker with the Posey Peddler's logo.

He looked as shy as a schoolboy, standing there with his baseball hat in his hand. He'd always been so sweet to her. Spontaneously, she reached up and gave him a peck on the cheek.

His face bloomed as pink as the carnations. She smelled the flowers, breathing in their fresh, sweet scent.

"I heard you were driving down to Asheville today. Didn't know if I'd catch you before you left."

"I'm not going 'til after work." She hoped he hadn't mentioned her birthday to Jackie. But even if he had, her friend wasn't one to take note of things like birthdays.

"Apple Festival's coming up soon," Boone said, shifting his weight.

"Believe me, I know. We've been having apple pie for two weeks straight." And they'd probably be having it for the next month as Aunt Lola refined her recipe.

He grinned. "Aunt Lola took second to Nettie again last year."

"So I heard."

"So everyone in Shelbyville heard. Nettie wore that blue ribbon for a month."

"Aunt Lola's determined this is her year. Her pie is already a big seller for our store. Don't know why she has to have that silly ribbon."

"Well, I hope she gets it. Nettie's head is getting too big for that straw hat of hers."

Duncan snorted down the donuts noisily, and they watched in silence for a moment.

"You sticking around for the festival then?" Boone asked.

Josie shrugged. The good harvest would take them past the festival this year, which was fine since she wanted to be here when the babies were born. She hadn't made plans to attend the festival, but with the cost of gas and her draining funds, she'd probably be trapped here most weekends. "I suppose."

Boone set his cap back on his head. "Well, save me a dance on the square, ya hear?"

"Will do."

• • •

Grady pulled the coffee carafe from the maker, poured the brew into the thermos, then took a sip and unplugged the machine.

He'd done more research the night before and was eager to share with Josie how they could utilize the newer method of training the trees on a trellis. Instead of planting trees eight or ten feet apart, they could plant them eighteen inches apart and prune them to grow no higher than they could reach without a ladder.

He'd been wanting to move toward this method for a couple of years, but the orchard hadn't been profitable enough to make it feasible. They could start with a few hundred saplings though, and go from there. It would take several years before they produced apples, but it would be a start.

Grady put on his work boots, grabbed his thermos, and headed to his truck. He was thinking of asking Josie over for a movie. *Just so we can talk about the orchard.*

It wouldn't hurt to soften her with a chick flick before he broached the tricky subject.

Yeah, that's why you want her to come over.

He turned over the truck engine, and it rumbled loudly, breaking the morning silence. *You have all day, minus the afternoon, to talk about the orchard with Josie.*

Dawn was waking the night sky, and when he approached Duncan's pen, he saw Josie and Boone

173

near the fence. They were standing close together, then Josie reached up and kissed Boone. On the cheek? The lips? It was hard to tell from here.

Either way, the gesture filled his gut with lead and something else even less comfortable. Hadn't she been moony-eyed with Grady only a week ago? Now she was getting affectionate with Boone?

Just like Danielle.

Maybe she has an ulterior motive for getting into your head, did you ever think of that?

The thought had nibbled at him before, but he'd dismissed it before letting it settle in. She wanted to sell the orchard, and sure, she could do what she wanted as long as Laurel agreed. But it wouldn't hurt to have him on her side. Is that why she was being so nice to him, why she'd taken refuge in his cabin last week?

That was the thought that was circling his brain when he pulled his truck alongside Josie and Boone.

Josie turned a smile up at him. "Good morning."

He couldn't miss the bouquet she held. He lifted his chin in greeting.

" 'Morning," Boone called as he got in his car. "Well, y'all have a good one."

Josie waved, then turned toward Grady, but he was already easing his foot on the accelerator.

"See you in the field." He didn't care if she was put off by his abruptness. He'd been stupid to think she might like him and even more stupid to let a woman like her too close.

twenty-one

I wish you weren't leaving after supper,"
Laurel said.

Josie finished setting the table and took a seat
beside her sister. Grady and Nate hadn't arrived
yet. She felt guilty at the sight of Laurel's crest-
fallen face.

"You know I never cared much for birthdays."
The sooner it was over, the happier she would be.

Laurel looked like she wanted to say something,
but the door opened and Grady and Nate entered.
Her sister knew about her twin who had died, but
they never spoke of it. The topic had been avoided
throughout her childhood as if the mention of it
would be the final straw that broke their dad.

Guilt pressed down hard on her heart, a feeling
that had grown so familiar it was a constant com-
panion. A feeling that had only gotten worse when
Ian had died. *Died saving you. Saving someone
who'd never been meant to live in the first place.*

"Happy birthday, Josie," Nate said, settling into
his chair.

Grady's chair grated across the floor. "Oh, I
didn't know." His eyes bounced off hers. "Happy
birthday." The words were a reluctant concession.

Once they were seated, Aunt Lola started a
prayer. "Our dearest heavenly Father, we thank
thee for the many blessings . . ."

Grady's hand was warm and rough against hers, his grip just tight enough for their palms to be touching. He'd been distant all day. After their connection at his cabin, they'd been on friendly terms, but he'd been back to his old self in the field, speaking only when necessary.

". . . For it's in your good name we pray, amen."

Josie pulled her hand away, missing the contact. Aunt Lola and Laurel kept the conversation rolling during supper. Grady was quieter than usual, and Josie was counting the minutes until she could leave.

Just after supper was finished, Aunt Lola brought out the Mississippi mud cake with one candle flickering on top. It was like every birthday throughout her childhood. She could almost smell her dad's pipe and his Old Spice cologne. She could almost hear his footsteps as he walked away from the table.

Josie pretended to make a wish, then blew out the candles. Aunt Lola served the cake, and when they were all stuffed from the sweet dessert, Laurel handed her a small, lumpy package.

The paper came off easily, revealing a handmade strap for her camera. Tiny colorful threads were woven tightly in a wide band that would hold her camera securely. A thicker piece cushioned the part that went around the neck.

"I wasn't able to go shopping . . . ," Laurel said.

"Are you kidding? I love it."

"I noticed your camera strap—"

"Is falling apart," Josie finished. "It's beautiful. It must've taken weeks." She fingered the intricate webbing of the threads.

Laurel grinned. "What else do I have to do?"

"You should sell these online. Seriously, you could charge a fortune for custom-made straps."

"She's right, hon," Nate said.

Some of Josie's photographer acquaintances in Louisville would love one of these.

"Well, I may have all the time in the world at the moment." She patted her belly. "But once these two arrive, I won't have time to brush my teeth."

"Don't you worry. You know we'll pitch in," Aunt Lola said. She handed Josie a box wrapped with gold foil and a pretty bow.

"The cake was plenty, Aunt Lola." Josie removed the bow and opened the package. It was a box of chocolate pecan patties from Confectionately Yours, the chocolate shop owned by two of Aunt Lola's church friends.

A smile tugged at her lips. "It's been years since I've bitten into one of these. Thank you."

"You're getting too thin," Aunt Lola said. "And so far, my cooking isn't helping. A man likes a little meat on the bones, doesn't he, Grady?"

Grady pushed his plate back, clearing his throat. "Whatever you say, Aunt Lola."

A change of topic was in order. "Well." Josie scooted her chair back. "Thanks everyone. But I need to get on the road if I want to make it to Asheville before dark."

After kissing Aunt Lola on the cheek, Josie headed up the stairs for her bags, almost giddy with the thought of the weekend trip.

twenty-two

Josie wiped the sweat from her forehead with the back of her hand and reached for another apple. The sun was climbing high in the sky and its rays beat down relentlessly. Since she was perched at the top of the ladder, the sun had full access to her back, and she felt a trickle of sweat carve a path between her shoulder blades.

She could even smell the heat. Was it too much to ask for a little breeze? The crew started a slow tune, Hernando's bass voice carrying over all the others. She bagged another apple, grimacing when the branch snapped back and smacked her cheek.

It was one of those days. She'd left Asheville early this morning and made the trek home. Her stomach had felt unsettled all morning. She was hot and tired and drained. She'd enjoyed spending time with her friends, but she'd had a nightmare that clung to her like an itchy wool sweater. In her sleep she'd relived the night Ian had died. But this time, instead of the creek being frozen, it was a watery grave with rippling arms that sucked him under. She could see his face, his eyes.

Josie shook the haunting image from her head. Why had he done it? Why, when all she'd ever done was push him away? It was an unsolvable riddle that spun around her mind all the time.

The migrants' tune ended and no one started another. It was too hot to sing. Josie pulled a rubber band from her shorts pocket and gathered her hair in a ponytail.

Even so, the air that assaulted her bare neck was thick and heavy with humidity. She longed for the air-conditioning at the house or at least a cool breeze. Her throat was parched, her tongue clinging to the roof of her mouth.

Maybe she needed a water break. Josie checked her watch. It was nearly time to relieve Aunt Lola, but she might as well finish the tree. She reached for a distant apple.

The motion disoriented her, and a wave of dizziness washed over her. Her head swam. She blinked hard and swayed.

Josie grabbed for the ladder, but she was already falling. Her arms reached for the ground even as her feet tangled in the rungs.

She hit the ground with a thud. The ladder crashed beside her, clanging as it landed.

"Josie!"

She heard her name in that instant before her brain registered the pain in her knee and on her palms. She took stock of her body parts.

Does anything else hurt? She rolled over and sat up. Her hands had broken her fall. *You're okay.*

"*Señorita* Josie!" Miguel was the first one to her side.

"I—I'm okay."

Grady was there, kneeling at her side. "Don't move." He poked around her knee, dusting away the grass clippings and dirt.

It was scraped and already red. It hurt like the dickens.

"Does anything hurt?"

My pride? It was sprained at least, possibly fractured.

"I'm fine. Just let me up." She brushed his hands away and pulled herself to her feet.

Miguel was picking up the ladder. Hernando gave her a bottled water.

"*Gracias*, Hernando." She uncapped the bottle and drew from it, feeling sillier by the moment.

"Can you walk?" Grady asked.

Josie capped the bottle. "Of course I can walk." She took a step and her leg nearly buckled under her.

He reached out as if to catch her, but she caught herself and batted away his hands. "I'm fine." She took a few steps. Her knee was fine. Just a little sore.

"You get dizzy, Miss Josie?" Miguel asked. "You need to get out of heat."

Her dizziness wasn't from the heat, but it was a

convenient excuse. "Maybe so. It's time to relieve Aunt Lola anyway." Josie started for her car.

Grady caught up to her. "I'll drive you."

What, he was being so nice all of a sudden after ignoring her all day? "I can drive myself." She tried to walk without favoring her good leg and winced.

"Stop being so stubborn." He took her elbow and steered her to his truck and opened the door.

Fine. Have it your way. She didn't understand the man. One week he was distant and brooding, the next he was teasing her, and the week after that he was back to being distant and brooding. *Like I need more complications in my life.*

Grady started the truck and it roared to life, covering the thumping of his heart. Josie had given him the scare of his life.

He'd seen her climbing the ladder over an hour ago and had almost stopped her. A woman in her condition shouldn't be working on a ladder. He'd bit his tongue though, and now look what happened.

When he'd heard the sickening thud of her body hitting the ground, heard the smash of the ladder falling behind her, his stomach was in his throat. He should've said something. He shouldn't have let his foolish pride stop him.

He slapped the steering wheel, then felt Josie's sharp glance.

"I could've driven myself. I'm fine." He couldn't help but notice the way her hand lay protectively over her flat stomach.

"You shouldn't have been on the ladder in the first place."

"It's a little hard to pick the top of the tree without one."

"You're in no condition for that job."

He rounded a bend, then gunned the engine, taking them up the hill. In the rearview mirror, dirt rolled out from the wheels, making a plume of dust.

"Condition?" she asked.

Well, he'd done it now. Stepped right in a pile of cow dung. There was no going back now, and it served her right anyway. How long did she think she could conceal it? She wasn't showing yet, but in another month or two . . .

He unlocked his teeth. "I know about the—the baby." He didn't dare look at her. She might see the things he was working so hard to hide. But, darn it, why didn't the woman take better care of herself?

"The *baby*?"

"I might be a man, but I'm not stupid. I saw Laurel go through all that, remember? The dizziness, the nausea, the fatigue—"

He was interrupted by a bark of laughter. "What is it with everyone?"

He glared at her. She was laughing? Wasn't she the least bit concerned for the—

"I am not pregnant." She pressed her fingers to her temple, mumbling. "Are you kidding me? My last date was . . . too long ago to remember."

"Why the nausea? The dizziness, the fall off the ladder?"

She looked out the window, the smile fading.

"It's hot, in case you haven't noticed. I guess I don't tolerate it very well. And I'm not used to working outside all day in the heat."

"That's all?"

She turned and looked him squarely in the eye. "I am not pregnant. Not now, never have been."

She looked sincere, her eyebrows raised, her head tipping slowly forward, waiting for him to reply.

She held up two fingers, locked together, a sarcastic smile on her lips. "Scout's honor."

He applied his foot to the brake as he slowed for the turn. His lips twitched as he pulled into the drive. She'd probably never been a scout. Even so, he believed her.

A slow whoosh of air drained from Grady's lungs. Relief that she wasn't involved with someone. His reaction should've scared him, but instead left him buoyant and hopeful.

twenty-three

*J*osie grabbed the tire swing, put her legs through the opening, and pushed off. The scent of lilacs carried on the breeze from the bush at the corner of the house, and she inhaled the familiar smell. Four days after her fall, the pain in her knee had subsided, and even the dizziness and nausea had faded.

Maybe I will make it through harvest. If she could just get the job done, convince Laurel to sell, and get back to Louisville before her health declined further. She didn't want Laurel to see her like that, didn't want to be a burden on her sister. And she didn't want anyone to stand in the way of her decision.

"Hey there." Nate came through the back door and sat on the stoop. He'd shed his dress shirt in favor of a beige T-shirt.

"Hey." The swing's motion was starting to affect her equilibrium. She dragged her feet through the long grass, scraping to a stop.

Nate looked like a dog who'd been kicked to the curb. Laurel hadn't been in the best of moods over supper, and to give Nate credit, he'd spent the evening trying to make her comfortable.

"Needed an escape?" she asked.

"This isn't her best side. Poor thing, she's miserable."

"The hormones don't help."

He nodded thoughtfully. "She enjoyed making that camera strap for you. She showed me her progress every night."

"It's beautiful and unique. She really could sell those, you know." Josie wrapped her arms around the tire and propped her chin on it. The faint smell of worn rubber reached her nose.

"I think it's reviving her dream of selling crafts."

"Really?" Maybe the bed rest was what she needed to remember her passion. She'd been so busy meeting all her obligations that she'd forgotten what she loved. Laurel used to talk all the time about owning a shop where she sold her hats, scarves, and handmade accessories. Maybe she couldn't open a shop for a while, not with the babies coming, but these days selling things was as simple as having an eBay account.

"Maybe it would be a good time for you to mention selling the orchard again," he said. "She might be open to it now."

"Or *you* could mention it . . ."

Nate stood slowly, shoving his hands in his pockets. "Or *you* could . . ."

"Coward." Josie pulled a face. "All right, I'll do it. But I'm waiting for a better mood."

He tossed a sardonic grin over his shoulder. "Smart move."

After he left, Josie closed her eyes. A gentle breeze cooled her skin. The tree above her shimmied, its leaves rustling, and somewhere on the hill two birds tweeted back and forth in conversation.

A distant rumble grew louder until she heard the popping of gravel and the squeal of tired brakes. When she opened her eyes, Grady was pulling his truck to a stop, his elbow protruding from the gaping window.

She hadn't expected to see him after supper. He wore a clean T-shirt and a timid smile.

"That's a precarious place for a nap," he said.

"Not as precarious as in there." She jerked her chin toward the house.

His grin widened. Did he have any idea how handsome he was? No, that was part of his appeal.

"I think I owe you a movie if you're up for it." He reached for something, then held up a white plastic bag.

"Whatcha got? Let me guess. *Jaws 2*."

"Give me some credit. I promised you a chick flick."

This ought to be good. The thought of him facing Berta Combs at the Pick-a-Flick checkout with a chick flick amused her. That must've put a dent in his masculinity. "You picked a movie for me?"

"Three of them. And you'd better say yes because I'm not going through that process again."

She untangled her feet from the swing. "How can a girl refuse an offer like that?"

Josie hopped in the truck, and he drove her to the

cabin. Once there, he opened the door for her, then disappeared into the kitchen.

"Popcorn?" he called.

"No, thanks. I'm still full from supper."

A few minutes later, he returned with two glasses of soda.

"Been to the grocery, I see."

He shot her a look and handed her the bag with the DVDs. "Take your pick."

The bag yielded a surprisingly good selection: *The Lake House*, *While You Were Sleeping*, and *You've Got Mail*.

"You totally had help with this." Josie sank onto the sofa.

He perched on the recliner's edge. "I'm in touch with my feminine side."

The remark, a sharp contrast with the bulk of his frame and the manly squareness of his jawline, drew a cynical smile from her.

"Okay, so I had a little help." He flipped on the TV.

"Well, whoever advised you has impeccable taste. I love all three."

"You've seen them all?"

"I could watch any of these a dozen times." Josie shuffled the cases in her hand, deciding.

"We probably have time for two if you want."

She handed him *You've Got Mail*.

He looked at the cover. "Tom Hanks and Meg Ryan, huh?"

"You're in for a treat."

He humphed.

While he put in the DVD, she set her soda on the end table and propped her bare feet on the stuffed ottoman. Her toenails bore the remnants of pale pink polish that Jackie had loaned her upon seeing her neglected feet. When he started the movie, she flipped the light switch and the lamps went dark. Evening light filtered through his bare windows.

He settled in the recliner, but she wished he'd opted for the sofa. He seemed so far away. *Get a grip, Josie. You're here for the movie, to escape the hormonal path of your sister, not to cozy up on the couch with Grady.*

She shifted sideways so the TV was her focus.

Almost two hours later, she'd forgotten everything but the growing romance between Kathleen Kelly and Joe Fox. By the time Brinkley trotted around the bend in the park, Josie was hugging a pillow, wishing the movie wasn't almost over.

Her heart softened as the two came together. *"Don't cry, Shopgirl, don't cry."*

"I wanted it to be you. I wanted it to be you so badly."

The couple embraced, Brinkley jumped on Joe, and the camera floated upward, looking down on them as the soundtrack played "Over the Rainbow."

Ah, what a movie. Josie slowly became aware of

her surroundings as the credits rolled. She glanced at Grady, wanting his take on the movie.

Before she could ask, she heard a snort over the soundtrack. The night had colored the sky inky black and only the flickering TV lit the room. Even so, she could see Grady's eyes were closed, his mouth open.

She squeezed the pillow with her fist and hurled it at him Frisbee-style. It hit him square in the chest.

He jumped, opening his eyes, looking around.

"You have got to be kidding me," she said.

"What? Why'd you do that?"

"Have you no shame? *You've Got Mail* is a *classic*, arguably the most romantic movie of all time."

He sat up straight. "I was just resting my eyes."

"You were snoring."

He stood and stretched. "I think I'd better go make some popcorn."

If he was tired, maybe she should leave. "We don't have to watch another one."

"Might as well," he said over his shoulder. "I have to return them tomorrow." She watched him walk to the kitchen, his long denim-clad legs taking their time.

She decided on *The Lake House* and put it in the DVD player. It was more guy friendly.

"Ready for popcorn?" he called.

She remembered the bland variety from last time and was about to turn it down.

"I got the good kind."

She was tempted, especially now that the buttery smell of popping corn wafted into the room. Still, she didn't want to get nauseated. "No, thanks," she called.

When Grady returned he started the movie and settled into the recliner, munching away.

It took her awhile to get caught up in the movie. She was too conscious of Grady sitting across the room. When he finished his popcorn, he thrust his legs out on the leg rest and laced his hands together across his stomach.

Focus on the movie.

Awhile later, she peeked at Grady again. He was still awake, a good sign.

As the movie zinged back and forth through time, Josie felt her limbs getting heavy. It had been especially hot, and she was used to turning in early these days. The sun sapped her energy, and the long days in the orchard were taking a toll on her body.

She sank deeper into the sofa and laid her head back on the soft cushion. She was going to regret staying up late when the alarm sounded in the morning. Still, it was Friday night, and a girl had to have a life. At least it wasn't a scary movie.

Grady still seemed to be watching with interest. It was a movie you had to follow closely or the movements between time became confusing.

Josie curled her legs under her, and when her toes grew cold, she tucked them between the cushions, feeling the nubby material of the sofa against the balls of her feet. She grabbed the other pillow and put it under her cheek. With each breath, she smelled the unique combination of pine and musk that was all Grady.

Before she could stop herself, she inhaled deeply, wanting to hold the air in her lungs for a while longer.

The cushions of the couch seemed to envelop her, and her tired bones sank gratefully into them. The movie played, and out on the porch, a cricket kept time with a hypnotic rhythm.

After a while, a quiet hush replaced the chirping.

Then someone was calling her name, but she didn't want to answer. The soft peace of the world where she lay was not easily abandoned.

"Josie." A man's voice.

Then a whisper of a touch across her cheek.

Her eyes opened and she stared up at Grady. Credits were rolling on the muted TV. She was sprawled on his couch. He was perched on the edge, his hand stretching across her to the sofa's back.

"Resting your eyes?" His words barely broke the silence.

She'd slept so hard she'd forgotten where she was. But now that she remembered, now that Grady was so close, his hip grazing her thigh . . .

• • •

Grady watched Josie register her whereabouts. He'd known she was asleep the last thirty minutes of the movie. He'd lost interest in the story, taking the opportunity to observe her unnoticed. He'd watched her breathing, her limbs going loose around the pillow, her face softening. A lock of hair had fallen across her cheek, and he'd wanted to brush it back, tuck it behind her ear.

It was the first thing he'd done when he'd come to wake her up. Now, as she stared at him with those sleepy eyes, he wanted to do more than wake her.

He reached out again and brushed the hair off her shoulder, wanting to feel the soft silkiness between his fingers again.

When he looked back into her eyes, there was a question. He had plenty of his own, but right now, he didn't want to think about that.

Right now he thought about how gentle Josie had been with Ted Barrow. He thought about the way she waited on her sister, the way she sassed him sometimes with her sarcasm.

But underneath it all, in the depths of her eyes, there was an indefinable sadness. Even now, her eyes locked on his, he saw it.

And wanted to eradicate it. He closed the distance between them, brushing her lips with his. The barely-there touch sent a jolt of something electric through him.

She returned the kiss, yielding to him. He pulled her closer. His heart felt like it might explode from the confines of his rib cage. He hadn't felt this way since . . .

Had he ever felt this way? Even in the early days with Danielle?

Danielle.

The memory of her betrayal tainted the moment and he pushed it away.

Josie touched his face, her fingers gliding down his jaw, leaving a hot trail.

Slow down, man. You have got to slow down. Think.

But it felt so good, the way she returned his kiss. Being wanted again, he'd forgotten how heady it could make a man feel.

Danielle made you feel wanted too, remember? Then she slept with your best friend.

Josie wouldn't do that. She's not like that.

Isn't she? How much do you really know about her?

It was true. He'd only known her a matter of weeks. Gathering all the restraint he could muster, he pulled away.

Josie's eyes opened, filled with questions again. Different ones. Ones he didn't want to answer.

He looked away before he could be drawn back in. Somewhere on the porch a cricket chirped, and over the thudding of his heart, he gradually became aware of the faint strains of the crew's music.

He shouldn't have kissed her. They had to work together. She was going to leave in a matter of weeks. She wanted to sell the orchard.

"I'm sorry." He ran his hand over his face, trying to erase her touch. It was the movies, all the romance. It got him thinking wrong.

Josie was still and silent. What was she thinking? God only knew.

twenty-four

*S*orry? *He's sorry?*
Josie lay on the couch, a ball of mortification curling in her gut. Clearly she hadn't been sorry. That had been evident in her feverish response to his kiss.

Sorry?

Not exactly the magical movie ending to their first and probably only kiss.

He stood and distanced himself from her. And that's what he was doing; it didn't take a genius to see it.

She cleared her throat, sitting up, then swung her feet to the floor. She wanted to escape, but the humiliation was going to follow her like the stench of a skunk.

"I shouldn't have done that," he said, apparently not realizing he should quit while he was ahead. Or at least no further behind than he already was. Didn't he know it was the last thing she wanted to hear after he'd kissed her socks off? It was like taking a beautiful Ansel Adams photograph and smearing it with ink.

"It's okay." It was the only thing she could say at a time like this. What else was there? *Really? I'm not.* Pride removed the option of honesty.

Standing, she found her Birkenstocks by the door and slid into them.

"No, really—," he continued, making a half-hearted effort to approach her.

He was going to say it again. *Stupid man.*

"I should be going," she cut in quickly. "It's late. We're tired." Yeah, that's what it was. Fatigue. It made them connect like supercharged magnets and then forced those lame words from Grady's mouth.

"Josie—"

"It's okay. See you in the morning." She slid out the door and pulled it behind her. She took the porch steps quickly and hurried outside the halo of the porch light as if she'd disappear when she reached the darkness. If only.

She hugged herself against the chill in the air. There was no moon to light her way tonight, and her foot hit the corner of a flagstone, tripping her. As her foot caught her weight, her knee buckled, igniting the pain that had nearly healed from her fall off the ladder.

I'm sorry.

What was he sorry about anyway? Sorry he was

attracted to her? Sorry he'd shown a little emotion? Sorry their kiss had lit a bonfire under him?

Or maybe it hadn't. Maybe it had only lit a fire under her.

Oh, there's a nice thought.

If that was the case, he had plenty to be sorry about.

It was just a kiss, Josie. Just a stupid, ordinary kiss between two consenting adults. A kiss he was sorry about.

Her feet swished through the grass as she passed the side of the house. The swishes seemed to repeat the word she wanted to forget. *Sor-ry, sor-ry, sor-ry.*

She was relieved when she reached the porch and left the echo of the word in the yard. Upstairs, she readied for bed, tossing aside the hoodie she still hadn't returned to Grady, and flipped off her lamp. Upon closing her eyes, her traitorous mind reviewed the kiss in slow-motion detail. Her breaths thinned at the memory.

Aggravated with herself, Josie flopped over hard, punching down the pillow.

She was the one who should be sorry. Why get attached to Grady? He was tied to a place she wanted to escape—a place she needed to sell.

There was no future here. No future at all.

She was the one who was sorry. She humphed aloud as if the punctuated sound could make the statement a reality, then pulled the sheet over her head.

· · ·

"Okay, spill," Laurel said the next afternoon, the second the door closed behind Grady. Nate had gone to mow while there was still daylight, and Aunt Lola was cooking supper.

Josie eased onto the couch beside Laurel and flipped on the TV. "What do you mean?"

"Don't play innocent with me. The tension was thicker than a valley fog in here."

"Don't be melodramatic." To the contrary, the day had been anticlimactic. Josie had tossed in bed all night, fretting, yet Grady hadn't said a word about the kiss.

Laurel grabbed the remote and flipped off the TV.

Josie noted the frown lines between her sister's hazel eyes.

"Listen here. I'm stuck in this house all day and night with nothing but my knitting needles for company, and if you have a juicy detail or two, I think you should show a little mercy and share, don't you?"

"When you put it like that . . ."

"Did something happen last night?" Laurel turned toward her, tried to pull her knee up, then gave up when her stomach got in the way. She leaned forward, eager like a cat that just heard a can opener.

"We watched a movie. Two, actually."

"Yeah, yeah. What happened after?"

Josie sighed. "Don't you want to know which movies we watched?"

"Fine. What were they?"

"You've Got Mail and *The Lake House."*

She nodded. "Good picks. Go on."

Josie's thoughts went back to the night before for the hundredth time. The way Grady's lips had felt on hers. He'd been so gentle, his touch the barest of whispers. Just the thought of it sent a shiver up her spine.

"Earth to Josie." Laurel wore an expectant grin.

"Sorry. Okay, after the second movie, or actually, during the second movie, I kind of dozed off."

"You fell asleep?"

"Well, he dozed during *You've Got Mail."*

"Never mind. Keep going."

"Well, I'm trying, but you keep interrupting."

Laurel made a zipping motion across her lips.

"Okay, so I dozed off, and next thing I know, I wake up and the movie's over." He'd been perched there, so close, and the look on his face . . . Ah, if she could bottle that look and sell it, she'd be a millionaire.

"Anyway, he's sitting there on the edge of the couch."

"Wait, where are you?"

"On the couch. When I woke, I was lying on my side and he was sitting, like, in the cradle between my arms and knees. Sheesh, you really are desperate."

"Shut up. No, go on."

"He was looking at me like . . . I don't know. I can't explain it. And then he brushed my hair back and kissed me." She shrugged. "That's it."

"That is so not it. Was it just a touch? Or was it more passionate? Where did you put your hands? How long did it last?"

Josie shrugged. There was no way she was going to admit it was the best kiss she'd had. "It was nice." *Liar. It was way more than that.* "*Was* being the key word."

"What do you mean?"

Even now the memory put a hole in her stomach. "Remember when you waited all summer for Evan Rodgers to notice you? Remember when he finally kissed you?"

Laurel's brows knotted. "Yeah . . ."

"Remember what he said afterward?" Her sister had been devastated. Especially when Evan had gotten back with his ex-girlfriend the following week.

The lines eased off Laurel's forehead and her mouth tightened. "Grady did not say he was sorry."

Josie nodded.

Laurel leaned back on the cushion and laced her hands over her swollen belly. "Men can be so stupid. What did he say this morning?"

"He acted like it never happened."

Laurel seemed to be digesting this bit of information. Well, if she could figure it out, more power to her.

"He may not have said anything," Laurel finally said. "But I'm telling you, there were vibes bouncing all over the room a minute ago. Trust me, pregnancy has boosted my intuition."

Pregnancy had done more for her moods than her intuition, but Josie wasn't going to be the one to say it.

"No, really," Laurel said. "It's true. Anyway, there ought to be something positive to balance out all this other stuff. Speaking of which, I gotta go to the bathroom again. I swear I have a bladder the size of a peanut. Don't go anywhere, we're not done yet."

Josie helped her off the couch and Laurel waddled across the room and down the hall.

Josie went to the kitchen and offered to help Aunt Lola, but she was shooed away. When she returned to the living room, Laurel was plopping back in her spot next to the end table.

"Need anything? More tea?" Josie asked.

"No, thanks. So, why do you think he was sorry?" Laurel switched gears with the delicacy of a Ford beater.

Josie sighed. "I don't know." *As if I haven't been circling that thought all day.* Circling like a vulture, round and round and round, never finding a spot to land.

"Were you?"

"Was I what?"

Laurel gave her a *hel-lo?* look. "Sorry. Were you sorry, or were you hoping it would lead somewhere?"

Josie gave it some thought. Actually, she'd given it thought all day, picking apples, trying to ignore Grady's presence. Who was she kidding? He was her focus all day, whether she'd wanted him to be or not.

Was she sorry? "It's complicated."

"How so?"

Josie turned so her back was against the armrest and cradled a pillow in her lap. "Part of me is sorry. The part that thinks logically and long-term. The other part of me enjoyed getting my socks knocked off."

A grin widened on Laurel's face. "He knocked your socks off?"

"Both of them," she admitted. "Or would have, if I'd been wearing any." It was a humiliating admission after Grady's lack of enthusiasm.

"So, what's the problem? Other than that he's sorry, I mean."

Josie shot her a thanks-for-the-reminder look. Did she really want to get into this now? She'd told Nate she would, and Laurel wasn't going to get better anytime soon.

"Grady's committed to the orchard, in case you haven't noticed." Josie said the next as gently as she could. "And I don't want to stay here, honey. I know you want me to, but there's just too many . . . too many reasons I can't."

How could Laurel understand? It had been so much easier for her. Her dad had accepted her. And she wasn't the one who lived with the guilt and shame from Ian's death.

"You still want to sell."

Now was her chance to push hard. "We're bringing in a great harvest. The land will go for maximum value if we move quickly."

Laurel looked away.

"You could continue to make your accessories and sell them. I'm telling you, that camera strap you made would be a hit with photographers."

Laurel seemed to be mulling over the idea, and it buoyed Josie's hopes.

"Imagine not having the worries of the orchard. The pruning, the picking, the mowing, the payroll, the hiring of migrants, the uncertainty of the weather . . . you'll have enough on your hands with the twins."

Laurel sighed. "I know."

"You'd still have the house and we could keep a few acres around it. We wouldn't be losing our heritage, you know. It's just land and trees. Our heritage is right here." She placed her hand over her heart.

Josie continued. "You could knit and sew in your spare time and sell things on eBay without having to leave the house."

Laurel ran her hand over her belly. "I don't know."

"Are you at least considering it?"

Laurel's sigh seemed to come from deep inside. "I am, I promise. And I'm sorry if I came across bossy when I asked you to stay before. I know you're a grown woman now, but old habits die hard." She gave a sheepish smile.

"Supper's ready!" Aunt Lola called from the kitchen.

"Apology accepted." Josie stood and pulled Laurel to her feet.

Josie squeezed her sister's hand. "I'll call Nate in." As she went out the back door, she recognized the relief for what it was. Laurel was close to giving in. Little did her sister know that if she insisted on hanging on to the orchard, it would end up being a burden she carried alone.

twenty-five

*I*t was a bad day from the moment Josie awoke. First, it was Monday, which meant she had six days in the orchard to look forward to. Second, her stomach was unsettled before she untangled her feet from the covers. Third, she had to face Grady again.

She took an extra-long shower, noting how dark her skin had become. She'd strived for a tan in her teen years. But this darkness wasn't from her long hours in the sun so much as a symptom of her illness. She knew this because the tan didn't stop at her clothes.

Deciding to skip breakfast, she filled a thermos with coffee and set out to the orchard. On her way out the door, she found Duncan in the yard, standing over Aunt Lola's flowers, and realized she must've left his pen open the night before. The yellow pansies and orange marigolds lining the walk were crushed. It took fifteen minutes and a slice of leftover apple pie to get Duncan corralled. She'd have to worry about Aunt Lola and the flowers later.

The crew was just arriving as she pulled her car into the Winesap grove. They would start and finish that variety this week. The bulk of the remaining apples ripened in mid-October and would be ready for picking next week: Fuji, Goldrush, Granny Smith, Pink Lady, and Limbertwig. They'd be busy getting those off the trees through November, hoping and praying for the absence of wind and rainy periods that brought fungus.

Josie greeted the crew and grabbed a bag, starting on a semidwarf toward the top of the hill, far away from Grady's trailer. The day promised to be cooler. Already a thick layer of clouds hung low in the sky, shadowing the mountains, and the air smelled vaguely of rain.

She picked for two hours before her stomach set-

tled enough for coffee and by then she had a caf-
feine headache. Taking a break with the others, she
dug two Advil from her purse, swallowed them
with a gulp of coffee, then perched on the open
tailgate of the pickup truck, grateful for the
reprieve.

The crew spoke in rapid Spanish. A slow drizzle
started as they returned to work, but that didn't
stop the men from singing.

Within five minutes Josie's hair hung in limp
clumps. The coffee had unsettled her stomach and
the Advil wasn't working. Her muscles ached
more than usual. She checked her watch, hoping
time was going faster than she thought. No such
luck. It was three more hours until her turn to stay
with Laurel.

She reached for another apple, twisting it from
the branch, then she bagged it. Her stomach was
not pleased that she'd forced coffee upon it. It
churned and cramped, offended.

Was she going to get sick? Her stomach spasmed
in response to the thought. Josie scanned the area
for a private place just in case. Behind the trailer?
She didn't want to be sick in front of everyone.
Especially not Grady. He was facing the other
direction on a ladder at a semidwarf, the trailer just
beyond him.

But if she went over the ridge and down the hill,
she'd be out of sight. Hopefully it wouldn't come
to that.

She reached for the next apple and the next. Before she got the third apple in the bag, she felt the unmistakable sensation of impending disaster. She shrugged off the bag and scrambled up the hill, then down the other side.

She was ten feet from the top when her stomach expelled its contents. She bent over, heaving.

Her stomach cramped, her pulse pounded at her temples. She caught her breath, hoping it was over. She was out of sight, far enough down the hill, and the migrants' singing had covered the sound of her retching.

Her legs shook like a sapling in a windstorm, and her hands trembled as she straightened and wiped her leaking eyes. That's when she saw Grady standing near the top of the hill.

Grady had tried not to notice Josie all day. He hadn't seen her since Saturday when they'd carefully avoided the subject of the kiss. But no matter how hard he'd tried, he'd been aware of her every movement.

He'd followed her with his eyes so often, it was a wonder he'd gotten any work done. But he couldn't seem to stop. He'd known something was wrong when she dashed up the hill, her shoulders stiff.

Now, as she straightened and turned, her eyes still glassy from her ordeal, apprehension cast a thick shadow over his thoughts.

She swayed slightly and he rushed to her side, taking her elbow.

"Sit down." His voice was gruffer than he intended. He pulled her under the nearest tree and helped her sit.

"I'm fine." Josie wiped the raindrops off her face and turned away.

She wasn't fine. A week ago she fell off a ladder and now she just puked up coffee. Had she lied to him about being pregnant? He squatted beside her, studying her. She was still shaking as she wiped her mouth with the back of her hand. He was torn between fetching her a glass of water and interrogating her.

"You're not fine," he said.

She shrugged. "It's just the—"

"Don't even say it's the heat, Josie. It's seventy-two degrees and raining."

She looked away, her eyes scanning the dozens of trees as if she might pick an answer from one of them.

The migrants ended a tune and started another in the gap of silence.

Josie's head fell against the bark of the tree as if her neck hadn't the strength to support it. Her eyes were bloodshot, tired-looking.

Fatigue, nausea, dizziness. She had all the symptoms, even if she had denied it once. Maybe it was none of his business, but he needed to know the truth. "Are you pregnant?"

That roused her. Her head rolled toward him and her eyes narrowed. *"No.* I already told you I wasn't." Somewhere she'd found the energy for anger.

But if it wasn't that, what was it? He'd seen signs of illness all along. And if the dizzy spells weren't from the heat, what was causing them?

"You need to see a doctor."

She leaned forward, readying to stand. "I don't need a doctor."

"Like heck you don't." He took her elbow, stilling her. "I've watched you get dizzy and fall off a ladder and puke your guts up. Where I come from, that means you're sick."

She pulled her elbow from his grasp. "I'm fine. I was just a little queasy. I should've eaten breakfast."

She had to know something was wrong. He stood and held out his hand. "Come on. I'll take you now."

Josie took his hand and stood, dusting off her damp jeans. "I don't need a doctor." As if belying her words, she swayed suddenly, reaching for the tree.

Grady grabbed for her waist, steadying her. Water dripped from the leaves above onto her face.

"You can walk to my truck, or I'll pick you up and carry you. Your choice."

He saw something in her eyes before she closed them. A flicker of something. He thought he was going to have to follow through on his threat.

A shadow passed over her green eyes, turning them stormy gray. She leaned against the tree. "I'm sick, okay? I already know that."

The words, her tone, planted a seed of fear deep in his bones. Sick? What kind of sick? He watched her, looking for a sign that this illness was some passing food poisoning or harmless virus. The clues he saw, the frown tugging her mouth, the furrow between her brows, weren't reassuring.

"What's wrong?" he asked, suddenly unsure he wanted to know.

He could hear Hernando's deep chuckle in the distance over the rain pattering on the leaves. Wind ruffled the tree branches and he heard the familiar sound of a few apples thunking on the ground nearby.

"I have a disease. It makes me sick sometimes, that's all."

But that wasn't all. He could see it on her face. She wasn't telling him everything; she was a terrible liar.

"How sick?" Dread stilled his heart, made the air catch in his lungs.

Josie pulled away from the tree. "It doesn't matter."

Grady grabbed her arm. "It matters to me." He didn't know how much until now.

She looked at him finally, one corner of her mouth pulling into a wry grin. "Let's just say you don't want to get too attached."

What did that mean? She couldn't mean it the way it sounded. She was going to . . . die? But the sadness he'd seen all along, rooted in her eyes, began to make sense. Grady felt something deep in his gut he hadn't felt since he'd found Danielle cheating with his best friend. An ache that started small and expanded painfully.

"Now you're really sorry about that kiss, huh?"

How could she be so nonchalant? Didn't she know he was coming to care for her?

The disease, whatever it was, angered him. Josie, so flippant and sarcastic, angered him. He wanted to scold her, yell at her.

But the look in her eyes stopped him. For all her bravado, for all the degrees her chin had tipped up, for all her sarcastic words, her hollow eyes gave her away. The rest was just a front. The rebuke that had formed on his tongue slid quietly down his throat.

She crossed her arms over her chest, a defensive gesture that made him want to pull her into his arms.

"Is it cancer?" Maybe there was something she could do. Some rock unturned that he could help her find.

"No. It has to do with the endocrine system." She turned and took a couple of steps away, putting space between them. "I don't want to talk about it."

"Why didn't you say something? Why didn't

Laurel or Nate tell me?" This last was a question to himself. What would it have mattered? Would he have kept his distance from her to protect himself?

Josie mumbled something just as the sky opened up and the drizzle turned to a steady shower. She looked small hunched over in the rain.

He wished he had a jacket to drape over her. He took a step closer. "I didn't catch that."

She looked over her shoulder. "They don't know. And I don't want them to, understand?" Her words were firm, set in cement.

He couldn't understand why she'd keep something so important from them. They loved her. They'd be devastated, and even more so knowing that Josie had shouldered this alone.

Josie looked directly at him, looking strong for the first time since he'd found her hunkered over. "This is between you and me."

"Your family deserves to know. It's not fair—"

"It's not up to you to decide what's fair. Laurel is at a tenuous point in her pregnancy. She doesn't need the additional stress."

Maybe she had a point, but still. Family was family, and you didn't hide things like this.

"Promise me you won't say anything," she said.

Could he make such a promise? But what did he know of this illness? She may have years left, and if that was the case, what did a couple of months matter one way or the other?

"Promise," she said again.

Whether he agreed or not, in the end, the decision belonged to her, didn't it? And at least he knew now. Josie had someone to confide in if she needed to. "Promise."

The rain continued steadily. Josie was soaked to the skin.

"You should go on to the house."

She squared her shoulders. "I'm feeling better now."

Stubborn woman. The crew picked in the rain unless it was a downpour. It was just short of that today, but he didn't want her out in this.

"I'm calling it quits for the day." He turned and walked up the hill before she could argue.

twenty-six

*F*or the next few days, Josie watched and waited, worried Grady wouldn't keep his word. At times, she couldn't believe she'd told him. With a few words to her sister, he could ruin everything. Yet, what choice had she had when he'd threatened to put her over his shoulder and take her to the doctor?

Throughout awkward suppers and tense business discussions, he'd kept silent about her illness. She'd told him her secret and nothing had changed.

Except for one thing. She felt him watching her in the orchard. He took her heavy bag from her, brought her water, tended quietly to her. Part of her wanted to reject the hovering, the independent part that wanted no handouts. The other part savored his tender care.

Laurel was getting antsy for the babies' arrival and, in her impatience, her mood worsened. She'd mentioned that their parents' graves needed tending—a job Aunt Lola had been too busy for since Laurel had been put on bed rest.

If Josie didn't get up there and do the job, she was going to come home one day to find her pregnant sister up there on her hands and knees.

Even so, she balked. Maybe she could ask Nate or Aunt Lola to do it, then thought twice about that. Her aunt had enough to do with the housekeeping and the store, and Nate had enough of his own pressures with running his business and taking care of Laurel. *Just suck it up, Josie. It'll be over before you know it.* Besides, there was nothing up there but overgrown plots.

On a Sunday morning after the others had left for church, Josie climbed the hill behind the house with a bag of gardening tools. It was Laurel's first time at church in weeks, the doctor having given her permission for the once-a-week outing.

A layer of gray clouds shrouded the sun and the wind blew in from the west, making the tall grass on the hill bow and shimmy. There was news of a possible windstorm the next afternoon. Grady was keeping a close eye on the weather, and if the storm looked likely, every hand he could find would be out gathering apples later today. Otherwise, many apples would drop and be wasted.

When Josie neared the top of the hill, the cemetery came into view. Surrounded by a split-rail fence, the family markers rested under a giant oak tree whose branches stretched out in an enormous canopy over the area. She walked through the opening, remembering her last visit here.

The sky had been spitting sleet and icy rain on the day of Ian's funeral. He was the only one buried in the cemetery who wasn't a blood relative.

The grounds showed signs of being well tended. Aunt Lola had planted ivy along the fence, and it had climbed and crawled obediently along the split rails. Perennials bordered each tombstone. Yellow roses for Grandma Mitchell, white creeping phlox for Grandpa, and myrtle for Uncle Otis. The flowers' smell thickened the air with sweetness.

She walked toward the back and started there, saving the difficult ones for last. Nate had kept up with the mowing and had even used the Weed Eater recently. Weeds grew in the flower beds though, and dead buds needed plucking.

She worked quickly even though the effort tired her and made her back ache. The sooner she was done, the sooner she could get out of here. When she finished the back rows, she moved on to the front, starting at her mother's plot. Aunt Lola had planted red roses, her mother's favorite, around the tombstone.

Josie pulled the weeds and pruned the bush, then sat back on her heels and read the words on the marble marker.

Katherine Mitchell
Beloved Wife and Mother

She tried to call up a picture of her mom but all that came to mind was the image of the photo in her old locket. Josie had been so young. She wasn't even sure whether the memories she had of her mom were her own or someone else's hand-me-downs.

Her dad's grave was next, and Josie could put it off no longer. Newer shoots of ivy poked from the ground at the base of his tombstone. Her aunt would coax them up toward the marble marker as they grew. The mound of earth over his grave site was sparsely covered with new grass. Aunt Lola was tending his grave as carefully as Laurel had tended him after his stroke—not that he'd deserved it. He'd been so selfish to burden Laurel that way.

Well, Josie wouldn't follow in his footsteps. As soon as the harvest was in, she'd go back to Louisville. Her sister wouldn't see her health decline or be burdened with her care.

Her eyes swung back to her father's grave. The marker matched her mother's.

Warren Mitchell
Beloved Husband and Father

Josie could think of a few adjectives to add to the epitaph. But then, she hadn't been here to help Laurel with the arrangements. Hadn't been here for the funeral either. She reached out and tugged at a dandelion that seemed to have endless roots. She should've come home to help Laurel. Lord knew she'd tried. She'd even packed her bags. But in the end, she couldn't do it. Couldn't face the memory of her disapproving father or the guilt over his disappointment. And her anger. She couldn't face that either.

Now, hunkered over his grave, she was face-to-face with the feelings. Her dad had left, was forever gone, and she'd never told him how she felt, had never even hinted at it.

And now it was too late.

It wasn't fair. She wanted to scream at him for the way he'd made her feel. He deserved to know, and she deserved the chance to say those things.

"Why?" she whispered toward the heavens.

The only answer was a dove's call. *Ooh-OOH. Ooh-ooh-ooh.*

"Why did you make me feel so . . . unwanted?" Josie sat back on her heels. "Why wasn't I enough for you? I was just a little girl and you made me feel . . . like I was nothing."

She was going to have her say now, even if he couldn't hear it.

She raised her voice. "And I still feel that way, Dad. You know that? I'm still not enough. It's ingrained so deeply in me, it can never be changed."

Her eyes connected with the gravestone on the other side of her dad's. Her baby twin brother. She wished he'd lived instead of her—that's what should've happened. Even as she thought it, she realized the idea stemmed from her dad's attitude and the way he treated her.

"That's what you wanted, wasn't it? You wanted him and not me. And then Ian came, and you wanted him and not me."

For so many years she'd tried to prove her worth by working hard, by trying to please her father, by trying to make him proud.

But it had never been enough. *She* had never been enough. Not for him, and not for her.

Then Ian had died. And her dad had grieved over him as if he were his own son, while he ignored the fact that he still had two daughters who were alive and needed him. She wanted to spit it out. She wanted to tell him the truth about Ian's death. It had all been her fault. Ian's death was on her hands. In those days after his death, watching her father walk around half-dead himself, sometimes, deep inside in a place she'd hidden from everyone else, she was glad Ian was gone.

But guilt always came on the heels of those feelings. How could she have such horrible thoughts? What kind of person was glad when someone died? Someone who'd shown her nothing but kindness? Someone who'd willingly given his life for her?

Maybe her father had been right. Maybe she was unworthy. Unworthy of love, unworthy of joy, unworthy of life.

Her breath seemed trapped in her expanded lungs, and her pulse pounded in her head. She had to get out of here. Out of this place full of memories better dead and forgotten.

Josie tugged off the gloves and dropped them at the base of her dad's tombstone. She wasn't ready to face this. Maybe she never would be. Maybe it needed to stay buried deep in her heart. Maybe she needed to take it to the grave with her.

But it was too late. She'd uprooted the memories and now she stood clutching them in her hands, wishing she could shove them back into the gaping holes.

Her breaths came quickly now, drying her mouth, rushing past the hard ache in her throat.

Josie stood, leaving the tools where they lay. She couldn't face this now. She had to escape. Before she finished the thought, her legs were carrying her away from the place.

twenty-seven

he news had been all over church. Grady changed into his work clothes as soon he got home. Nate had gone to tell Josie and gather the crew.

The windstorm alert had been upgraded to a warning a few minutes before church. It was due in the area the next afternoon with high winds and driving rain. They needed every hour of daylight and every hand they could muster to pick the apples most susceptible to dropping.

Once the wind started, the fruit would fall to the ground at an alarming rate where they would lie bruised and useless. Not even processors accepted drops that could carry E. coli or patchulin. A big windstorm could destroy the remainder of their crop.

Grady shoved his feet into his boots and jogged to his truck. When he reached the orchard, Mr. Murphy and a few other men from church were arriving to help, and Nate was arriving with the crew in tow. Some of them had brought their wives to help.

Grady had been picking for ten minutes before he noticed Josie's absence. When the first bin was full, he used the lift tractor to move it into the trailer. He exited the lift as Nate passed with a bag full of apples.

"Where's Josie?" Grady asked.

Nate emptied his bag into the bin. "Don't know. Her car was gone when we got home. Laurel tried to call her cell, but she left it at home."

Maybe she'd gone to the grocery or something. There were only so many options on a Sunday in Shelbyville. She'd be home soon. Lord knew they could use every hand they could get. It was killing Laurel to be on the sofa when the remainder of their crop was at stake.

Josie must not have watched the news and been aware of the weather update. If she was in town, someone would tell her and she'd be back quickly.

Grady and the crew moved at lightning speed all afternoon, barely pausing for water breaks. Aunt Lola fixed sandwiches for an early supper, and the crew worked on. As the afternoon slipped away and there was still no sign of Josie, Grady began to worry.

No one knew where she'd gone. Aunt Lola said her camera was on the desk where she kept it. They weren't worried as they knew Josie liked to stay busy and frequently went off on the weekend. She'd made more than one last-minute trip into Asheville, and he was told Ashley had called the day before. They'd probably made plans for a visit. Josie was a grown woman; it wasn't like she had to leave a flight plan every time she left the house.

But she'd known about the potential windstorm. Even if she did want to sell the place, she wouldn't take off when they needed her.

Grady grew more concerned as the evening passed. His imagination ran wild even while his hands did their automatic work.

What if she was sick? What if she'd gotten dizzy—or worse, passed out—behind the wheel? What if her car had careened off the road, and she was even now lying at the bottom of a gorge?

The sun sank lower in the sky until it disappeared behind the hills. The crew began packing up. Grady put the last bin in the trailer and drove them home. Darkness had fallen, and the porch light was on at the Mitchell house. Josie's car was still absent from the driveway.

Grady slowed as he passed Nate on the drive.

"Got a lot done today," Nate said. "Hopefully we'll be okay."

Grady nodded. "Josie's not home yet." He couldn't quell the knot in his gut that told him something was wrong. The heavy weight of responsibility pressed down on him. He was the only one who knew she was ill.

Nate's lips tightened into a flat line before he spoke. "She knew the storm was coming. But then, she's not exactly been dependable in the past. Probably drove to Asheville for the day."

A defense rose in Grady's throat, but he pushed it down. "Probably." They said good night and

Grady accelerated, easing down the lane toward his cabin.

Her family might worry later if Josie didn't appear by morning, but they'd be worried now if they knew about the illness. Maybe she had driven to Asheville, but she'd never done a day trip. She always stayed overnight. He wondered if Laurel had thought to check for her overnight bag.

Surely Josie would've left a note if she were planning to stay overnight. And she knew about the windstorm. She knew he'd need her help. Regardless of Nate's assessment of Josie's attitude, Grady knew she wouldn't desert them without good cause.

As he reached the turn toward his cabin, he made a split-second decision and passed it, accelerating up the incline toward the main road. On the way, he dug his cell from his pocket and found Boone's number. He'd call Boone's sister in Asheville and find out if Josie was there. He should've done it earlier when he started worrying.

He stopped when he reached the top of the hill and made the call.

"Yep?" Boone's voice sounded in his ear.

"Hey, Boone, it's Grady."

"Hey, Grady. What's up?"

"I was wondering if I could get your sister's number in Asheville. I need to reach Josie and I think she might be there."

Grady put his window all the way down and rested his elbow on the ledge.

"I can give you Jackie's number, but I don't think Josie's there. I passed her in town coming home from church."

Would she have gone to Asheville that late in the day?

"She wasn't heading toward the highway," Boone said. "Everything okay?"

Last thing he needed was to get Boone suspicious. "Yeah, just needed to talk to her is all. Can I get Jackie's number just the same?"

Boone rattled off his sister's number and they hung up. When Grady reached the end of the driveway, he stopped and punched it in.

Someone answered on the second ring. "Hello?"

"Hi, uh, is Josie there?"

"Josie Mitchell?"

"Yeah, this is Grady from Shelbyville. I thought Josie might be down there this weekend."

"Oh, hey, this is Ashley. No, she didn't come this weekend. Is everything okay?"

Grady assured her it was, then hung up, his stomach tightening as each moment passed.

What are you going to do, Mackenzie? Drive down every dark road in Shelbyville looking for her car?

Where would she go? Would she have gone to a friend's house? He couldn't think of anyone in town she was close to.

There was nothing open on a Sunday night in town except the grocery store and Joe's Tavern. But she'd never gone to the tavern before that he knew of. And she couldn't have been there all day.

When he reached the crossroad, he turned toward town. A light rain had begun to fall. He drove slowly along the main road, looking down each street that he passed. There were hairpin curves and deep ravines off the roadside. What if she'd had an accident? It was too dark to see. *Where is she, Jesus? Help me to find her. Keep her safe.*

Maybe he should call Laurel and tell her about Josie's illness. Her life may depend upon being found. They could call Sheriff Roberts, and he could be on the lookout for Josie.

He entered town. Shelbyville was a mere blip on the map, snuggled between two stop signs and a traffic light the town had been proud to install three years earlier.

It was dark and deserted now. Only the park-style streetlamps were lit, an embellishment that had taken three town meetings to decide upon. The storefronts' darkened windowpanes reflected his headlights.

Across town, the lights of Ingles glowed like a big-city stadium. He'd check the grocery last. Maybe someone in there had seen her.

The only sign of life was the corner of Main and Penny Avenue where Joe's Tavern squatted. Music leaked from the wood-paneled building, and neon beer logos shined through the shaded glass. Parking was behind the building, so Grady swung his truck around the corner and slowed at the gravel lot lit by a single streetlamp. His eyes swung through the haphazard rows of vehicles and stopped when they came to the second row.

Almost hidden, tucked between a pickup and an SUV, was Josie's little brown Celica. He turned his truck into the lot, relief battling with anger. Had she been here all day? Been here drinking and partying when he'd been worried she was in a ditch somewhere?

He exited the truck and reached the rear door of the building with long strides. Inside the tavern, smoke gave the interior a hazy glow. A twangy country song poured from the jukebox in the corner. He'd never been in the place but recognized Ray Blackford behind the varnished bar.

"Hey, Grady." Ray filled a mug from the tap and set it in front of a customer.

Grady nodded. "Ray." His eyes swept the dim confines of the bar. He was surprised there were fifteen people in Shelbyville who wanted to be out on a Sunday night.

Ray leaned on the bar. "Looking for someone?"

It was hard to see around the tall booths. "Josie Mitchell. She around?"

Ray nodded his head toward the back of room. "Thataway."

"Thanks."

Adrenaline still coursed through his veins from the worry, from scouring ravines for her knotted-up car. He'd been worried for her, worried for her family. What would they have done if something had happened to her? He'd been afraid on their behalf.

Who are you kidding? You were afraid on your own behalf. You were worried you'd lost her.

He clenched his teeth together, his jaw working. He tried to deny the thought, but it would be a lie, and what good did it do to lie to yourself? He *had* been worried for her, blast it all. Worried on his own behalf.

He turned the corner and spotted her in a booth, her chin propped on her palm, listening to some guy who sat across from her. She blinked, her eyelids moving in slow motion.

The guy was Hispanic, probably a migrant worker on one of the other orchards. He was leaning forward, smiling, too close.

Grady suppressed the desire to pick him up by the collar and remove him from the booth. Instead, he stopped at the table.

Josie straightened. Or tried to. "Grady." Her smile and diction were sloppy. He noted the empty glass on the table by her elbow.

Grady stared the man down until he squirmed, then slid across the booth, standing. "I will see you later, Josie."

Josie waggled her fingers at him.

Grady was torn between sliding into the vacated spot and hauling Josie up from the booth, tossing her over his shoulder, and carrying her to his truck. Exercising restraint, he lowered himself into the seat.

Josie reached out and took his hands, patting them. "I'm so glad y're here."

Grady pulled his hands from hers. He was disappointed in her, running to the tavern and loading up. And of all the days to get skunked, she'd picked today.

What really rankled wasn't her supreme lack of responsibility, but the fact that he'd had her injured or worse in his own mind. He'd seen her hurt and bleeding, unconscious. The adrenaline rush was gone, leaving him shaky in its wake.

"Do you have any idea how worried we were about you?"

A frown tugged the smile from her face. Confusion knitted her brow. "What?" She strung the word into two syllables.

"We needed you at the orchard. Nobody knew where you were."

Her bloodshot eyes opened wide. "Laurel . . ."

"Laurel's fine. It's the windstorm. It's coming."

She blinked. Then she moved suddenly, scrambling up from the table. "The apples . . ."

Grady grabbed her wrist. "It's ten o'clock, Josie."

He was wasting his breath. She was three sheets to the wind.

"Gotta get 'em off the trees . . ." She tried to pull her arm away.

He tightened his grip. "It's too late. Sit down."

"Everything okay, Josie?" The Hispanic was back, stretching up to his full five feet three inches. He eyed Grady's hand, wrapped around Josie's wrist.

As if Grady would hurt her. But he was in no mood to explain himself. *Back off,* amigo.

He wasn't going to get anywhere here. Josie needed to sleep it off. Grady slid from the booth. "Let's go home." He thought the man might back off when he saw how Grady dwarfed him.

The man didn't seem to notice. "Josie?"

She swayed a little, and Grady and the other man reached out to steady her. Grady glared at him until he let go.

"I'm fine." She smiled, seemingly forgetting the apples, and linked her arm through Grady's. "He's taking me home." She blinked up at him, squinting. "Y're taking me home?" She looked at him with complete vulnerability, like a child at his mercy.

He softened at her confusion. God help him, she was getting to him. How could a woman frustrate the daylights out of him one minute and break his heart the next?

He led her past her friend and past the jukebox.

As they passed the dance floor, a slow country ballad began.

Josie turned abruptly, and he plowed into her. In the moment it took to steady her, she draped her arms around his neck and began swaying. "Love this song."

"Come on, Josie." He tugged at her arms, but they tightened around his neck.

"Dance with me." Her lower lip puckered out. "Please . . ."

The Hispanic was eyeing him from across the room. There was a bit of stubbornness in Grady that wanted to defy the man by marching Josie right out the door. But a little time to sober up wouldn't hurt. Aunt Lola would have a conniption if he brought her home like this. Maybe if he waited awhile everyone at the house would be in bed.

He put his hands at Josie's waist and swayed with her. He wondered if he should call and let them know she was okay. But then they'd wonder why she wasn't calling herself.

Why do you need to protect her anyway? She's the one who went out and got soused. If her family disapproves, that's no fault of yours.

Josie snuggled against him, laying her head on his chest. He was glad she was too drunk to notice the way his heart kicked into high gear. She stepped on his toes, the featherweight of her body barely impeding the movement of his feet.

The country singer crooned about drowning his

sorrows in a bottle of beer. Is that what Josie had done? Had the reality of her illness been too much? He thought of her all alone in the house while the others were at church. She needed someone she could count on, someone she could talk to. He tried to imagine what it would feel like to know some illness was going to take his life. Then he imagined going through it alone.

A quick pang of loneliness pricked him, just a taste of what Josie must feel. The residual anger drained away, leaving a heavy sadness in its place. He cradled the back of her head. If only she would open herself to the possibility of God. She didn't have to go through this alone.

God, have mercy on your child. Help her through this. Help me be to her what you want me to be.

He wanted to protect her, to shield her from the pain she was trying to drown out with alcohol. He laid his chin on her head, inhaling the scent of lilacs. He felt the breaths come and go from her lungs. Breaths that drew in life.

How long did she have? How could it be that all this life he held in his arms would soon be snuffed out? He tightened his arms around her.

What are you doing, Mackenzie? Where's this going to lead? You're gonna get hurt again. And there was no way for it to end other than hurt. Did he want to go down this path?

He dug deep for the courage to ask the question. *What do you want from me, God?*

Josie pulled her arms from his neck and wrapped them around his waist. Her hands grazed over his back, leaving a hot trail. The singer held out his last note and the song ended.

Just in time. Grady pulled away, hating the cool curtain of air that fell between them. "Time to go, honey."

He ushered her to the truck and helped her in. By the time he turned the key, she was snuggled into the door, her head on the window ledge.

Grady checked the clock. It was almost eleven. He didn't know if Laurel or Aunt Lola would be up waiting and worried, or whether they'd be sound asleep. He could only hope for the latter. Josie didn't need Aunt Lola's disapproving looks or her sister's pointed questions. She needed someone to take care of her, someone to look out for her.

The truck rumbled down Main Street, then he turned onto Stone Gap Road, his lights cutting a winding path in the darkness. From the other side of the cab, quiet snores escaped from Josie.

Sleep was just what she needed. Heaven knew she was going to feel bad enough come morning.

When they reached the house, he cut off his lights and turned off the ignition. The house was dark except for the porch lights, a good sign. Now if he could only rouse Josie.

He touched her arm. "Josie."

A soft snore was his only answer. He tried again, rubbing her arm. "Josie, we're home."

She didn't move, didn't so much as twitch. The glow of the porch light cast a pale yellow sheen over her face. Relaxed in sleep, her lips were parted. Her eyelashes grazed the tops of her cheeks, reminding him of an innocent child.

She was out cold, and he hated to disturb the peaceful oblivion she'd finally found. He exited the truck, closing his door quietly, and went to her side, opening the door slowly so he didn't jar her awake.

As the door slipped from under her, she turned and curled into the seat.

"Josie?" he whispered.

The wind rustled the branches above him, reminding him of the windstorm due in fifteen hours. They had a long day ahead of them.

Deciding to let her sleep, Grady slipped his hands under her and lifted her. She turned into him with a sigh, nuzzling her face in the cradle between his head and shoulder.

He closed the door softly with his hip, then climbed the porch steps and wrestled with the handle. Unable to stop the screen door in time, it slapped against the frame. He winced, hoping it wasn't as loud as he feared.

What would her family think if they saw him carrying Josie into the house? Drunk, no less. *It's a little late to worry about that, buddy.*

He thought he'd skirted the hall table, but one of Josie's feet connected with it. Her sandal thudded to the wood floor.

Way to go. You've probably woken half of Shelbyville by now.

But not Josie. A long, quiet snore erupted.

The stairs creaked as he carried her to the second floor. If the noise woke someone, hopefully they'd think it was Josie returning and go back to sleep. At the top of the stairs, he reached her door, glad the other rooms were at the far end of the hall. Moonlight shone through the gauzy curtains, enough to see by.

He carried her to the twin bed in the corner and laid her down, then went back to shut the door before he flipped on the tiny lamp.

Josie lay just as he'd left her, a floppy doll, arms and legs askew under the frilly canopy. She jerked, the bed quaking, her intake of breath audible.

He waited, praying she didn't wake. What would she think, finding him here in her room? Her hand lay open next to her face on the pillow. Dirt caked the creases of her palm and he wondered how it had gotten there.

She whimpered and her hand balled into a fist. Her head tossed on the pillow and her brows lowered.

He wanted to wake her now that her oblivion had turned nightmarish, but what would he say?

Josie curled into a ball, her dirty fingers clutching the pillow. She muttered something. A name? Ian?

She quieted, her breaths evening out. The bed

was still unmade from the night before, the covers shoved down in a wad. He picked up her foot and eased the other sandal off.

She was in jeans and a T-shirt and would have to stay that way. He lifted her other foot off the covers, eased it back down, then pulled the sheet up to her chin.

But before it settled over her shoulders, her eyes opened wide.

twenty-eight

*J*an was drowning. She could see his face through the crystal ice, looking up at her. His eyes were glacier blue. Cold and dead.

She woke with a start, the image haunting her. Within seconds, her rolling stomach snagged her attention. She was going to throw up. *Oh no.*

She pushed past Grady, barely questioning his presence in her hurry to make it in time. She leaned over the bowl and retched. It seemed to be coming all the way from her intestines. Her stomach cramped down hard, making her double over, even when she'd finished.

The light had come on, and she caught sight of Grady's denim-clad legs at her side. The commode flushed, sounding loud in the cramped room.

Her head throbbed in time with her heart, fast and hard, like blows of a hammer. The acidic taste of bile coated her mouth. She felt a cool washcloth settle at the base of her neck, and a glass of water appeared in front of her.

She took it, then stood, her legs wobbling beneath her. Why had she drunk all that beer? Didn't she feel bad enough without adding a hangover to her list of ailments?

She leaned over the sink and rinsed out her mouth. She felt like death warmed over, and she was sure she looked it too.

"Better?" Grady whispered.

She avoided the mirror as she straightened and nodded. She had a vague recollection of dancing with him at Joe's. Had that really happened or was it the precursor to her nightmare?

He flipped off the bathroom light and ushered her back to her room. *God, please let Aunt Lola sleep through this.* She'd never hear the end of it if her aunt caught Grady in her bedroom, and neither would he.

Her steps were slow, her balance unsure. Grady slipped an arm around her waist.

Why was he doing this? She lowered herself onto the mattress, remembering the windstorm. The entire day rushed back like a film in fast-forward. The cemetery, the long drive, the stop at Joe's.

Then Grady's arrival. That part was blurry. She closed her eyes, not able to think past her pounding head. The windstorm was coming, she remembered that part. They both had a long day ahead. It was late, and they both had to be up early. She couldn't believe he'd hunted her down at Joe's and stayed through this.

"I'm sorry . . ." She didn't know where to go from there. Sorry she'd been stupid enough to drown her pain with alcohol. Sorry she hadn't been there for him today. Sorry he'd seen her retching again.

Was it the beer or the illness? It was hard to know where one began and the other ended.

Grady pulled the covers over her and she turned her face into the pillow, wanting to hide. There would be plenty of time for mortification come morning.

"Go to sleep," he whispered.

She felt him turn the cloth on her neck, felt the coolness of the other side against her skin before she heard the click of the lamp, the sound of his footsteps on the floorboards.

She had a fuzzy flashback of dancing again. Of Grady's arms around her waist and the weight of his head resting on hers. Even drunk, she'd been aware of feeling something she hadn't felt in a very long time. Security.

It was the last thought she had before she sank into oblivion.

twenty-nine

A bluebird jeered outside Josie's window, rousing her earlier than usual. The sound of the bird was like a beak pecking at her forehead.

Her head throbbed and her mouth felt as if it were full of cottonwood fluff. Memories of the night before washed over her like a flash flood.

She closed her eyes, moaning against the inevitable confrontation with Grady. The windstorm was due in the afternoon, she remembered. They had a lot of apples to pick and not much time. They couldn't get them all, but if they could get the ripest ones, they might not lose too many.

Putting a hand to her forehead, she rooted through her purse for Advil and swallowed three of them. After a quick shower, she headed outside, deciding to skip coffee for the time being. The pounding in her head had diminished to a dull ache. The horizon was just now pinking up with the rising sun. A steady wind blew in from the west, a precursor of the coming storm. Already she could imagine the dreaded sound of apples thumping to the ground. Orchards expected some drops—ten to fifteen percent was normal. She wondered how many Grady and the crew had picked the day before.

If you'd been here, you would know. Guilt ate at her, feeding on her like a worm on a rotting apple.

Laurel probably had to be tied down to be kept at home and Josie had run off and gotten drunk.

Grady had counted on her, and she hadn't been here. Instead, he'd been there for her. The night before was blurry, especially the part at the bar. She didn't even remember how she'd gotten to her bedroom, but she remembered getting sick. She'd kept Grady up late being her nurse. So much for not being a burden.

He probably felt sorry for her. That thought bothered her as much as the guilt. She didn't want his pity, didn't need him feeling sorry for her.

When Josie turned the corner of the house, the spot where she parked her car was empty. It took a moment to remember. Her car was at Joe's. Before the implications sank in, she heard the roar of Grady's truck rumbling down the drive.

He stopped when he reached her side. "Climb in."

She eyed the door, the memory of the night before blazing across her mind like a forest fire. What did he think of her? Was he still angry that she'd deserted him?

Knowing she had no choice, she opened the door and slid inside, avoiding eye contact.

He put the truck in gear and accelerated. Gravel spit from under his tires. Outside a bluebird called. She needed to say something. Had she apologized last night?

She had an instant flash of snuggling against his

chest on the dance floor. Had he called her "honey"? She wished she could remember.

Or maybe she didn't.

"Feeling better this morning?" Grady asked.

He didn't sound angry. She was grateful for that and grateful he'd broken the ice, even if it did refer to the night before.

"Much." She remembered nothing after vomiting and falling into bed. She wondered what she'd said and done that she couldn't remember. How many other ways had she embarrassed herself?

His actions were above and beyond the call of duty. She owed him one. "Thanks for—" *Hunting me down at Joe's? Driving me home? Getting me to bed?* "—for taking care of me."

How long had it been since someone had taken care of her? She was used to being independent. Her father had never taken care of her. Laurel had tried to look after her baby sister, but Josie had bucked her sister's authority every chance she got. She hadn't been cared for like that since her mother had been alive.

"I'm sorry about taking off like that," she continued. "I didn't know they'd upgraded the windstorm." She gripped the crackled leather of the armrest as they rounded the bend toward the migrant housing.

"It worked out." She barely heard his words over the hum of the engine.

Unable to stop herself, she looked at him. His thick hands rested at ten and two on the steering wheel. His eyes still wore the remnants of sleep—and no wonder after she'd kept him up late. His hair was damp at his neck from his shower.

More than fatigue though, his face wore the mask of strain and she knew with certainty he'd been worried about her the night before. It was why he'd come looking for her at Joe's.

As if sensing her scrutiny, he turned. His eyes seemed to drink her in. They held her mesmerized.

His Adam's apple bobbed as he faced forward again. "Don't do that again."

The command should've made her defensive, but it didn't. She wasn't sure if it was the vulnerable tone of his voice or the look on his face.

"I won't."

The day passed in a blur for Josie. Laurel insisted she was fine at home alone, and even Aunt Lola closed the store for the day and helped in the orchard. By four o'clock, the wind picked up in heavy gusts that made ladder work treacherous. They'd done their best and could only hope the remaining apples would weather the storm.

Josie hadn't eaten breakfast or lunch, afraid the food would upset her stomach and interfere with her work. Her stomach gurgled loudly after she and Grady dropped off the workers. She folded her arms over her stomach, hoping he hadn't noticed.

"I told Aunt Lola I'd pick up a pizza from Crusty's. Figured we'd stop and pick up your car afterward."

"That would be great, thanks." She leaned back in the seat as fatigue settled over her like a heavy fog. She'd worked hard—they all had. Hard and fast, and the pace had gotten the best of her.

A gust of wind pushed the truck to the edge of the driveway, and Grady corrected it. The apple tree branches were waving, the apples on them diving like fishing bobbers under the tug of a bass.

"I hope they'll be okay." she said.

He looked out his window as a tree dropped half a dozen apples beside the drive. "We've done all we can. Now we just pray it was enough."

Prayer was mentioned so often in her family that Josie had stopped hearing it. Only after being away for several years did she have a fresh perspective. Did prayer work? Her own prayers had never seemed to accomplish anything. Not that she'd said many of them, but the last one she'd uttered in complete desperation had been ignored. Not ignored exactly, she reminded herself. After all, she'd been saved from the frigid water. But in many ways, she'd been lost there too. A loving God, a God who was capable of miracles, could've done much more if he'd wanted.

Her aunt would be appalled at her thoughts, but seeing as how her life would be ending sooner than later, the question of God was beginning to nag at her. What was there after death? Where was Ian right now? Had his faith gotten him to heaven? She wanted to believe in eternal bliss. But if there were such a place, would she make it in? Was believing in God's existence enough?

Probably not. It might be easier not to believe at all. Grady seemed so sure of his faith. Why couldn't she be that sure? Would it change anything if she were? Would the guilt be easier?

"Do you believe God answers prayers?" The question was on her lips before she could stop it.

He turned the truck onto the street, taking his time with the response. "I wouldn't waste my time with it if I didn't."

"But how do you know he cares? How do you know he hears you?"

Grady's shoulder lifted in a half shrug. "I've seen prayers answered. I feel his presence when I talk to him."

It wasn't enough. She was suddenly desperate for an answer she could live with. And die with. "Feelings are misleading."

He shrugged. "Do you believe in the wind?"

She looked out the window, seeing his point. Was it that simple?

"See how the branches are moving and the grass is swaying? You can't see the wind, but you can see its effects."

At the moment that wind was no doubt tugging countless apples from their trees. Was that how

God was? Carelessly wreaking havoc at his whim? She wouldn't voice the thought, but still it was there.

Grady was the one who changed the topic. "You skipped lunch."

She was surprised he'd noticed. She'd taken a break with everyone else and had pushed the coleslaw around her plate while the others ate.

"Do you always get sick?"

She shook her head. "It comes and goes." Lately it had been coming more than going. The fatigue was worse too. She was trying her best to hide it, especially from Laurel and Aunt Lola.

"I wanted to talk to you about something . . . I have a friend back in Chicago—a doctor," he said.

Josie shook her head again. "I'm done with doctors."

"He's an endocrinologist."

She needed to be careful. If he found out it was Addison's, he could find out it was treatable. And then what would she do?

This was hard enough as it was. Who did he think he was coming in and trying to fix everything? She nearly laughed out loud. Her problems were beyond fixing. The disease was the least of it. Her hand tightened on the armrest.

"I know you're trying to help, but just back off, all right?" After the words were out, she realized he might misinterpret them. She liked having him around, liked the way he looked at her sometimes, so deeply she wanted to sink into the brown depths of his eyes.

She hoped he'd ask what she meant so she could clarify. When several moments passed, Josie realized he wasn't going to, and her own tongue seemed stuck to the roof of her mouth.

thirty

The effects of the windstorm weren't apparent until the next morning at daybreak. They'd lost about forty percent of the remaining apples. Since the bulk of the orchard ripened late, this was significant. The mood was somber the rest of the week. A forty percent loss was heavy. Some of the orders Laurel had gotten would have to be canceled—a difficult thing when she worked hard for each sale.

The sale of the orchard had been on Josie's mind all week, and as Friday arrived, she realized something had turned inside her. Whatever decision was made about the orchard, she was going to do her best to make this season a successful one. No more trips to Asheville. No more running off and getting soused. If she had to strap herself to a tree, she was going to be out here every possible hour until the last apple was plucked. It was the least she could do for Grady and Laurel. Even with the loss of apples, they could still make the season a successful one so long as nothing else happened.

Grady was distant, whether from the apple loss or Josie's careless words, she wasn't sure. All she knew was that she missed him.

The bad week they'd had did nothing for Laurel's mood, and Friday night found Josie retreating to the tire swing. With Aunt Lola having gone out to eat with Mr. Murphy, Laurel and Nate probably needed time alone anyway.

Since Josie had made the decision to devote herself fully to the orchard, she'd only felt trapped. She had too much time to think while she worked and the evenings were even worse. Not having a trip to Asheville to anticipate pulled her mood even lower.

She needed to stay busy, especially in the evening when her mind was prone to wander places she didn't want to go. Josie shifted as the edge of the tire dug into her thigh. She couldn't just sit around and wait for time to pass.

The windstorm had brought down a thick layer of leaves, a crispy brown blanket that smelled of decay. She saw a rake leaning against the oak and untangled her legs from the tire swing.

She had a pile the size of a small car when Grady's truck rumbled up the drive.

As Grady rounded the curve that brought the house into view, he caught sight of Josie raking leaves. She'd looked half-dead over dinner and hadn't eaten enough to keep a robin alive. Was she trying to kill herself? The yard was Nate's job. Where was he? Grady pushed down the irritation, reminding himself Nate didn't know Josie was ill.

The fishing poles in the truck bed jangled against the metal bed as he hit a bump. He pulled to a stop, the notion of an invitation already sparking in his head. *She'll probably say no.* He'd kept his distance all week, but he figured that was the way she wanted it.

Grady leaned his elbow on the door frame. "Going fishing if you want to tag along," he said before he could reason himself out of it.

Josie leaned against the rake handle. Probably to keep herself upright. She seemed to be considering the idea as she looked over the pile that was high enough to tell him she'd been at it awhile.

"Got an extra pole?"

The jolt of joy was disconcerting. "Yep." A few leaves floated to the ground, landing in the patch of grass Josie had just raked.

She leaned the rake against the nearest tree. "Where at?"

He wondered why it mattered. "Murphy's pond."

She wiped her hands on her jeans as she approached.

Grady cleared the bench seat. Yesterday's newspaper, a cone wrapper from the Dairy Freeze, and a stray fry. He told himself the stutter of his heart was surprise and nothing more. She climbed in.

"You got permission?" she asked as he put the truck in gear.

"Helped him with a roof leak last year, and he lets me use it whenever I want. Why?"

She shrugged. "He's not real fond of me. I caught his bushes on fire, remember?"

He smiled. "I forgot about that. I thought it was his house though."

"Just the overhang."

"Well, that makes it better. He's still dating Aunt Lola, so he must not hold it against you too much."

She shifted, crossing her legs. The denim hung loosely around her knees. Had she lost weight in the weeks she'd been home? She seemed smaller. Her hands looked tiny all folded up in her lap, her arms actress-skinny.

She wasn't taking care of herself. She probably shouldn't be working in the orchard. Her body could be using all that energy to fight whatever disease she had. He wanted to tell her that. Wanted to insist she stay home and rest with Laurel.

But she'd already told him what she thought of him butting into her health affairs. And she was too stubborn to listen anyway. Maybe the best he could do was make sure she was resting when they weren't working. He already slipped in a couple of extra coffee breaks when he saw she was tired.

He'd thought a lot about the question she'd asked him on the day of the windstorm. Her family would be distraught to know she wasn't sure about

God. Especially if they knew about her illness.

If only he could pass his faith to her. If only it were that easy. At least she was searching, and that's where the journey began.

A few minutes later, he pulled into Murphy's drive and passed the farmhouse. The lane turned to a bumpy dirt road beyond the house, winding up a hill and through an evergreen forest. Murphy had a prime piece of land and a pond that was a fisherman's dream come true.

He slowed under the fanned branches of a Norway spruce and cut off the engine. They gathered the tackle and headed down the grassy slope where a flat rock jutted out into the water. His favorite fishing spot.

He grabbed a pole and opened the container of worms, threading one onto the hook for Josie. When he finished, he handed it to her. But she had the other pole and was already threading her own hook. Danielle wouldn't have been caught dead with a squirmy worm in her hands. Shoot, she wouldn't have been caught dead fishing in some backwoods pond.

"What?" She set the pole down, rinsing her hands in the pond's clear water.

"Nothing." They settled on the rock, a tight fit for two. The windy weather had moved out, leaving the surface of the pond as smooth as glass. The evergreens reflected back, casting dark shadows over their bobbers.

The only sound was the rustling of dead leaves and pine needles from a squirrel or bird moving along the forest floor. "Sure is peaceful here."

"The air smells so clean." She closed her eyes, inhaling. "Pine sap and autumn leaves and earth."

Her bobber dipped under the surface. "You got a bite."

She opened her eyes and watched the red and white globe, waiting. When it sank, she gave her pole a swift tug and reeled in.

The line was taut, the end of the pole slightly bowed. "You got him."

She reeled in until the fish cleared the water. A nice-sized largemouth bass. She pulled the hook from his mouth and put him in the mesh basket like a pro.

"I think you earned yourself a fish dinner."

She rinsed her hands in the water, wiped them dry on her jeans, and rebaited her hook. "Is that an invitation?" She tilted an unsure look his way.

His breath caught in his throat. Have mercy, she was beautiful when she looked at him like that, all vulnerable and uncertain.

He cleared his throat. "I'll skin them if you fry them." Frankly, he'd skin *and* fry them if only she'd agree to come over.

She cast back out in the same spot. "Deal."

He watched her from the corner of his eye, remembering how soft her hair had felt the night he kissed her. Remembered how pliable her lips had been, how she'd felt against him.

What are you doing, man? Trying to drive yourself crazy?

"Tell me about you," she said suddenly. "I don't know much other than you were married before and studied agriculture."

Anything to change the direction of his thoughts. "What do you want to know?"

"What was your wife like?"

"Just bring in the heavy artillery, why don't you?"

"You mind?"

What was there to hide? It was Josie. She wouldn't judge, and he had nothing to be ashamed of. But when you were betrayed, it somehow left you feeling as if you did.

"We met in college. She was attractive and dangerous."

She almost smiled. "I can relate."

Now there was a comment to follow up on. He pulled his line in a couple of yards and locked the reel. "That song, 'Maneater'? It was written for her."

She cocked her head. "Not good."

"Sadly, I didn't realize until I found her in bed with my best friend."

Her lips pulled down. There might've been pity in her eyes, but he looked away before he could decide.

"I'm sorry."

"I was too. But that was a long time ago."

They were quiet so long, her bobber had floated close to shore before she spoke again. "We all have our demons. How long were you married?"

Too long. It was on his tongue, but that was sarcasm speaking. It had been pretty good in the very beginning. "Less than two years."

He wondered if Josie had ever been close to marriage. He was sure there'd been no lack of male attention.

"Do you miss her?"

He might have dismissed the question with a laugh, but the seriousness of Josie's tone stopped him. "No. I do miss the companionship though."

He missed coming home and having someone there. Having someone in bed beside him when he woke in the middle of the night. Having someone to call when he had good news.

It was time to move on. "How 'bout you? Serious relationships? Ever engaged?"

She reeled in her line to pick up the slack. "None of the above. Lots of dead-end relationships and broken hearts. Mostly mine."

He found that hard to believe. What kind of man wouldn't want a woman like Josie? "Tell me about your job back in Louisville."

She shrugged. "I work with a small group of photographers, and we're assigned events, birthday bashes, anniversary parties, reunions, and the like."

251

"You enjoy it?"

"Sure. It's nice to be present for happy events and watch the families interact, try and capture some of that excitement on film."

"Doesn't it make you lonely for your own family?"

Josie's gaze skittered away from his. "It's different when it's other people's families. I'm on the outside looking in, and that's not all bad, you know? It's safer." She bit her lip as if afraid she'd revealed too much.

Through the haze of his vision, he saw Josie's bobber go under again. She jerked the rod and reeled in another bass.

thirty-one

*T*hat's the last time I take you fishing," Grady said.

Josie flipped Grady's bluegill in the frying pan and it sizzled, spitting grease darts, one of them catching her on the wrist. She'd already cooked the four bass and one bluegill she'd caught, and had set the crispy brown fillets on a platter. The aroma of fried fish filled his house. Grady's fish stretched across the sad-looking pan he'd dug from a cabinet.

"At least he's big." Grady set the silverware on the corner table. It wobbled when he leaned against it. "Some might even say huge."

"Let's not get carried away."

"He barely fits in the pan."

"He's shrinking more with each second." She removed the fish with the spatula and turned off the burner.

"I'm trying to be a man about this."

"I didn't mean to wound your fragile male ego. That's the biggest bluegill I've ever seen. Better?" She set the platter on the table, and they seated themselves opposite one another.

"That's more like it."

While she arranged the napkin in her lap, he bowed his head in a quick prayer, then they dug in. The smell of frying fish hadn't nauseated her, and she was hopeful her stomach wouldn't rebel.

Grady nodded as he chewed. "Not bad."

The fish was tender and mild. She ate small portions and hoped for the best.

"I stopped by Pick-a-Flick earlier if you're up for a movie," Grady said a few minutes into their meal.

It was his turn to pick. But it wasn't the movie that tempted her to stay. "Let me guess. *Rambo*."

"Give me some credit."

"A compromise." He reached for a plastic bag and pulled a DVD from it.

"*Speed.* Oh, that's a good one. Another Sandra Bullock flick."

"You've seen this one too?"

What could she say? She had no life. She'd

rented every decent movie available the past few years. What else did she have to do on the weekends? After a while, the nightlife scene had worn thin, and the caliber of men she ended up with made a movie seem like a promising option.

"It's worth watching again."

When they were finished eating, Josie rinsed the plates and placed them in the ancient brown-paneled dishwasher.

Grady leaned around her to stash the silverware in the basket, and his chest brushed her back. When he pulled away, she missed the contact.

Josie cleared her throat. "I'll refill our drinks while you put the movie in."

By the time Josie entered the living room, the movie was ready, and Grady was seated on the sofa. She smiled at him as she settled in next to him.

She couldn't stop the thread of anticipation that worked through her. He wanted to be next to her.

"In case there are scary parts," he said as if his choice of seating required explanation. Even in the dim light, she could see the flush that climbed his neck.

The notion that he wanted to be close made her feel wanted—something she hadn't felt in too long. "It is pretty creepy at the end where the bad guy's on top of a train and—"

"Are you trying to ruin it for me?" He pushed Play, and the movie began.

The story was action-packed and tense, holding her attention most of the time. It had been several years since she'd seen it and she'd forgotten parts of it.

Grady watched intently, giving her an opportunity to study him discreetly. He had a strong profile with a perfectly formed nose and a strong jawline. His bangs, parted in the middle, hung beside his forehead, curling ever so slightly inward, almost touching his eyelashes. She let her gaze wander down the column of his neck to his shoulders and his arms, thick and tan. He was handsome and strong. Any woman would be lucky to have him.

His ex-wife was an idiot. How devastated he must've been when she betrayed him. Josie wondered if that was why he hadn't remarried, why he so seldom dated. Why he'd been sorry he'd kissed her. A thing like betrayal had a way of shaking you. Changing you. Trust was a fragile thing not easily restored. Was he afraid of getting hurt again?

What in the world are you doing, Josie? If he's afraid of getting hurt, you are the last thing he needs.

Grady put his arm across the sofa back, shifting her focus. The movie was coming to its dramatic climax, and the bad guy was on top of the train with Keanu Reeves.

Just before the character's decapitation, she turned from the screen. Grady curled his arm around her shoulder and pulled her in until her face was buried in the soft cotton T-shirt.

Mercy, but he smelled good. All piney and musky and manly. There should be a law. His fingers moved on her arm, drawing circles, making her skin tingle.

This is a bad idea. A very bad idea. And yet it was so nice she couldn't tear herself away. It felt good to be held and protected. Even if just for a little while.

"Bad part's over," he whispered, his lips so close to her ear that she felt the warmth of his breath.

Josie didn't want to leave her safe cocoon, but she lifted her head.

And there he was. So close. So tempting. Her hand itched to run up his chest and behind his head. Then she wanted to pull him toward her until—

Bad, Josie.

Bad, bad, bad. Where is this going? You're going to hurt him. He doesn't deserve that. Hasn't he been through enough?

But he was leaning toward her with that look in his eyes. She had to do something.

Josie turned away. "We can't." Her heart complained loudly, emphatically. *Yeah, yeah, I know. Believe me.*

Grady leaned his forehead against her temple, his warm breath tickling her ear. "Why not?"

Because I'm going to die. Because it will hurt

you. Because these feelings confuse me, make me question things, and I've already made up my mind.

"You know why," she said instead.

She felt him trace a trail on her back. Her body responded with a quiet shiver. *Not fair.*

"It's just a kiss."

She drew in a shaky breath. "This from a man who is downright dangerous in that particular department." Didn't it always start with just a kiss? A kiss with Grady was like having just one hit of a potent drug. Impossible. Already she wanted it more than she could bear.

And what then, Josie? Where can it go from there?

Maybe I could let it play out. Maybe there's a way . . .

Grady tilted his head. Or was it her? She didn't know, but suddenly their lips were touching. His were like a dove's wing, feathery and soft. It shook her to the core.

So good. Not only the kiss, but the way he wanted her. She wanted to relish that thought for these few minutes. What could it hurt?

Maybe things could be different. Maybe she could find the will to live if she were loved by a man like Grady.

What about the guilt? What about Ian? That won't go away, Josie. He died because of you, and nothing can change that.

She was exhausted from the weight of reality. Too tired of living a life she didn't deserve, trying to pay penance for a sacrifice she could never be worthy of.

And now she was pulling Grady into her mess. He was going to suffer along with her. Suffer, just as he had when Danielle hurt him. She wasn't going to be another Danielle in his life.

She pulled back, her eyes burning. "No."

He framed her face with his palms. "Yes."

"You don't understand." Was that her voice, all choked and raspy?

"I understand everything I need to."

She shook her head.

He brushed away a tear with his thumb. The tenderness of the gesture broke her. Everything bubbled up inside, ready to spill out. The desire for Grady, the need to end her life.

The maddening knowledge that she couldn't have both.

Could she live with the past if there was a hint of hope for the future? She didn't know. And how could she allow Grady to wade in deeper? Risking her own heart was one matter, but what right did she have to risk his when she was so confused?

She had to get out of there.

Josie jumped up from the couch. She was sliding her feet into her sandals before Grady spoke. "Wait, Josie."

She didn't dare look. Just the strain of his words

was enough to make her want to bury herself in his arms again. To hide from life as she'd hid from the movie. But scary scenes ended. The real-life ones just kept going, and she couldn't stay in the refuge of his arms forever.

"I have to go." She opened the door and escaped. Her feet shuffled across the porch and took the steps, outrunning anything Grady might say to make her stay.

thirty-two

*J*osie plucked an apple from the Fuji tree and dropped it in her bag. Her muscles ached with the movement, and there was nothing to explain the pain except the disease. It was slowly wreaking havoc on her body. Her knees ached when she walked, her back hurt, and then there was the nausea. How much longer?

The progressive symptoms were a needed reminder that she'd made the right decision the night before. Hard as it had been, it was best for both of them.

Grady had only nodded hello earlier. She felt his eyes on her, burning the back of her neck as she worked. It took all her focus to keep her mind on her job. How could she go on like this for the remaining weeks?

The sooner you get these apples down, the sooner you can go home.

Home to what? An empty apartment? An empty life?

No matter how empty Louisville was, it was easier than being here. Easier than being—

"Can we talk?" Grady's voice startled her.

His tired eyes hinted of a long night and she knew from his expression that he didn't have small talk in mind. She wanted to smooth the frown lines from his forehead with her thumb the way he'd smoothed away a tear the night before.

Stop it, Josie.

She twisted a ripened apple and dropped it in her bag. "What's the point, Grady?" Her tone betrayed her fatigue. She'd had a long night of her own and plenty of time to think. She'd reached a decision and was determined to stick with it. No matter whose love she had, it wouldn't be enough to change anything.

"The point is, I care about you."

Her stomach tightened, her hand paused on the next apple. The words played over in her mind, refreshing her. How could a few words sound so good, feel so good?

But what right did she have to them? Grady deserved better than what she could offer. She freed the apple from the branch with a twist and a snap, bagged it, and reached for another.

He grabbed her arm. "*Josie.*"

Could he see her chest rising and falling, heaving as her lungs kept pace with her heart? Why was he making it so hard? What could she say to make him understand what he should already know?

Maybe she needed to make it clear she didn't have much longer. Maybe he thought she had years instead of months. "There's no happily-ever-after here, Grady."

His eyes softened, melting like milk chocolate under the sun's warmth. Did his eyes tear up, or was it a trick of the shimmering shadows dancing across his face?

He swallowed, his Adam's apple bobbing. "I want to be here for you."

He'd already lost one love. Why would he set himself up for another loss? The sweetness of his offer, the selflessness of his desire made her eyes ache.

You could change your mind. Maybe Grady could make life worth living again.

This was the voice that scared her most, the one she was afraid to listen to. Afraid because it made her hope. And hope was a scary thing.

"Josie?"

She bolstered the courage to open the door a crack, just enough to let the idea in. She was a bottle of pills away from becoming healthy again. Put that way, it sounded so easy. Too easy.

What about the guilt? What about the burden of trying to make her life matter and failing over and over again? If only she could make it up to Ian. But he was gone. There was no reconciling that.

And this disease didn't happen on its own, remember? God had given her what she deserved.

"You don't have to go through this alone." Grady's fingers grazed her arm, sending prickles of awareness along every nerve.

What if?

What if she opened herself to the possibility of a new life? Being loved by a man like Grady could make a difference, couldn't it? Maybe it would wash away the guilt, make her forget.

It was possible, wasn't it? Looking into his eyes now, she wanted to believe it. Wanted to so badly. Still, this wasn't a decision to be made lightly. She needed to be sure before she committed to anything. It was only fair.

"I need time," she said. Her eyes fell down the column of his neck where his flesh disappeared beneath the crew-neck T-shirt. His shoulders were broad, the white material stretched across them, narrowing down to the waist of his shorts.

"How much time?"

She wasn't going to be rushed, for their own good. "As much as it takes." She was going to take her time and do the right thing for once, whatever it was. Those brown eyes staring into hers only made it more difficult.

"Hurry up." His tone was a caress. "I miss you."

A loud pounding pulled Josie from a deep sleep. She blinked the haze from her eyes. The clock read nine thirty. It was Sunday, and the others were at church. Most of Shelbyville was at church.

Another knock sounded.

Who in the world?

Josie untangled herself from the covers and threw on a robe. A wave of dizziness assaulted her at the top of the stairs, and she grabbed the railing, pausing on the wood step until it passed. The pounding had stopped.

When she reached the door, she pulled it open, but there was no one there. Strange. She stepped out on the porch, belting her robe, feeling mildly annoyed. A green Buick she didn't recognize was parked beside her Celica.

A tall man in a cap was walking away from the house toward the hill.

Josie clutched her robe at the neckline and walked to the edge of the porch. "Hello?" she called.

The man turned, then lifted a hand. "Didn't think anyone was home." He walked back toward the house.

As he approached, Josie recognized him. Hank, their former manager. Ian's father. Panic welled up inside her. What was he doing here?

Maybe he knows.

But there was no way he could.

He was walking up the hill. He's carrying a cluster of flowers. He's only come to visit the grave.

"Josephine Mitchell." He removed his cap, revealing a hairline that had receded several inches. His face had aged, the tired lines around his eyes a permanent stamp of grief.

"Mr. Leland, how wonderful to see you." The lie slipped out easily.

His booted feet stopped just shy of the porch. His Wranglers hung on his frame. The potbelly she remembered was gone, his jeans held in place by a wide brown belt.

"You're all grown up," he drawled.

As opposed to Ian, who's rotting in his grave. She shook away the thought. It wasn't what he'd meant. "I suppose I am. Laurel told me you moved to Tennessee."

"Yep, that's where I am now." His dark eyes, shaped like almonds and slightly turned up at the corners, were so much like Ian's.

Maybe he'd remarried. Maybe he'd found happiness in the hills of Tennessee. Maybe he'd made peace with his loss and moved on.

"Have a little cabin set back off the road a ways. It's small, but there's just me."

"Sounds nice."

"It's home. I come back here every year on Ian's birthday though." He gestured up the hill. "Put flowers on his grave."

Ian's birthday. She'd forgotten it was in October. How could she have forgotten? It was right before the festival.

How hard this day must be for Hank. Josie cupped her elbows. She should invite him in. It was the hospitable thing to do.

"Your aunt takes good care of his grave. It's a solace for me to come back and see it well tended."

Josie nodded, unsure of what to say. Unable to untangle her thoughts enough to pull a few coherent words from the mess.

"My boy loved you like a sister, Josephine. Hope you know that."

Bile churned in her stomach. She worked to keep a smile on a face that felt more like plastic than flesh. *Speak, Josie. Say something.*

"Thank you. He was—he was a special boy." And yet she'd never felt anything for him except resentment. Never took the time to get to know him at all.

Did Hank know that? Had her adolescent envy been obvious? Ian had never seemed to realize, but he'd been a boy, desperate for a friend. Adults perceived things that children were oblivious to. Was Hank trying to pour salt in her wounds? No, he wasn't that kind of man. But death had a way of changing people.

Maybe he does know.

Josie averted her eyes.

"That he was. He would've been twenty-one today."

An ache swelled inside her, massive and heavy.

Twenty-one. Legally an adult. Instead, he'd died on the brink of manhood. *Because of me.*

Hank set the cap back on his head. "Well."

She didn't know what to say. She wanted to beg his forgiveness, tell him it should have been her. Tell him it was all her fault. *I'm so sorry.* Instead, the ache inside swallowed up her words and expanded.

"I'll be on my way. Tell Laurel and your aunt I'll stop by and see them before I head out of town."

He was coming back. The thought brought dread, and she felt guilty for her selfishness. Blue Ridge Orchard was a connection to his only child.

Josie pried her tongue from the dry roof of her mouth. "Will do."

With a wave, he turned toward the hill.

Josie went into the house and shut the door behind her, her breaths coming unnaturally fast. Just when she thought maybe . . .

The reminder of what she'd done and who she was came rushing back. What right did she have to life when she'd taken someone else's? What right did she have to love when she'd yanked away the only thing Mr. Leland had left in this world?

She thought of his face, all sunken and hollow. He looked ill instead of looking like a man enjoying the fruits of his labor. Ill and lonely.

What right did she have to happiness when she'd deprived Ian of it? The disease was justice. God's way of evening the score. And who was she to stand in his way?

She returned to her room, her mind fixed on the thing she should've done weeks ago. Maybe she hadn't had the courage until now. Maybe she'd clung to a futile hope that was buried like a seed deep inside her. Maybe Grady had been all the temptation she'd needed.

But now there was nothing to stop her. She grabbed her purse from the dresser and dug deep until her fingers closed around the injectable cortisol and the two bottles. She went to the bathroom, wrapped the shot with a wad of tissue and tossed it into the waste can, then she twisted off the lids and upended the bottles over the commode. With the flick of her hand, the pills were spinning, spinning, swirling through the water, and then they were gone.

thirty-three

*T*he autumn foliage was Josie's excuse to disappear with her camera for the day. She spent a fortune on film and stayed out until twilight drew its heavy curtains across the hills. She'd left her rolls of film at Ingles to be developed while she was out snapping more photos, then she'd picked them up, eager to see her work.

She sat in the deli booth where she and Grady had sat before and opened the packages, surveying the images she'd captured. A couple of them were blurry, but there were a few she was pleased with. One of them was of the creek water rippling over a rock, the water frozen in time, each drop in perfect focus. Maybe she would enlarge that one. The covered bridge over the gap was also good. The shadow of a tree fell across the entrance, darkening the interior.

She was proud of her work, and she found herself wanting to show someone. Leaving the world of her photos, she looked up and saw she was alone in the deli. She'd been alone all day, wanting to avoid Hank and her family.

It was getting late though, and Hank would surely be on his way by now. She packed her prints and returned to her car.

Within minutes she was pulling into the driveway and longing for her bed. She wanted to erase Hank from her thoughts, and sleep was the only way that was going to happen. She hadn't been able to get his tired, gentle eyes out of her mind all day. Eyes so like Ian's.

She forced the image from her mind as she crested the hill and glided down the slope. Would she ever go down this hill without thinking of that night? Her eyes darted to the left where her sled had gone over, where Ian had trudged down when she'd fallen through the ice.

Stop it, Josie. Stop thinking about it.

How much worse can I feel? How much sorrier

can I be? There's nothing I can do to make it right. Nothing.

Yes, there is. You're doing it now, doing the only thing that will make it right.

But Ian was gone and she couldn't bring him back. If she could reverse time, she'd do things differently. She wouldn't go down the hill. Wouldn't let Ian jump into the frigid water. She'd rather she'd died herself. Her father probably would've too.

Josie accelerated down the hill as if she would escape the memory as soon as she left the area. But there would be no escaping the memory until she left this property for good. Once harvest was over, once Laurel had the twins and she could leave, it would be better.

The thought was heartening until she realized it was a lie. Had she been able to forget in Louisville? In Columbus? In Pittsburgh? There was no escaping the memory until life was over.

And what then? What waited for her on the other side? What if she would be eternally punished for what she'd done? Anxiety rose inside her with the speed and force of a hurricane.

Maybe there was no escape at all. Maybe there was a price to be paid for her sin. A price inescapable even through death.

The thought shook her to the core. It was easier to think of death as an end. Oblivion, or at least the cease of existence. But what if her family was right and there was more? What if God punished her eternally for what she'd done, for who she was?

She pulled up to the house, her mind so far from her whereabouts, she didn't notice the Buick until she was beside it.

A heavy sigh filled the car. She was beginning to believe God was hanging around, if only because somebody had to be orchestrating this bad string of events.

She let her head fall against the headrest, looking up to the heavens through her roof. "Are you serious?" Her voice rang out in the darkness.

Her engine hissed and snapped. Apparently so.

When she opened the front door, she heard the sound of chatter from the dining room. If she could just sneak up to her room.

"Got a plate for you, Josie," Aunt Lola called. "Come say hi to Mr. Leland."

So much for that. Josie entered the dining room, avoiding eye contact with Grady. She greeted Mr. Leland again and took a seat.

"We were just talking about the time we went up to Grandfather Mountain and Ian got stuck on the middle of the bridge," Laurel said.

He'd been terrified of heights. It had been Josie who'd convinced him to go across. Dared him. Laurel had been the one to get him.

Mr. Leland laughed. "So much for facing your fears. He wouldn't go past the second rung on a ladder after that."

I was so mean. I wanted him to fail. I wanted him to make a fool of himself.

Josie picked at the meatloaf, wishing she'd turned down supper. Now she was stuck at the table until they were finished.

"Nate said you had a good year, Grady," Hank said.

Grady scooped a bite of peas onto his fork. "Yes, sir. Good crop, our best since I've been here. Would've been even better except for the windstorm, but we'll still turn a profit."

"Good you've moved back home, Josephine. Looks like Grady's making more work for everyone." He smiled.

"Oh. I'm just back 'til the end of harvest. I live in Louisville now." She saw Grady's fork pause on the way to his mouth.

"We're hoping to change her mind," Nate said.

"If only she weren't so stubborn." Laurel poked her with her elbow. "I keep telling her I'll need her for aunt duty." Hank's visit had turned her mood around.

"I'm so happy y'all are being blessed with babies," Hank said.

"Won't be long now," Aunt Lola said.

"How much bigger could I possibly get?" Laurel said.

Josie wondered how long she needed to wait before she could excuse herself without being rude.

"What are you doing up in Louisville, Josephine?"

She cleared her throat. "I'm a photographer."

He nodded. "Always did have that camera around your neck. But I thought sure you'd stick around and run this place. You had a knack for it."

That's what she'd thought too. She'd seen a bumper sticker once: "If you want to make God laugh, make plans."

"Ian had hopes of helping you run it someday. He sure loved this place."

A sharp knife wedged between her ribs, sinking deep into her flesh.

"He'd be proud to see it prospering," Hank continued.

Panic bubbled up inside her, begging escape. She chewed a mouthful of peas, hoping someone else would speak. Couldn't they talk about something else, someone else? Then she felt guilty for the thought. It must bring Mr. Leland joy to talk to people who knew Ian. Who was she to rob him of that?

Finally, Grady mentioned the vine-style method of growing apple trees, and the two started talking shop. Josie remained quiet for the rest of the meal and excused herself when Aunt Lola brought out another apple pie.

"It's the recipe that's going to win me the grand prize," Aunt Lola tempted.

"Save me a slice, and I'll have it tomorrow." She

said good-bye to Hank and slipped from the room, to the stairway, feeling Grady's eyes burning the back of her neck.

He caught her on the second step. "Josie."

So close to escaping. She sighed, turning around. He was eye level.

"You okay?" The concern in his chocolaty eyes was the only thing that stayed her irritation.

Her bed beckoned. She wanted to sink into its quilted softness and pull the covers over her head. "I'm just tired."

A strand of hair brushed the side of his eye and caught in his eyelashes. "Can I get you anything?"

"I just need sleep." Oblivion, really, but sleep would suffice for now.

He nodded. "All right. 'Night, Josie." He touched her chin with his index finger. Just a whisper of a touch, but it melted her. Made her want to sink into his embrace and find her escape there.

"Good night," she said, then bolted up the stairs before her weakness led her further astray.

thirty-four

*Y*ou still look tired."

Josie swallowed the sip of hot coffee and scooted across the tailgate to make room for Grady. The others sat a distance away under a shade tree, enjoying a coffee break after a long morning.

"I'm not sleeping well." The illness had its repercussions, but Hank's visit hadn't helped either. When she had slept, visions of Ian had haunted her.

Hank's words echoed in her mind all night. *"He'd be proud to see it prospering."* This year's crop would've made Ian proud. Even with the loss from the windstorm, it was a good year. She could picture Ian now, scanning the orchard, his scrawny shoulders pulled back, a silly grin on his freckled face. He'd taken pride in his work here.

Josie was going to make sure she was doing everything in her power to produce a harvest that would make Ian proud. That's the one good thing she could do with the time she had left. She owed Ian. Maybe she couldn't work off the debt, but she could even the scales a little.

"You're working too hard."

It was the least she could do. And in truth, staying busy was easier on her mind, just harder on her body. Grady's thigh pressed against hers, made her forget there was anything wrong with her body. The contact made her feel whole, connected.

Which was all wrong. She shifted, pulling her knees to her chest.

"We only have a couple of weeks to go on harvest. You could stay with Laurel all day, and Aunt Lola could keep longer hours at the shop."

Did he have to be so concerned for her? It only made it harder. Made her decision to stay away more painful. His suggestion was tempting. Being at the house would mean less contact with Grady, but it would also mean too much time on her hands. Besides, she was determined to see this harvest through, work as hard as Ian would have if he were still here.

"I'd rather stay busy." It was the only thing that would make the time pass quickly. Would keep her mind from filling with thoughts of Ian and Hank and her dad. "Besides, I like it out here." It was the one place she knew what she was doing.

"Your body needs rest."

Why couldn't he just leave her alone? "Don't tell me what my body needs." It felt good, snapping at him. But just for a moment. Then the familiar pang of guilt crept in.

She set the thermos down, then rubbed the back of her neck as if she could massage away her guilt.

Grady let Josie's sharp tone roll off his back. She wasn't feeling well and it made her irritable. She wasn't so different from her sister. Why did she have to be so stubborn about the work?

"Sorry," Josie said, barely meeting his eyes before flickering away. "I know you're just trying to help."

She looked so small tucked into a ball on the edge of the tailgate. He wanted to wrap his arms around her and protect her. But he couldn't protect her from everything. Wasn't sure she wanted him to try.

He wanted to ask why she'd acted so strangely over dinner. There was something she wasn't telling him. Her face had turned ashen when Hank was talking. She'd picked at her thumbnail with her middle finger the way she did when she was upset or anxious. The way she was doing now.

Maybe if he figured out what was worrying her, it would take off some of the pressure. "Hank seems to be faring well."

Josie stopped picking and sipped her coffee. "Mhmm."

"His son was about your age, wasn't he?"

Josie stirred, looking restless. "A few years younger." She checked her watch, let go of her legs, and set them dangling over the end, poised for flight. "Probably should get back to work."

"It's only been three or four minutes." There was something bothering her, and his hunch that it had to do with Hank was right on. It was all starting to make sense. The way she kept busy all the time, never sitting still until she was about to drop. The way she wanted to run off to the city. The way she'd run from the orchard even though she'd always wanted to stay and run it.

He was tired of beating around the bush. "What is it, Josie? What are you running from?"

Her answer was too quick. "I'm not running from anything."

He knew she'd left shortly after Ian's death. Had that factored into her decision? Maybe he shouldn't press her. She had enough problems, didn't she? And yet sometimes talking helped. She kept everything to herself, all bottled up.

He pushed a little harder. "It must have been hard when Ian died."

She froze for an instant, her dangling legs stiff. "Stop it." Her skin had blanched. "All right. We all have our ghosts. And maybe I *am* running from them."

He felt bad for pushing so hard. But running didn't help. He knew it better than anyone. His voice gentled. "How's that working for you?"

She hopped off the truck, a dismount that was surprisingly agile until her legs buckled on the landing.

Grady was off the truck and grabbing her before her knees gave way.

She brushed him away. "I'm fine."

She was so stinking independent. Couldn't she let him in just a little? "You're not fine. You should be at the house."

"And you should mind your own business."

"You are my business."

Her chin went up and she crossed her arms. "How do you figure?"

This wasn't going the way he wanted. Why did he have to get so pushy? And why did she have to be so prickly when all he wanted was to help? When he just wanted to take care of her because he . . .

What? Cared for her? It was what he'd told her two days before. The phrase seemed hollow compared to the feelings she stirred in him. Was he in deeper than that? Had he fallen in love with her?

Did she return those feelings? Is that why her lip quivered for just a moment before she stilled it with her teeth?

Her chin had come down just a notch, though her hands still gripped her own biceps like a lifeline. A strand of hair came loose from her ponytail and a breeze caught it, dragging it across her face.

He reached out to tuck it behind her ear.

She flinched away before he caught the strand. That one movement told him more than anything she'd said. He felt the rejection down to his bones.

"I can't do this," she said.

He didn't have to ask what. Still, he waited for some kind of elaboration. Was it the illness? The certainty of—what was it she'd said? *There's no happily-ever-after here.*

Or was it something else? That thing from the past—whatever it was—that she ran from?

Hernando's boisterous laugh cut through the silence.

"Harvest is nearly over," she said. "I'll be going home soon, and until then, I just need—"

Her words halted; her lips worked, seeking the right word. He wished he could fill in the blank for her. *You.*

"I just need to be left alone."

The ache in his bones spread. "Left alone?" *It's not complicated,* amigo*, that makes it pretty clear.*

In the grove, the crew rattled off Spanish faster than he could follow even if he were paying attention.

She let loose of her arm long enough to tuck the wayward strand behind her ear. "A relationship is out of the question right now."

"You've made your decision . . ."

"I hope you understand."

There was understanding, and then there was accepting. But it was her decision, not his.

The words she'd just said rang in his head. *Left alone.* What did that mean? They worked together, they ate supper together. Was he not supposed to talk to her, look at her, help her?

He was only willing to cooperate so far. "I guess I'll have to be content with friendship." Assume the sale. His dad had taught him that.

"Grady . . ." Her head tipped sideways, and he could see another rejection poised on the end of her tongue.

What? A moment ago he was hoping for love, now he had to beg for friendship? It was a little humiliating.

But he was going to fight for whatever he could get. "We have to work together, lead this crew together. Friendship is the bare minimum, don't you think?" He tossed the words out as casually as he could, shamed by how desperate he felt for her consent.

The chatter between the crew wound down as they finished their coffee and made their way back to the trees.

"Friends?" He put out his hand.

She looked at it as if it were a rotten apple. Finally, she extended her own.

"Friends," she said, the word wobbling ever so slightly on her lips.

thirty-five

*W*hat is going on between you and Grady?" Laurel's question made Josie wish she'd retreated to her room after supper instead of taking pity on her sister.

"I don't know what you mean." Denial was the best defense. For the past two days, there'd been tension between her and Grady. She felt every weighted glance he sent her way.

"Baloney. The way he looks at you . . ." Laurel fanned her face, her knitting needle waving. "Heaven have mercy."

Josie felt a need to fan her own face as heat climbed her cheeks. "Your hormones are affecting your reasoning skills."

"On the contrary, my perception has never been sharper. Spill it."

Her sister was easy to talk to, but Laurel didn't

know enough to understand why the relationship was impossible. And she couldn't tell Laurel everything.

"You have the hots for our manager, admit it."

The crass expression didn't begin to describe her feelings. Feelings that made everything harder, more complicated. Feelings she had to put from her mind if she was ever going to survive these remaining weeks.

And she hated what this was doing to Grady. Her decision had hurt him, and she regretted that. She wished she could do something for him. Something that would make it—

The orchard. He'd always wanted one of his own, and she could see to it that he could buy it. She weighed the cost, the extra burden on Laurel during the years it would take him to buy her shares. She trusted Grady now. He was a hard worker, and if her family had managed to keep it going for three generations, she was sure he could too.

Maybe she could even sign some of her shares over to him in her will. The thought of leaving Grady something he treasured buoyed her spirits.

Now Laurel's voice startled her from her thoughts. "Are you all right?"

"I'm fine." She lifted the corners of her lips, hoping for a convincing smile. She wanted any idea of a pairing between her and Grady banished from her sister's thoughts. "We're just friends." It was what they'd decided on. Or rather, what she'd reluctantly agreed to.

"I never had a friend look at me the way Grady looks at you . . ."

"We're *friends*."

Laurel shrugged and her needles clacked together as she worked the yarn. "Whatever you say."

"We're just friends." Grady loaded a crate of Granny Smiths for the farmer's market. They'd hired a high school student to man the stand.

"Sorry to pry." Nate adjusted the crate in the bed of the pickup. "That's what Josie said, but Laurel's concerned. She says Josie doesn't seem herself, and hasn't been since she's come home."

Grady felt a prick of guilt. How could she be herself? He hated that she was going through this alone. He'd hoped that being her friend meant she'd spend time with him, confide in him. He was half tempted to tell Nate about her illness. She needed her family right now, especially since she wasn't letting him in.

But then there was Laurel's condition. Josie was right that she didn't need the stress. She needed to carry those babies as long as possible.

Grady pushed the crate onto the bed and shoved the tailgate closed. "Laurel doing okay?"

"She's bored and uncomfortable, but the babies are healthy. She's got the furniture all picked out, but I need to finish painting the room. Probably ought to do that tomorrow night."

"Must be getting close to delivery time." The closer, the better. Once the babies were born, Josie could tell her sister, and then she'd have the support she needed. Surely she wouldn't go back to Louisville as she'd said. He didn't like the thought of her being alone.

"Her due date is in three and a half weeks, but she'll likely deliver early since it's twins. Still, the longer she carries them, the better."

Every day the delivery was delayed was another day Josie suffered in silence. He knew it was the right thing, but that knowledge didn't make it any easier. In the meantime, he'd just have to see to it that being friends with Josie meant being a shoulder for her to lean on.

thirty-six

*J*osie was minding her own business, her thoughts far away, when Laurel set her sneaky plan in motion.

". . . So I was wondering if you could pick it up tonight, Josie," Laurel was saying.

Josie chewed a mouthful of green bean casserole. "What?"

"The baby furniture? I just told you it's on sale now and I was wondering if you could pick it up tonight if you don't have plans."

As if she ever had plans. At least it would get her away from the house. "Sure."

Laurel beamed. "Great. It's all settled."

Grady scooted his chair back. "I'm ready whenever you are."

She stared up at him. "What?" *You have got to pay better attention.* Her eyes fell to his trim waist, then she looked away.

"To leave for Asheville . . . ?" Grady said.

Grady was going too? Josie set down her fork and wiped her mouth, stalling. An hour there, an hour back. Lots of time. All alone. "Oh, I thought . . ."

That she was going to haul furniture for twins in her Celica? Of course they'd need Grady's truck.

"Pick you up in ten minutes?"

She checked her watch. If they were going to get there before it closed, they'd have to hurry. "Sure." He left, the screen door slapping against the door frame as he exited.

Josie nailed Laurel with a glare, which her sister missed entirely.

"I'll get started on the trim." Nate pecked Laurel on the cheek.

"Chicken," Laurel murmured.

Aunt Lola began gathering plates. "Better get the dishes done." She disappeared into the kitchen.

Josie pushed away from the table and stared her sister down. "I see right through this little plan of yours, missy."

"Don't be paranoid." Laurel rubbed the small of her back, arching. "The furniture I wanted finally went on sale today, and I'm about to pop here, in case you haven't noticed."

"You know perfectly well Grady could've gotten it himself."

Laurel sighed. "I have some female things I need you to get while you're there. I couldn't very well ask him to pick up a few nursing bras, could I?"

As if she couldn't have asked Nate to do that. Her sister was up to no good and Josie knew it.

"Stop looking at me like that. I'm just a bored pregnant lady in need of a little excitement. Humor me."

The thought of a trip alone with Grady was providing a measure of excitement for Josie too.

Twenty minutes later they were on their way. The truck rumbled and bumped down the highway, filling the awkward silence and jarring the contents of Josie's stomach.

Did Grady know they'd been set up? If so, he didn't seem to mind. He flipped on the radio and whistled along to the country tune. Josie watched the trees, clothed in vibrant autumn hues, march by in the fading light. October was passing quickly, bringing a crisp chill to the air that warned of winter's approach.

Josie leaned back and forced herself to relax. She was finally escaping the orchard, only she wasn't escaping at all. Instead, she was trapped in a vehicle with the man who made her want to throw all caution aside and embrace life.

It was dangerous stuff. *And you've already been down this road, Josie. Already made your decision. Now you just have to stick to it.* This was the easy part, right?

When the song ended, Grady turned down the radio. "Tell me about your life in Louisville. You haven't said much about it."

Because there wasn't much to say. "I lived in an apartment near downtown, second floor. I chose it because it had this wonderful veranda that faced east. I have an impressive garden out there with lavender and strawberry, wisteria . . . Well, I did anyway."

"How long did you live there?"

"Eight months." It was the longest she'd stayed anywhere since she'd left the orchard. She found herself unsettled after staying any one place awhile. Maybe it was time to get a new place anyway.

"What about friends?"

"I've only been in Louisville eight months. I was in Columbus before that. And Pittsburgh before that. I guess I like to move around, experience new things." Running, just like Grady had said. Being on the go was easier. She got stir-crazy when she stayed in one place too long.

"Doesn't sound like you have many roots."

"Roots are overrated. If you aren't careful, they climb right up and strangle you whole."

She felt his eyes on her. "Really? You think so?"

"It's not like you have so many roots yourself."

The singer crooned about a lost love and a dog that died. If Grady had any relatives, he never talked about them. He was as much a loner as she.

"I have my mom, she just lives too far away. But the man she married has a business in Chicago, so she's not moving anytime soon. I guess I'm trying to grow roots in Shelbyville. That's why the orchard is so important to me."

She'd never told him she'd changed her mind about selling. It was the least she could do for him. How could she take away what he'd worked so hard for? She'd called Allen, her attorney, the day before and made sure fifteen percent of her shares would go to him. That would leave Grady with thirty percent and Laurel with seventy. Her sister and Grady could work out the buy from there. Between him and Nate, they'd make things right, make sure Laurel was taken care of after she was gone.

If she asked him to, he would. The song was winding down, and Josie worked up the nerve to ask. "Would you do something for me?"

He looked at her. "What's that?"

She had to think about after. It was the most important thing. "You know the orchard was never Laurel's thing. She assumed the responsibility because I left and then Dad had the stroke."

The song on the radio ended and the DJ started talking. Grady snapped it off.

"Laurel always dreamed of selling her crafts, and I'd like her to have that chance if she still wants it. Either way, I don't want her to worry about the orchard. That's why I was so adamant about selling it."

An ache started in her throat. "At the same time, I respect what you've done with Blue Ridge and the plans you've made for its future success. I wondered if you were still interested in working out a buying arrangement. Something long-term that would give you time to buy it out." She didn't mention the shares she'd left him. She'd let that be a surprise. Her gift to him.

Grady braked at a stoplight. It was what he'd wanted so badly. She didn't expect the long silence that followed. Maybe he didn't want it anymore. Maybe he'd changed his mind. Her gaze found his.

She couldn't quite read the look in his eyes. The shadows were pressing in around them. Something flickered in his eyes before he looked away. The light changed, and he accelerated.

His Adam's apple dipped. "I didn't want it like this."

Something in his tone bothered her. He felt sorry for her. He wanted to buy the orchard, but not because she was dying.

"You wanted to sell it so it wouldn't be a burden

to your sister after—" His words choked to a halt.

"She never wanted it to begin with. Not really. It was my fault for leaving." And her dad's fault for dumping it on her.

"You couldn't have known your dad was going to pass."

But she hadn't come home even then. Couldn't face the guilt of Ian, didn't want to face the unresolved issues with her dad. She didn't want to think about this now, much less talk about it.

"Are you still interested in buying it?"

His jaw clenched, the shadows dancing across his face. "I don't want to talk about this."

It wasn't as if she had all the time in the world. "I need to get this settled, Grady."

His hands worked on the steering wheel as if he wanted to strangle it. He blinked rapidly, emotion drawing his facial muscles into a hard plane.

Maybe he didn't want it anymore and was afraid to tell her. "If you're not, I'll figure something else out." She didn't want to dump the orchard on Grady any more than on Laurel. He deserved to be happy. To find those roots he wanted. A place that was home, someone to keep the loneliness at bay.

The thought tightened her stomach, made it twist painfully. She didn't want to think of him with someone else. It should've been her. If fate hadn't intervened, she would've stayed on the orchard all along and would've met him after Hank retired.

She and Grady and Ian would be working the orchard together.

She and Grady would've fallen in love. Maybe they'd be married by now. Maybe they'd be driving to Asheville to pick up their own baby's furniture.

Stop. What are you doing to yourself?

"I'll work something out with Laurel, if she wants to sell," he said. "I won't let the orchard be a burden to her." He placed his hand on hers and met her gaze. "I promise."

The warmth from his fingers enveloped hers as he stared into her eyes. The connection felt good, made her feel whole and healthy and content. She could pretend, if she wanted, that they *were* married. That they *were* picking up their own baby furniture.

That she'd never caused Ian's death and hadn't been on the run from the truth ever since.

"Thank you." She slipped her hand from under his and looked away. She tried to enjoy the relief she should be feeling now that everything was in place. She was sure Laurel would let him buy her out once she got a taste of life after the twins were born. Nate would help convince her.

It was all taken care of. She just wasn't sure why the relief she had expected never came.

By the time they reached The Baby Loft, the mood had lightened. Grady had turned the radio back on, and when he started singing along to a hit tune, she joined in, which only made it sound worse, if that was possible.

Somewhere between Burnsville and Weaverville, her stomach settled, and though her energy level was still low, her spirits were higher.

Grady let her off at the door and got out to shift a few things in the back. Josie grabbed the nursing bras and a few other items Laurel had written on a list while she waited for the worker to load the boxes: a pair of cribs, a changing table, and a matching bureau.

She wished she had time to stop and see Ashley and Jackie, but it was getting late, and they probably had plans anyway. Besides, it would be late by the time she and Grady got home as it was.

Her cell phone rang as she exited the store. A man was helping Grady heft one of the boxes into the truck bed. She pulled out her phone. Ah, five bars of reception. Welcome to the city.

"Hello?"

"It's Nate. You might want to get home as soon as you can. Laurel's in labor."

Josie's feet stopped on the sidewalk outside the store. "But we just left."

"Her back's been hurting all day, but apparently that was the beginning of labor. We're at the hospital and the doctor says she's progressing quickly."

Grady approached. "What's wrong?"

"Laurel's in labor."

Two seconds later he was shoving the other boxes into the truck and slamming the tailgate in place.

"Everything is okay," Nate said. "The babies are positioned right and the doctor expects a smooth delivery." He covered the phone and Josie heard a muffled voice, then he was back on the line. "Laurel said to get your heinie back here."

Josie smothered a smile, excitement building inside. "Tell her it was a fine time to send me after her furniture."

A rustling sounded through the line. "Uh, she's in a bit of pain now. Gotta go."

Josie flipped her phone closed and hopped in the passenger side as Grady turned the key, released the parking brake, and eased onto the street.

"Come on, come on, step on it."

He tossed her a bemused smile. "Patience, Auntie Josie."

She couldn't help it. Somehow the whole baby thing hadn't seemed real until this moment. What if Laurel gave birth before she got there? She didn't want to miss the big event.

Worse, what if something went wrong? What if something happened to one of the babies? Or to Laurel? Nate hadn't said it was too early. He'd even said the doctors expected a smooth delivery. But what if—

"Stop worrying. Everything's going to be fine."

"You can't know that." Grady turned a corner and slowly worked up to the speed limit. "Could we put the pedal to the metal, please?"

Within minutes Grady was accelerating onto the freeway, the distance between Josie and her sister growing shorter by the second.

thirty-seven

Josie rushed to the desk, braking only when her hands hit the sharp edge of the counter. "Is Laurel okay? Has she had the babies?"

The woman's hazel eyes peered over a pair of black, heavily framed reading glasses. "Are you a member of the family?"

Josie narrowed her eyes at Aunt Lola's friend. "Verna Mae Pridemore, you know very well I'm Laurel's sister."

The woman pursed her lips, then smoothed her flippy cartoon hair. "Laurel's doing fine. She's in delivery, but you'll have to wait in the lobby just down the hall."

"Thank you." Josie rushed down the hall and found Aunt Lola in the nook of cushioned chairs flanked by tables.

"She's doing fine," her aunt said in greeting, then gave her a sturdy hug. "They took her into delivery about twenty minutes ago."

What a relief. Somehow she didn't quite believe it until she saw Aunt Lola's peaceful countenance.

Josie took a seat on the edge of a chair and set her purse on the table. "I tried to call Nate on the way over, but I guess he turned his cell off."

"I think he's got his hands full with Laurel. Where's Grady?"

"Parking the car."

Aunt Lola filled her in. When Grady appeared and sank into the seat next to Josie, Aunt Lola sat on his other side and caught him up too. As silence settled between them, Aunt Lola bowed her head, her lips moving in a silent prayer.

A moment later, Grady joined hands with Aunt Lola and Josie and bowed his own head.

Josie closed her eyes. It had been so long. She didn't know what to say, how to begin even. It seemed to come so naturally to everyone else. Maybe God wouldn't mind if she just sat here quietly. She was sure Aunt Lola's and Grady's prayers would have more effect anyway.

Grady squeezed her hand and let it go when he was finished, then Josie grabbed a magazine to occupy her mind. She flipped through one after another, looking up each time the doors leading to the delivery rooms opened. An hour passed, then two. At times, the hands on the utilitarian clock seemed stuck.

At one thirty, Josie set down the copy of *Carolina Country* magazine she hadn't been able to read. Grady was slumped in the seat beside her, his arms folded across his chest, his eyes closed.

Aunt Lola watched a rerun of *Judge Judy* on the ancient TV in the corner.

"What's taking so long?" Josie asked. She thought the delivery was the short part of labor.

"She's delivering babies, not mail, Josephine. These things take time."

She only hoped everything was okay. There was always a possibility of a C-section with twins, and she knew Laurel was hoping to avoid that.

"You took twenty-some hours yourself, you know, and as I recall, the delivery part was no walk in the park for your mama."

She hadn't known that. Her mom hadn't said anything, and that wasn't something her dad would've passed on, especially given the memory of her twin's death.

The thought sent a shiver of fear through her. What if it happened to one of Laurel's babies? Was this sort of thing genetic? And why didn't someone come out here and tell them what was going on?

Josie's back ached and she shifted, facing Grady, trying to get comfortable on the chair. She'd already flipped through every magazine on the table. She laid her cheek against the back of the vinyl chair and pulled her knee up, careful not to jostle Grady.

Grady let out a soft snore, drawing her attention. His dark locks fell in waves along his face. He looked serene and vulnerable in sleep.

She let her eyes rest on the planes of his face.

The harsh fluorescent lights cut across his features, highlighting pencil-thin shadows that fanned out from his eyes. She noticed a tiny crescent-shaped scar at the corner of his mouth and wondered how he'd come by it.

His skin had darkened under the autumn sun and looked golden brown against his black crew-neck T-shirt. His neck and jaw sported a five o'clock shadow that made him look rugged. She remembered her initial impression of him as Marlboro Man and felt a smile tug at her lips. She'd been attracted to him from the beginning, and that was before she knew the man beneath the handsome exterior.

He was gentle and caring, always watching out for her. He was a man you could count on, a rarity in her experience. Her eyes fell to his lips, slightly parted in sleep. His upper lip had a bow that made her want to dip her finger into the valley of it, and his lower lip had just enough fullness to make him ripe for kissing. She could nearly feel the kiss now, feel the feathery softness of it.

She sensed a change, an awareness, and when her gaze trailed upward, she found Grady's eyes open. Their gazes locked, a steady current of something strong connecting them. She wanted him that moment in a way she'd never wanted a man. She wanted all of him, completely. She wanted to jump inside his mind and curl up with his thoughts. She wanted to love him and let him love her.

The thought startled her, and she broke eye contact, sitting up in the chair. She was weak, so weak! She had to stop thinking about what she wanted. She had to think of Grady, of what was best for him. And she wasn't it.

The delivery door busted open and Nate appeared, a silly grin spread across his face.

Josie shook herself from her thoughts and stood.

"We have two healthy baby girls!" Nate said.

Girls! Josie embraced Nate, relief making her legs go wobbly.

"Laurel okay?" Aunt Lola was right behind her.

"She's fine. Exhausted, but fine."

"Congratulations, Nate." Grady shook his hand.

"Thanks. They're identical, can you believe it? I'm going to have to put their initials on their feet or something."

Josie was so happy for Laurel. She'd always imagined her sister with girls. Now it was a reality. And two of them . . .

"When can we see them?" Josie asked.

"I'm not sure. They're doing all that after-birth stuff, but the girls are breathing just fine and got high scores, whatever that means."

"I think it means those babies will be going home with Laurel," Aunt Lola said.

Nate pushed on the door, clearly eager to return to his wife. "She was worried about that. I'd better get back to her. Just wanted to thank you guys for praying and let you know all is well."

After he left, they sat down and waited again. Any fatigue Josie had felt before had been washed away by the wonderful news. She was almost shaking with it.

"You could probably go on home and get some rest, Grady," Aunt Lola said. "Josephine and I will want to stay awhile."

Grady tossed Josie a look. "I'm not leaving until I get a peek at those future troublemakers."

"Suit yourself. Shouldn't be long anyhow."

I'm an aunt. Josie let the idea soak in. There hadn't been a baby in the family since she'd been born. And now Laurel was a *mom*. Everything was changing.

A wave of dizziness washed over her, and she leaned back in the chair. She laid her head against the wall and closed her eyes a minute, hoping it would pass. Instead, closing her eyes and tipping her head made it worse. Her head felt weighted with lead as she pulled upright and opened her eyes. Her vision swam.

"You're not feeling well," Grady whispered.

I will not pass out. Not here. Not now. She licked her lips and gathered enough breath for an answer. "I'm fine." She could feel his eyes on her. The last thing she needed was for him to call attention to her illness here in the hospital.

"Liar."

The door swung open and a nurse appeared. "All

right, family, you can come see your little darlings now."

Josie feared she might faint when she stood, and then what would happen? She had to hide it from her aunt.

Seeming to realize her predicament, Grady reached out and took Josie's hand. Fortunately, Aunt Lola was in a hurry toward Laurel's room, her sneakers squeaking against the hospital tile.

Grady helped her to her feet. "All right?"

The initial wave of dizziness passed after a few seconds. She nodded, and they followed in Aunt Lola's wake.

Laurel was propped in the bed holding a bundle when they arrived. Her hair was damp around her forehead, her face flushed.

Josie leaned down and placed a kiss on her forehead. "Congratulations, Mommy." She looked down into the tiny face of her niece. Her blue eyes peered into Laurel's face. "Oh, look at her! She's so tiny." An impossibly small fist curled next to her cheek. "I wish I had my camera."

"This one's five pounds two ounces," Laurel said. "And Hefty over there weighs five pounds seven ounces."

Nate transferred the other infant into Aunt Lola's waiting arms.

"I can't believe they're identical," Josie said. Her legs still shaky, she grabbed the handrail for support.

"Want to hold her?" Laurel asked.

Her arms ached to hold the baby, but what if she fainted or fell? Grady pulled a chair from the corner and placed it behind her.

Laurel transferred the baby into her arms and Josie sank into the rocking chair. The infant was so little and helpless. Her eyes were shaped like Nate's, but she had Laurel's dark head of hair. What a little miracle. That Nate and Laurel's love had created a tiny human being full of potential. One day this little one would grow into a full-fledged adult with all her own capabilities and strengths.

And you won't be around for it.

She felt an ache at the back of her eyes and the baby's face blurred.

"Did you finally decide on some names for the little rug rats?" For all her snap, Aunt Lola's voice was choked.

The one in Josie's arms blinked, her eyes opening wide. Josie pulled her close, cradling the back of her head.

"We did," Laurel said. "You're holding Katherine Marie . . ."

"After our mom," Josie explained to Grady.

"I'm sure she would've loved that," Grady said.

"And Josie's holding Corinne Josephine."

"You named her after me?" Josie looked down at the bundle in her arms, feeling awed and proud, and grossly undeserving of the honor.

"Katie and Corie for short," Nate said.

"I like that," Grady said.

"Your mama would be so proud, Laurel," Aunt Lola said.

The words faded as Josie watched her niece suck in her lower lip. "Hey, little Corie," she whispered. "It seems we share a name." She could only hope this one had a brighter future. "You deserve so many good things. Your mama and daddy are going to be the best parents ever. You'll see." A rock lodged in her throat.

Corie blinked up at her with somber eyes as if she heard and understood Josie's words.

Grady peered over her shoulder. "Amazing."

He didn't have to say anything else. She knew exactly what he was feeling because she was feeling it too. New life. New hope. A renewal of all things good, wrapped up in the tiny bundle of a baby. It was enough to renew her hope in a loving God.

God, if you're listening, could you look out after these two? Bless them with a long, happy life and lots of love.

How long had it been since she'd prayed? She wasn't sure, but she had the distinct feeling this prayer made its way past the hospital ceiling, maybe into the very ears of God himself.

thirty-eight

*J*osie slept hard and late, waking to the whirring motor of an electric tool. The clock read ten forty-two. Her body ached all the way to her bones, especially her back, and she was already nauseated.

Today was the apple festival and the orchard work would be put on hold for the biggest event of the year. By now, the parade would be well under way if not over, and the downtown streets would be lined with people. The square would be filled with carnival games for the children, and tonight it would be converted to a dance floor with a live band. A loud and colorful display of fireworks would conclude the big event. Until then, vendors on the sidewalks would sell everything from apple dumplings to crafts, and clusters of neighbors would chat about the harvest, the latest gossip, and the windstorm they'd all survived.

Josie suddenly realized they had no one to man their own apple booth now that the twins had arrived and Nate was otherwise occupied. She needed to get down there fast.

After her shower, Josie followed the whirring sound and found Grady on the nursery floor amid crib rails, tools, and what looked like a million screws of varying lengths. It was sweet of him to assemble the furniture. Nate wasn't too good with tools.

"'Morning." Josie took the rubber band she'd grabbed and pulled her hair into a ponytail.

The drill stopped. "'Morning." His eyes raked over her, and she wished she didn't look so frumpy and tired. "Sorry if I woke you."

She pulled her ponytail tight. "You should've woken me earlier. Someone needs to be at the booth."

"Aunt Lola's got it covered. You needed some sleep."

Aunt Lola had stayed up as late as she. "Where's Nate?"

"He was up around seven and left to check on Laurel and the babies."

Just the mention of the twins made Josie crave them, long to cuddle them against her chest. To smell the sweet baby scent and feel the slight weight of them in her arms. She couldn't wait to photograph them.

She'd love nothing more than to zip over to the hospital, but Laurel and Nate deserved some time alone. This was a huge moment in their lives, and they needed privacy.

Grady shifted the nearly assembled crib, setting it upright, testing its weight. "Good stuff."

"It would've cost a fortune if it hadn't been twenty-five percent off. Need some help?" With the orchard workers off for the day, and the booth at the festival covered, Josie had nothing but time on her hands.

Then she remembered the apple pie bake-off. "Oh no, Aunt Lola's apple pie. She should be here baking." She checked her watch. The judging was at two. "I'll go take over the booth."

Grady checked the time. "I offered to take the booth this morning, but she said the contest didn't matter. Anyway, by the time you got down there and she got back, she wouldn't have time to make it."

He was right. "She worked so hard on that recipe, and we all agreed it was the best one yet. It means so much to her. And now Nettie Albert will win again and hold it over poor Aunt Lola all year."

Josie wasn't going to let that happen.

"Where you going?" Grady called as she rushed from the room.

"I got a pie to bake."

Josie chewed off the last of her pinkie nail as she watched Sheriff Clem Roberts stroll to the microphone under the big tent.

Beside her, Aunt Lola shifted, wiped her sweaty hands down the legs of her jeans. Grady had taken over the booth so Aunt Lola could be here for the awards.

Across the tent, Nettie Albert straightened her straw hat and smoothed her khaki shorts where the pleats parted to make room for her rounded stomach.

"Look at her," Josie heard Verna Mae whisper into Aunt Lola's ear. "She thinks she's a shoo-in."

"She probably is," Aunt Lola said.

"Stop that." Josie nudged her aunt. "Think positively and have a little faith."

"I'm saying a heartfelt prayer as we speak," Aunt Lola muttered in reply.

Josie wasn't sure God cared about apple pies, but he cared about Aunt Lola, didn't he? She felt silly as she offered up a silent request. She'd followed Aunt Lola's recipe to a T. The fluted crust wasn't quite as neat as her aunt's work, but she thought it looked pretty good.

Banjo music poured in through the open tent flaps, and the smell of baked apples and fried elephant ears wafted in on a crisp breeze. A fly settled on Josie's arm, and she brushed it away.

Clem tilted the microphone and a loud squeal followed. When he spoke, he made a production of the award announcement, as if the five minutes at the microphone were his five minutes of fame for the year, and he wanted to make the most of it. He thanked everyone from the judges to the hovering flies.

Finally, he got around to the awards. "Third place in the pie category goes to Maggie Lou Sparks." A brief patter of applause accompanied

Maggie to the front as she accepted her award. Sometime in the last few days, her hair color had gone from red to black, with chunky blonde highlights.

"Good for her," Aunt Lola said. "It's her first time finishing."

"In second place we have . . ." Clem held the paper arm's length away, tilted his head back, and read over the flat top of his glasses. "Nettie Albert."

Josie smiled. "You won, I just know it."

"Hush, you're getting my hopes up."

Nettie's smile was as flat as a pressed leaf. After accepting her red ribbon, she made her way to the back of the crowd.

"And finally, we have our grand prize winner in the apple pie category . . ." Clem held up the ruffled blue ribbon.

Every muscle Josie had was stiff with anticipation.

"Lola Mitchell!" he said with a flourish.

"You won!" The applause was thunderous as Josie hugged her aunt, then watched her approach the stage and take her ribbon. The smile on her aunt's face was priceless. It had meant so much to Aunt Lola to win, just once. Josie's eyes burned, threatening to spill over. She remembered the little prayer she'd whispered and wondered if that had any bearing on the outcome.

Aunt Lola returned, showing her ribbon to

Josie and Verna Mae. "A little prayer goes a long way, ladies."

"And a great recipe don't hurt either," Verna Mae returned.

thirty-nine

*J*osie took over the booth for Grady so he could go home and finish the furniture. After Aunt Lola showed off her ribbon, she went to check on Laurel and the babies and came back in time to hear Mr. Murphy's performance on the mandolin. He played his sweet-sounding rendition of "Redeemed."

The afternoon sped by as Josie stayed busy selling apples and caramel dip. Boone stopped by the booth and reminded her she'd promised him a dance later.

Once the booth was closed, she went home for her camera, then visited Laurel and the babies. She snapped two rolls of photos and was eager to get them developed. Laurel was rested and antsy to go home and get settled with the babies, but the hospital wanted to keep the three until the next day.

By the time Josie left Nate and Laurel at the hospital, she was exhausted. The excitement from the night before and the hours selling apples had drained her. She hadn't eaten all day, afraid it would only make her sick.

If she had her druthers, she'd drive home and

curl up in bed, but she didn't want to miss the best part of the festival and she'd promised Boone a dance. As darkness crept over the hills, they would turn on the string of lantern lights lining the dance floor and gather to catch up with neighbors over a cup of apple cider. She smiled thinking of how little girls would dance with their daddies, and Ray and Connie Blackford would waltz around the floor, bumping into everyone. Some things never changed.

Tired or not, she was in for the long haul. Josie parked her car at the end of Main Street and started the long walk toward the town square. Streetlamps glowed in the darkness, and in the distance, the colorful lantern lights shimmied in the breeze. Strains of a fast country song carried on the breeze. Her body seemed not to have recovered from the excitement of the night before. She felt as if she were moving through quicksand. Her legs trembled as she walked, and she wondered if she had the strength to dance. Maybe best to stick with slow dances tonight.

As she approached town, she walked under the banner that stretched across Main Street: "52nd Annual Shelbyville Apple Festival." Triangular flags, strung from the lampposts, lined the street, dancing in the wind.

When she approached the square, she scanned the crowd and located Aunt Lola on one of their big quilts under a tall oak tree. Josie navigated the lawn chairs and blankets, greeting friends and neighbors as she went. When she reached the quilt, she lowered herself and leaned back on her elbows, stretching out her legs.

Her aunt's blue ribbon was pinned to her floral blouse. Her apple pie would be available at the store and would be the pie of choice to serve at family gatherings and the like. It had been a weekend to remember.

"Quite the weekend, huh, Aunt Lola?"

"I should say."

A breeze sent dried leaves scuttling across the sidewalk and caused a chill to run through Josie. She should've gone home for a sweater.

Mr. Murphy approached, his booted feet stopping at the frayed edge of the quilt. " 'Evening, ladies."

Josie complimented him on his performance, then he invited Aunt Lola to dance. Josie watched them go, Mr. Murphy's beefy hand on the small of her aunt's back. Maybe she'd finally found someone to love. Judging by the way her aunt looked at him as he pulled her into his arms, she'd say the answer might be yes. She was happy for Aunt Lola. She'd been alone far too long.

Dancing beside her aunt and Mr. Murphy was Maggie Lou's little girl and Boone. He twirled her around, her sundress ballooning and her thin blonde hair fanning outward. If she were photographing this event, she would capture that moment on film. Boone would make a wonderful father someday. Maggie Lou watched from her lawn chair near the swing set.

Josie's eyes scanned the crowd, skimming along the low stone wall that circled the square. People were perched in groups of two or three. She stopped when her eyes ran across Grady. He leaned against the wall, watching the dancers, his long legs crossed at the ankles.

Beside him, Harmony Schneider said something and laughed, touching his arm. Josie felt a prick of jealousy. She'd known since that night at the grocery that, for a chance with Grady, Harmony would turn in her cashier's apron in a heartbeat.

She watched for Grady's response, but he barely spared Harmony a glance as he crossed his arms and continued watching the action on the dance floor.

As if sensing her scrutiny, he scanned the crowd until he found her. Without breaking eye contact with Josie, he said something to Harmony, then straightened and walked her way, tucking his hands into his jean pockets.

Heaven have mercy, he was handsome. From the top of his dark head to the soles of his booted feet. No wonder Harmony was smitten. She took a mental snapshot and hoped it was imprinted on her brain for later so she could pull it up and linger over it awhile.

The smile he'd saved just for her only reinforced

the thought. He lowered himself beside her, and she sat upright, hoping to ease the crick in her back. They sat in silence for a few moments, listening to the band's tune, watching the dancers.

The Apple Queen and King, chosen earlier in the day by a panel of judges, took a spin around the floor. The teenaged girl's tiara tipped sideways and her partner steadied it.

Grady must've been watching them too. "Aunt Lola told me that was you a handful of years ago," he said.

It had been her senior year in high school, just before her world fell apart. "It seems like a lifetime ago."

The tune ended, and Boone approached moments later, still a little winded from his frantic turn around the floor with Maggie's girl. " 'Evening, Josie. Grady." He extended his hand to Josie. "May I have the pleasure?"

Josie took his hand, reluctant to leave Grady. Her legs wobbled as she stood, and Grady reached out to steady her, but not before Boone swept her away.

The band was playing a fast tune, much to her dismay. Nonetheless, she put on a smile and let Boone twirl her until she was dizzy—it didn't take much these days.

She was grateful when the band started a slow song. Her heart raced faster than the tempo of the previous song. Boone took one of her hands and set his other at her waist. He looked boyishly cute without his hat, his curls damp at his neck. He'd gone home and spiffed up, changing into a white polo and a crisp pair of jeans.

"Aunt Lola said Laurel and the twins are doing great," he said when they were moving in a slow circle.

"They are." She couldn't help but smile as she thought of her sweet nieces. "So adorable."

"New twins and a blue ribbon all in one weekend. Can you stand it?"

"It's been pretty exciting."

He turned her gracefully. "Mr. Murphy seems pretty taken with Aunt Lola."

"I was noticing that. She deserves someone who'll cherish her."

Many couples joined them until the floor was packed with dancers. Boone's mom and dad danced at the edge of the floor. Mr. Barrow was having a good day, seemed to have come out from under the Alzheimer's enough to recognize his wife. Josie thought how hard it must be for them both.

Josie looked at all the familiar faces. People she'd known since she was old enough to have a thought. People who'd given her lollipops and gum, people who'd looked out for her when she was out of Laurel's sight, people who made this town special.

It was a great place to grow up. A great place to belong.

Boone seemed to read her mind. "Tell me you don't just love Shelbyville."

Once upon a time she had. Now the memory of Ian haunted it. "If you like small-town living."

"Which you do."

"Fine, I do, but I'm still going back to Louisville."

He leaned back. "What? With those new nieces coming home and all?"

"Don't start on me, Boone Barrow. I've been getting enough grief from Laurel and Aunt Lola." Not to mention Grady.

When the band ended the tune, the dancers applauded, then the band started another slow song. Her arms ached, but Boone moved them in a quick circle before swaying in time to the ballad.

"Just 'cause you're so stubborn," Boone said.

"Am not."

"Are so."

She shook her head, giving up. Much as Boone might think they were right for each other, she couldn't think of him as anything more than a brother.

"Cut in?" Grady was beside them, towering over them with his broad shoulders and set jaw.

She was about to suggest a break, but Boone was smiling graciously and stepping back, letting Grady assume his spot.

His right hand held hers the same way Boone's had. His left hand rested in the same spot. How come it felt entirely different? Why did she have these impossible feelings? Why did he have to be so difficult to resist?

Grady's feet shuffled, landing partly on her toes. He winced. "Sorry. Not much of a dancer."

Her legs trembled against his. These feelings he evoked were exhausting. "Why'd you cut in then?" She stared into the vee of his shirt where tiny dark hairs peeked out.

"Couldn't stand seeing you in Barrow's arms."

Why did he have to say things like that? Things that made her stomach go all tight and hard?

"He's just a friend," Josie said. And that was a fact.

Grady squeezed her hand the tiniest bit. "I know the feeling."

She breathed a wry laugh because Grady didn't know at all. There was nothing the same in her feelings for the two men.

She watched the other couples swirling around them. Boone passed on the other side of the floor with Harmony Schneider. Her head tilted back in a deep laugh at something he'd said, and Josie thought they looked good together.

Her stomach gave a growl loud enough to be heard over the music.

"Have you eaten?"

Since when? And what was the point when she'd only feel sick for hours? "I'm not hungry."

Grady studied her, seeing right through her. "You

can't stop eating. Maybe the doctor can give you something for the nausea."

She didn't want to talk about this tonight. She was weak and chilly, and getting very tempted to lean into his chest and let him hold her. They were barely swaying now, which was more in keeping with Grady's skill level.

She was leaving in a week anyway, once the harvest was complete. It wasn't as if she was going to kiss him or lead him on. She just wanted to snuggle against the cool night air. He wouldn't mind that, would he?

When his hand moved to the small of her back, she lowered her own aching arm and wrapped it around his waist.

He pulled her close, and she didn't resist. She laid her head on his chest, letting the thud of his heart drown out the band's bass. His embrace was warm and safe.

He rubbed her back in small circles, sending a shiver up her spine. She felt his chin resting atop her head, and had a brief flashback of dancing at Joe's the night before the windstorm. But she was fully sober this time and in way deeper than she had been then.

As weary as she felt, she no longer wanted to go home. She wanted to stay here, to linger in his embrace as long as she could. *Keep playing the slow ones, guys,* she instructed the band.

His thighs swept against hers as they shuffled.

Josie closed her eyes and inhaled the scent of him. She wanted to embed it in her memory so she could carry it home to Louisville and unpack it like a favorite pillow. Pine. Musk. Man.

Utterly intoxicating. As she shifted her weight, her knee buckled.

Grady grasped her elbows, a frown catching between his brows.

"I'm fine." She just wanted him close again. But as she moved toward him, he held her away so he could look into her eyes.

"You're shaking."

Maybe her hands trembled a little. Maybe her legs were a little wobbly.

"Let's take a break," he said.

She wanted to whine like a tired three-year-old, but he was leading her through the throng and back to the blanket. He sat, propping his back against the tree, then pulled her into his side. One tug of the quilt, and she was covered to her waist.

"Better?" he asked.

She nodded against the material of his shirt. By morning there'd be bets on how long until they walked the aisle, but even that thought didn't deter her.

She was giving in, but she couldn't seem to stop herself. *I'm not feeling well. Can't a girl weaken a little at times like this?* She closed her eyes and let her head rise and fall with each of his breaths, breathing in the scent that was all Grady.

But the motion made her dizzy and she opened her eyes until the world stilled again.

"You want to go home?"

She should. But what was there but an empty house, an empty bed? "No." She knew she could use the sleep, but tomorrow's light would bring the realization of her foolishness, and she wasn't ready to give up the fantasy just yet.

"Want something to eat?" His voice rumbled through his chest cavity and into her ear. "I could run to The Corner Café and grab something bland like dinner rolls from Peggy."

Her stomach twisted at the mention of food. Another thing that would keep until morning. "Un-uh." She turned her head into him. The softness of his T-shirt contrasted with the hardened muscles beneath it. A delectable combination.

"It's getting worse, isn't it." It wasn't a question.

And it was true. The decline seemed sudden, but maybe it was only the excitement of the weekend. The doctor had said something about stress, and even good moments brought a kind of stress.

"All the excitement from last night, I think," she said. "It's been a long day." They sounded like excuses. She'd slept late this morning and baking an apple pie was hardly as wearing as working in the field.

"At least you won't have to hide it much longer."

She could make it another week until harvest

was over. Once she was back in Louisville, she wouldn't have to pretend anymore.

"When are you going to tell them?"

She realized he wasn't talking about her going home. He was talking about telling her family. She'd used Laurel's pregnancy as an excuse, but the twins had arrived safely and there was no reason, from his perspective, to keep the illness a secret any longer.

But Laurel wasn't even home from the hospital yet. Plus, there would be raging hormones and feeding schedules. Her sister didn't need this right now.

"I'm going to wait a bit," she said finally.

He shifted so he could look at her. "Wait for what?"

She could see it wasn't going to go down so easily this time. "For things to settle. Laurel has enough going on right now without dumping this on her." Feeling Grady stiffen, Josie sat up and instantly missed the closeness.

"*You* have enough going on right now without having your family's support."

She felt suddenly alone. A cold wind enveloped her in a frosty hug. Josie wrapped her arms around her waist, shivering. "I'm fine."

"Do you realize the absurdity of that statement?"

He looked as if he wanted to shake her. "Don't be angry." She didn't want his wrath. She wanted the warmth of his arms, but that was lost now. Like so many other things.

"How's Laurel going to feel when she finds out? How's she going to feel knowing you kept this from her? She might understand about the pregnancy, but there's no reason now, Josie. No reason at all that justifies you keeping the truth from her."

What was she going to do? She couldn't tell her family. They'd want to know all the details, and then they'd find out her disease was treatable. They couldn't know that. It would ruin everything.

"Look at me," Grady implored.

But she didn't want to look at him. Didn't want to get caught up in those eyes that cared too much, that did things to her reasoning skills.

She couldn't tell her family and she couldn't explain why. And Grady wasn't going to let her off the hook.

"Your family needs to know. Not just for you, but for them."

Who was he to tell her what she needed? What her family needed? It was *her* illness, her life. In a week, she'd be back home, and he could wash her from his memory. The thought disturbed her. *That's what you want, isn't it?* She was so confused. And the way her head was spinning wasn't helping.

"Mind your own business, Grady."

She pulled her feet under her, poised for flight.

He leaned toward her, adamant. "You need their support."

She gave a half smile. "How much support can they be from three hundred and fifty miles away?"

Her reply stopped him cold, made him freeze in place. Not so much as a blink. Finally, he straightened and his brows slowly knotted together. "You're going back?"

His confusion baffled her, annoyed her. It had been the plan all along. Why did everyone seem to think she'd changed her mind? Why did she feel as if she were continually explaining herself to everyone? And to Grady of all people, whom she hadn't even known three months ago.

"You're going back?" His voice was louder this time.

Well, she could be snippy too. "Yes, I'm going home. Louisville is my *home*, remember?"

"You pretty much said before that there's no one and nothing there, that about right? What's there to go home to? You have family here. People who—" His face twisted, shadows dancing in the hollows of his cheeks. "People who love you."

She looked away before she could drown in the depths of those eyes, before she could let herself believe he was talking about his own feelings. She had to get out of there.

"I want to go home." She made to stand.

He held her with a firm hand. "You are not going through this alone. I won't let you." His eyes locked on hers, held her every bit as tightly as his grasp did. "If I have to tell them myself, I will."

Panic swelled inside, pushing the air from her lungs. There were boundaries, and he was overstepping them. She never should've told him about the illness, never should've let herself get involved with him at all. Now he was usurping her right to choose, forcing her hand.

How dare he think he had a right to force her into this? He had no right. No right at all. She jerked her arm away and was on her feet before he could say a word. And then she was walking as fast as her feet would carry her across the darkened square.

forty

*J*osie made her way blindly through the square, navigating chairs and blankets and people she didn't really see. What was she going to do now? What was she going to do if he told them?

Why are you doing this to me, God? This is what you want, isn't it? For me to die like Ian?

She couldn't even die right. Her dad was right. She really was pathetic.

The throng of people opened to a spacious field of grass. The sound of the band faded. Her legs trembled, buckling every few steps on the uneven ground. She had to keep going, had to reach her car. Why had she gone this way? The street would've been faster.

Maybe she should drive all the way back to Louisville tonight. She wouldn't have to face Grady and his unfair ultimatum.

It was a grand fantasy, but there were too many

obstacles. Her body would never make the trip without a night's rest, and there was her family to consider.

Besides, what would it change? Grady would tell them anyway, and he would be forced to do so sooner than later as an explanation of why she'd up and left.

The creek gurgled beside her, running as fast as she was, chasing her. Above the whoosh of the wind, a voice called her name.

Grady.

Go away. She didn't know whether to hide behind a tree, turn around and tell him off, or quicken her steps. Who was she kidding? She couldn't walk any faster if she wanted. Her lungs choked on the oxygen that rushed in and out, burning her chest.

The toe of her sandal caught a tree root, and she tumbled in the darkness. The impact forced the air from her lungs, making her grunt. She pushed against the ground, damp and spongy, fringed with long grass.

"Josie!" He was there quick as the snap of a flag.

She rolled over, sat up, heaving from exertion. She felt the ache of frustration clogging her throat in a massive lump.

She batted away his hands, striking him. "Go away! Just leave me alone." Why was this happening? Why now when she was so close to leaving? "You have no right to make my decisions for me. You don't understand anything!"

He sat back on his haunches, giving her space.

She gulped in air, the dampness of the earth seeped into her jeans. In the distance, the bass of the band kept tempo with her heart.

Beside them, the creek trickled, whispering secrets as it had that night. She could almost feel the cold, steely fingers pulling her under. Could see Ian's face disappearing under the watery grave as she'd seen so many nights in her sleep.

"Then tell me. Make me understand."

Her eyes burned, ached. All of her ached, from the inside out. She was so tired. So tired of carrying this impossible burden. She just wanted it to be over.

"It was my fault," she whispered. Her hands clutched at the fringe of grass. Some of the strands snapped in her fist.

"What was, honey?"

The gentleness of his voice was her undoing. She could tell one person, couldn't she? She could unload this burden on Grady; maybe it would alleviate the pressure building in her.

"We were sledding," she said. *Just get it out. Say it, and get it over with.* "I—I did something stupid. I went down the hill into the gap, toward the creek. I thought it was frozen."

The night crashed in on her. The frosty smell of cold, the slice of the runners cutting through the snow. The sickening crack of splitting ice.

"The ice gave way with this horrible sound, and then I was falling. I was so cold and I couldn't reach the bottom and I couldn't get out. He couldn't get me out."

"Who couldn't?"

She didn't want to say his name. As if saying it aloud had some kind of power that would pull her under as easily as the creek.

"Ian?"

She nodded, grateful he'd spared her that one thing. "He kept trying, but the ice kept giving way and I was getting so cold. Too cold." She didn't want to say the next part. The hard part. Her throat closed up, refusing to surrender the words.

"What happened?" He ran his thumb across her face, smearing the wetness.

Just say it, Josie. Saying it won't make it any truer. "I was panicking. I didn't think I would make it much longer. He jumped in." She looked Grady in the eye, needing him, needing someone, to understand what Ian had done. "He knew. He knew he wouldn't make it. He gave his life to save mine."

Once the words were out, there was no stopping the rest. "He had to have known. We were so far from home and the water was so cold. I was numb. He jumped in and lifted me out. He saved me and he knew—there was a look on his face—" She covered her own face as if she could hide from the memory of it. She would never forget the look on his face.

"He knew he was going to die. Why did he do it?" *Why?* She screamed the question in her mind as she never had before.

Grady took her wrists, pulled her hands away from her face. "It was an accident. That's all. You didn't mean for him to die."

"It should've been *me*." She jabbed her finger into her sternum. "I was supposed to die."

"*No.*"

"Yes! It was my foolishness and it should've been me. Ian was—good. He didn't deserve to die."

Grady was shaking his head. "Neither did you."

"How can I ever be worthy of his sacrifice? Grady, answer me that. I can't. There's nothing I can do to earn it." God knew she'd tried, tried so hard. Some debts were too big to pay off.

"You don't have to be worthy—"

He thought he had all the answers. "You don't know what you're talking about, what I've lived with since it happened. You don't know how it feels to be so utterly, completely unworthy." How could he? He was Grady, whom everyone loved and respected. So good, so worthy.

"You're wrong, Josie. Someone gave his life for me too."

She cleared her vision with a blink. Was it true? And if it was, how had he coped? She searched his face for answers.

He wetted his lips. " 'While we were still sinners, Christ died for us.' "

It took a moment for the words to sink in, for the words to ring the bell of her memory. He was quoting Scripture? She didn't need a Sunday school lesson, she needed someone to understand.

She backed away from him, angry. "That's not the same."

"Isn't it?"

"No." She knew it wasn't. But all the reasons, the words, twisted around in her mind unassembled. She tried but couldn't make sense of her thoughts, much less express them.

She said what she did know, what she'd come to understand through the whole ordeal. "That God you worship gave me this disease, Grady. He's punishing me for—"

"No, honey."

She looked away so she couldn't see the look on his face, so she wasn't tempted to believe what he was saying.

"He's punishing me for what I did. I should've died then and I didn't, so he's making sure I die now." She felt the weight of the penalty crushing her, so heavy she thought it might press her flat on the ground.

"God doesn't work like that. He loves you."

She shook her head, wanting to cover her ears.

"He does." Grady pulled her into his arms.

She pushed at him, but he was too strong. And she was too weak. She finally stopped fighting and crumpled in his lap, crying. She was so tired. Tired of fighting, tired of feeling unworthy.

He brushed wet strands of hair off her cheek, off her forehead.

"Shhh. He loves you," Grady whispered in her ear. His fingers brushed the soft flesh of her cheeks. "And God help me, so do I."

She opened her eyes, staring up at him. He looked as tortured as she felt. Her precious Grady. He loved her? She could scarcely believe she could stir those kinds of feelings in a man like Grady.

But if he really could love her . . .

If he could love her, maybe God could too. It was possible, wasn't it? She wanted to believe it so badly.

"I don't know the purpose for this disease," he said. "But it's not his punishment, honey. He wants you to find him. He wants you to let him love you through it. He wants you to find peace."

Peace. A foreign word. Something she hadn't felt in so long. Maybe never. Why was it so hard to believe what Grady said? To stop fighting and surrender? What was the worst that could happen?

What do you want with me, God?

She closed her eyes, her chest aching with each rise and fall. Her heart beat slow and hard against her ribs. Grady believed what he said, she knew that with certainty. But was it true? Did God really love her and want her to find peace? Could it be as easy as surrendering to him?

Why not? She'd tried everything else. She'd fought, she'd run, she'd given up.

All right. All right, Jesus, you win.

You win.

Josie opened her eyes and stared into Grady's. Her head felt as if it were filled with helium. She tried to lift her hand, steady her head, but she couldn't seem to make it move. The world still tilted and swayed. Grady blurred.

"Josie?"

Everything was going dark, tapering down to a pinpoint of light. She blinked, trying to regain her vision.

"*Josie.*"

She opened her mouth. *I'm not feeling so good.* Her head floated, spinning, spinning. And then the tiny pinpoint of light was swallowed by darkness.

forty-one

*G*rady paced across the waiting area in the ER where he'd sat with Josie when Laurel had gone into early labor. It seemed so long ago, much longer than a couple of months.

The blue carpet swallowed the thud of each step. In the corner, a news program carried on as if his world hadn't just come to an abrupt and jarring halt.

The ambulance had arrived within minutes of his 911 call, and they'd let him ride with Josie as they assessed her situation and questioned him. The paramedics hadn't detected a blood pressure or a pulse.

He'd told them all he knew. "She has an endocrine disease of some kind. No, I don't know what it is. She's been sick. Nausea, some vomiting. She's been achy and tired. Can't you do something?"

Once they arrived at the hospital, they'd wheeled her still body on the gurney through the double doors, and he hadn't heard a thing since. He checked his watch and saw it had only been twenty-eight minutes. It seemed like much more. He'd called Nate once he'd arrived and left a voice mail. Aunt Lola didn't own a cell, so he'd called Mr. Murphy and asked him to bring her over.

He ran his hands through his hair, then jumped when his cell rang.

He fished it from his pocket. "Yeah?"

"It's Nate . . . your message, and I'm . . . way down. Any word?"

The signal was breaking up and Grady struggled to hear. "No, nothing." Couldn't they at least send someone out with an update?

"Shoot. I . . . give Laurel something positive . . . on to . . . wanting to keep her upstairs . . . hear something."

"You're breaking up."

Nate said he'd be down in a minute and Grady pocketed his phone.

Maybe it was his fault. Maybe it was the stress of reliving those memories she'd been running from. *She's already sick, Mackenzie, did you have to go and push her like that?*

Maybe the stress was all she'd needed to send her body over the edge. He ran a cold palm over his face. *Oh, God, please save her. Please. She can't die this way.*

He reminded himself that he'd known she was dying. But knowing it and living through it were two separate things. And now that he'd seen the full weight of the burden she carried, he wished for more time. If nothing else, he wanted her to find peace, to find God before the arms of death carried her away.

"Not getting a pulse."

"No blood pressure either."

The paramedics' words rang in his ears. Were they trying to pull her back from the clutches of death even now?

Please, God.

He hoped the plea was enough. He couldn't formulate more words, couldn't get them untangled from the snarl in his mind.

Nate appeared, running toward him, his shoes squeaking on the hospital tile.

"Still nothing," Grady said as Nate slowed.

Before he could respond, the exit doors opened and Aunt Lola whooshed in, her face drawn, Mr. Murphy on her heels. Aunt Lola looked as if she'd aged ten years since this morning. "How is she?"

"No word yet," Nate said, then caught her up on what Grady had told him. He heard Aunt Lola's gasp when he told her there'd been no pulse in the ambulance. Mr. Murphy set a hand on her shoulder.

Grady turned and walked away, ran a hand through his hair. *You've got to tell them about the disease. They need to know.* It was the right thing to do. Maybe he should've told them long ago, Laurel's pregnancy notwithstanding.

Yeah, and look what happened to Josie when you forced her hand. Guilt rode him long and hard. He'd never forgive himself if—

He turned back to Aunt Lola, saw her wilted shoulders and glazed eyes. Her blue ribbon hung askew on her shirt like a forgotten painting on a wall. He had to tell them, forewarn them.

He walked toward them, reluctance paving the way for his slow steps.

The double doors behind him swung open, and they all turned to face a small middle-aged woman in teal scrubs. Grady recognized her as one of Peggy Tackett's daughters. She barely came up to Grady's chest as she approached.

"Lola, Nate." She nodded, tucking her mouse brown hair behind her ears. "Grady." She wore concern between her clear blue eyes.

"How is she?" Aunt Lola asked.

"She's holding her own."

Grady released a breath he didn't know he'd held and closed his eyes. *Thank you.*

"We've given her hydrocortisone and saline through an IV, and she's starting to come around."

"Thank God," Aunt Lola said. "Do you know what's wrong with her?"

She glanced at Grady. "You mentioned to the paramedics that Josie has an endocrine disease."

He could feel the heavy weight of Aunt Lola's appraisal. He didn't even want to look her way. She was going to give it to him later, and he probably deserved it. But right now, he was too thankful Josie was still alive to worry about it.

"She has a disease?" Aunt Lola asked.

"It's called Addison's," the doctor continued. "It's a disease that results in your body producing insufficient amounts of cortisol and sometimes another hormone called aldosterone."

"Is it serious?" Nate asked.

Grady wished he could protect them from the truth, but he'd already done that too long and it wouldn't change the facts. He was glad Aunt Lola had Mr. Murphy there for support.

"Left untreated, the disease culminates in what's called an Addisonian Crisis, which is fatal if the patient doesn't seek medical treatment. This happens when there's a severe adrenal deficiency. It's difficult to diagnose," she said, addressing Grady, "but your knowledge that she's suffering from an endocrine disorder helped me to diagnose quickly."

He remembered Josie's lack of a pulse in the ambulance. "Did you have to revive her?"

The doctor shook her head. "During a crisis, patients can present with no pulse or blood pressure. It's quite strange, really, and rare. I've only diagnosed one other case in my career."

"But she's going to be okay?" Aunt Lola asked.

"We need to run more tests, but she's coming around. We'd like to keep her a couple of days. Addison's patients have to take replacement hormones orally and have to be vigilant about their health. Otherwise, they can lead a pretty normal life."

It took Grady's fuzzy mind a minute to digest the words. Where was the bad news? Where was the prognosis Josie told him about? Maybe this doctor had it all wrong.

"Wait," Grady said. "Are you sure that's what she has? Addison's disease?"

"Josie confirmed the test results when she was awakening."

He didn't understand. Josie was going to be okay? The disease wasn't a death sentence?

"Can we see her?" Aunt Lola asked.

"We're getting her into a room now. I'll send a nurse out with the room number in a few minutes."

It was quiet as the doctor exited through the doors.

"Thank you, Jesus," Aunt Lola whispered.

"I need to tell Laurel the good news," Nate said.

"I'll go with you," Aunt Lola said, with a look toward Grady that promised she wasn't finished with him. "Give us a call when they have a room number."

Grady nodded, then they walked toward the hallway leading to the elevators.

He sank into a chair, his legs giving way under the pressure of his discovery. He turned the information around in his head, seeing it from every possible angle, trying to make sense of it.

Josie knew she had Addison's and had told him the disease was fatal. The doctor said it was easily treated. Which was the truth?

What had the doctor said? Something about the disease leading to a crisis if left untreated. She'd used the word *fatal* in there somewhere.

Fatal. Left untreated.

Why hadn't Josie been taking her medication if it were as simple as that? She knew she had the disease, the doctor had confirmed it with her. Surely her doctor had prescribed those hormones she needed.

Josie's words from earlier played in his head. *"God gave me this disease, Grady. He's punishing me."*

Reality hit like a solid sudden punch to the gut. *Oh, God.*

Is she letting this disease take her life because she—because she doesn't want to live anymore? Because she thinks you gave it to her? The slow suicide of a woman who thought she deserved to die?

He closed his eyes against the thought. Why didn't she tell him? Why didn't she tell him the truth so he could tell her how special she was? *This isn't your will for her, God. Let her know how much you love her.*

He tried to imagine the tremendous guilt and pressure she'd lived under. Thinking she was to blame for Ian's death and carrying that burden alone. Feeling unworthy of the sacrifice. Had anything he'd said helped, or had his words only weakened her body and nearly killed her?

Josie's eyes fluttered open. She squinted against the too-bright light. An IV bag hung on a stand at her side, its cord disappearing beneath the bandage on the back of her hand.

The metal bed railing was cold against her arm. She wore an ugly, speckled blue hospital gown. A monitor beeped beside her. She had a vague recollection of people bustling around her bed, of a doctor asking her questions.

Then she remembered the last moments before she'd passed out. Feeling dizzy and sick and . . . peaceful.

She remembered Grady's voice calling her name.

Grady. Where was he? She turned her head on the pillow, but she was alone. The door was open and a girl wearing peach scrubs passed by. She sucked in a breath, let it fill her lungs, and released it in a deep sigh.

Where was her family? Did they know about the disease? Did it matter?

Caroline Tackett appeared in the doorway. She picked up the chart and gave Josie a smile. "How are you feeling?"

"Better." Her throat was raspy and dry. "My family . . ."

"Is downstairs wearing a hole in the carpet." Her eyes crinkled at the corners.

She felt bad for making them worry. She had just come through the crisis she'd anticipated all these months. Only she hadn't expected to survive it. What would her family be going through if she'd had her way?

"Am I okay?" Did she want to be? Did she want to get better, go on? She felt different now that she'd come through the other side. She felt herself holding her breath, waiting for Caroline's answer.

"You'll be right as rain in a couple days." Dr. Tackett asked her questions related to her disease, then told her she was scheduling some tests for the next day.

When she left, Josie looked out the window where darkness swallowed everything but the lights in the parking lot. It was late. She was so tired. She'd just been through an ordeal, had barely come through, according to Caroline.

She closed her eyes, but instead of being claimed

by sleep, she found herself remembering the moments leading up to the crisis. Grady's words, her decision. And it had been a decision. Not the "sinner's prayer" she'd heard so many times in church, but a real decision.

Is this your answer, God? Do you want me to live after all?

It seemed unfathomable after so many months of believing she was going to die, was meant to die. Could she readjust her thinking and accept whatever God wanted? The notion was scary. Strange that life could be a scarier proposition than death.

And what of Ian and the guilt? What of the pain that his death had left her with? Could she find a way to deal with that? Would having God in her life make it bearable?

A shuffling sound awakened her. The doorway was filled with a sight more beautiful than the Blue Ridge Mountains on an October morning.

Grady.

Every nerve in her body sung with awareness. He stopped just inside the door, pocketing his hands, unsure. She wanted to grab him and pull him closer.

"He loves you. And God help me, so do I."

Were sweeter words ever spoken? Josie wet her lips. "Come 'ere."

Eyes locked, he took three steps and was at her side. Now that he was closer, she saw the fatigue that lined his eyes, rimmed his taut lips.

There was a somber look in his dark eyes, and Josie knew that he knew everything. That her disease wasn't fatal. That she'd been killing herself one day at a time. The thought shamed her now. Humiliated her. Why hadn't she considered how her actions would affect others? Wouldn't she have left them with the same kind of guilt she'd been trying to escape? She looked away.

Did her family know what she'd done? The thought made her want to pull the hospital sheets over her head.

"Look at me," Grady whispered.

Ashamed as she was, she was hungry for him, too hungry to resist his request.

His mouth opened and closed. He tried again. "You're okay. We're going to get you through this." He took her hand, the one with the IV, and held it, his warmth seeping into her cold flesh.

She drank in everything his eyes, his touch, his words said.

"I'm so sorry I upset you," he said.

She shook her head. "No—"

"It wasn't my place to—"

"Everything happened just as it was meant to." She didn't realize the truth until she verbalized it. She'd meant to be back in Louisville before the crisis happened. But God had different plans.

Her words left him speechless.

"Does my family know about the disease? About—" She couldn't put words to her actions.

He smoothed his thumb across her knuckles. "They know you have the disease and they know I knew about it." His smile wobbled. "I don't think Aunt Lola's too happy with me right about now."

She would have to tell them what she'd done. They wouldn't understand unless she told them everything.

And maybe it was high time she did.

"I guess I have a lot of explaining to do."

He pressed a soft kiss against her knuckles. "Later. Right now you need your rest."

She didn't want rest. She wanted to hear those words again, the ones that made her heart sing just thinking about them.

But he was leaning over, placing a soft kiss to her forehead. "One day at a time, honey."

forty-two

*J*osie crested the hill, then began the descent, her feet swishing through the tall grass. When she reached the bottom, winded, she stepped onto the rock that jutted into the water— the one she'd barely missed on that treacherous night.

Sweetwater Creek was running slowly today, a peaceful pool of water cradled in the gap. On both sides, the hills, clothed in vibrant autumn hues, rose majestically toward the heavens.

The air smelled like ripened apples and

autumn, and the cloudless sky was a shade of blue that matched the twins' eyes. Those two little dolls had stolen Josie's heart, and she was wearing the role of Auntie Josie quite well if she did say so herself. Laurel had taken to motherhood as naturally as a fish to water, just as she'd figured.

Josie sank onto the rock, her legs aching as she stretched them out. The harvest was complete; it was a day of celebration. They'd picked the last of the apples, finishing in midafternoon. Tonight they'd have a barbecue, then tomorrow they'd say good-bye to the crew.

When Josie had come home from the hospital two days before, she'd been ready to work, but Grady would have none of it. Only because today was the final day had he reluctantly given in.

"No ladder, no lifting. And lots of breaks. More breaks than work, actually, and if you get tired, you'll tell me right away."

A smile curled the corners of her mouth as she remembered his unwavering conditions. She had gotten tired today. And hot. It was unseasonably warm and she wasn't as recovered as she'd thought, though she wasn't about to admit it.

The water babbled against the rock, whispering an invitation. She slipped off her shoes and socks and lowered her feet into the creek. The water bubbled over them, washing, refreshing.

She'd had a lot of time to reflect at the hospital

between the testing and poking and prodding. She thought about Ian and that night and she thought about God.

Grady's scripture had replayed until it was etched into the recesses of her brain. *"While we were still sinners, Christ died for us."*

His comparison between Ian's sacrifice and God's hadn't been so far off target. They were all guilty of something, weren't they? There was no way to earn some gifts. At some point, you just had to receive it.

Why had it taken so long to realize it? She waved her feet in the water, feeling the current tug at her legs as if to say, C*ome along, Josie. There's more work to do.*

She'd told her family about Ian the day after she'd come home. Laurel's eyes had filled with tears when she found out what Ian had done for Josie. It had been a shock for them to realize Josie had wanted to die, but Laurel and Aunt Lola were taking it in one day at a time. They all were. She would call Hank in a day or two, as soon as she found the nerve. Ian's father deserved to know how selfless his son had been.

Last night she'd had a long overdue conversation with Aunt Lola about her father. There was still a lot of healing to be done there, a lot of feelings to process and hurt to work through. But she was beginning to understand that it was his flaws that had caused him to treat her as he did, and not her own. That would have to sink in a little at a time until she fully believed it.

Above her, she heard a voice calling her name.

"Down here!" she called, her eyes scanning the top of the hill for Grady's form.

When he appeared at the crest, she watched him take the incline, watched his long legs eat up the distance.

He stopped on the fringe of grass that edged the creek, tucking his hands in his back pockets. The sun hit the flesh of his arms, carving shadows under the muscles.

"Wondered where you'd gotten off to," he said.

She should've told him, but he'd been talking to Hernando when they'd finished, and she hadn't wanted to interrupt.

"Saved a seat for you." She patted the rock ledge beside her.

He tucked a smile into the corner of his mouth. "Best invitation I've had all week."

When he was beside her, pants rolled to his knees, feet in the water, they sat in comfortable silence. His thigh moved against hers, slow, subtle movements, as he swung his feet in the current.

Above them, a dove called from a tree on the hillside, and Josie tracked it to a maple, where its round gray body contrasted against the vibrant red leaves.

The dove called again. *Ooo-OOH. Ooh-ooh-ooh.* The sound reminded her of home. Of mornings in bed when she was young and her mother was alive. Of swinging on the tire swing after she finished her homework and was free for the evening. There were good memories here too. Those were the ones she needed to remember.

Grady's voice broke into her thoughts. "I do believe this is the first time we've been alone since Saturday night."

Half the town of Shelbyville had been to the hospital, usually outside visiting hours, much to Verna Mae's frustration. Ashley and Jackie had even driven from Asheville one evening to check on her.

"That right?" She'd been hungry for time alone with him, but even when she'd gotten home, there were her family and the babies. And much to her frustration, she was exhausted by dinnertime. It didn't help that two certain squallers were keeping her up nights.

"You've changed." He was staring at her, and her flesh warmed under his appraisal.

"How so?"

"You tell me."

She was different. She hadn't felt like running once since she'd left the hospital. Her mind hadn't been bogged down with guilt. Her focus was not on the past, but the future.

"I have peace." Such a simple word, yet what joy was there in life without it? Not much, as she'd discovered.

"That's a good thing."

"It really is." The lazy sounds of the water, the dove calling, and the warmth of the sun made her sleepy. She lay back against the flat surface of the rock, keeping her feet in the water.

"You're tired."

Josie closed her eyes against the sun. "Little bit. It's going to take time." She hadn't fallen asleep until eleven the night before, then she'd woken every two hours to the twins' cries.

"I'll tell you one thing," she said. "When I'm fully recovered, I'm going to help Laurel with the twins' feedings. Poor thing's going to be a walking zombie in a matter of weeks."

Grady's thigh stilled against hers, and she sensed a change in the quiet that followed.

She opened her eyes, shielding the light with her hand. "What?"

He was looking at her as if trying to read the fine print. "You're staying then?"

They'd never exactly had the conversation. The family had tiptoed around her the last few days, keeping the mood light, avoiding stressful topics, even when she tried to broach them. Probably doctor's orders, but completely unnecessary. As if she could convince them of that.

But yeah, she was staying. This was home, and the bad memories no longer had her in their grip. She was free, and planned to enjoy it.

"Think you can stand working with me every day?" she asked.

344

His mouth twitched at the corner. A sign of nervousness or pleasure, she wasn't sure. Learning things like that took time, but they'd have plenty of that. If he was willing.

"Are you going to be stubborn and sassy?"

"Probably."

He smiled. "What I figured. I guess I can put up with you."

She remembered his dream of owning an orchard. His plans to buy Laurel out. She wanted his dreams to come true too. "We can still work something out with Laurel's shares."

"Maybe I can work something out with the other owner." He reached over and touched her arm, drawing his finger down it.

A shiver ran up her spine at the contact. Heavens to Betsy, what he did to her. She closed her eyes and wondered if he could see her heart trying to burst from the confines of her rib cage.

"I don't mean to rush you. We can go slow as you like."

It had only been one harvest, after all, but it seemed like longer. They'd spent so many hours together, working.

"Shoot," Grady said, the word riding a nervous chuckle. "We can start over if you want."

She felt him shift and opened her eyes.

He was extending his hand. "Hi. I'm Grady." There was vulnerability in his eyes, the kind that made her want to kiss him silly. He gave a tiny one-shoulder shrug. "I'm kind of in love with you."

His words were a balm to her battered heart.

And she didn't want to start over. Not when there was so much to look forward to. "No." Her voice was barely audible over nature's sounds.

His smile fell, pulling the corners of his eyes with it. His hand fell to his side.

Josie pulled herself upright until her face was inches from his. She looked into the rich brown pool of his eyes. "I'd rather we pick up right where we left off." She found the courage to say the words. " 'Cause I'm kind of in love with you too."

His face transformed, softening. His gaze was like a caress on her face, so powerful she could almost feel it.

When his lips brushed hers, it was like coming home. The tiredness she'd felt moments before evaporated like a rain puddle under an August sun.

He made her feel alive. Loved. So much more than she would've expected from a man she'd once thought of as Marlboro Man. How could a first impression be so wrong?

A moment later, he drew back.

She laughed with joy.

"What?" The seriousness of his expression only tickled her more.

This was going to be an adventure, so much fun. She looked forward to every last bit of it.

"What?" he asked again. "I'm trying to be all romantic here, you know."

Heaven forbid she should stand in the way of romance, especially with the likes of Grady. "Shut up and kiss me, Marlboro Man."

One of his brows disappeared beneath his bangs. "What?"

"Oh, never mind." Before he could press her for an answer, she brushed her lips across his and Grady returned the favor with eagerness, the subject seemingly forgotten. There would be time to talk later, but for now she wanted to savor the moment there in the cradle of Sweetwater Gap.

acknowledgments

$\mathcal{I}$ owe many people a debt of gratitude for their contributions toward this novel.

To Karen Solem for her support and encouragement.

To Ami McConnell, editor extraordinaire. I am amazed by your insight, skill, and wisdom. All writers should be so blessed as to have an editor like you!

I am privileged to work with the entire Thomas Nelson Fiction team led by Allen Arnold: Amanda Bostic, Jocelyn Bailey, Jennifer Deshler, Natalie Hanemann, Ami McConnell, Becky Monds, Katie Schroder, Lisa Young, the creative cover design team led by Mark Ross, and all the copy editors.

Thanks to the Thomas Nelson sales force who make sure my books make it to the bookstore shelves.

Maureen Kercher from Kercher's Sunrise Orchards took time from her busy schedule to educate me on the workings of an apple orchard. Any errors are mine alone.

Thanks also to Dr. Ronda Wells who educated me on the symptoms, treatments, and diagnosis of Addison's disease.

Thanks to Kristi Etter for Aunt Lola's fabulous apple pie recipe which can be downloaded from my website.

Every story I write evolves from a brainstorming session with my dear friends and fellow authors from the Girls Write Out blog (www.GirlsWriteOut.blogspot.com), Kristin Billerbeck, Colleen Coble, and Diann Hunt. Love you, girls!

To Jessica Alvarez for helping me hone the story and fine-tune the wording. My readers thank you!

Thanks to my husband, Kevin, whose support and encouragement mean the world to me.

Thanks most of all to God who, twelve years ago, took my modest dream of finishing a novel-length manuscript and turned it into so much more than I imagined.

I love to hear from my readers! Feel free to send me an e-mail at denise@denisehunterbooks.com or visit my website at www.DeniseHunterBooks.com.

reading group guide

1.What role did each of these characters play in Josie's life: Aunt Lola, Laurel, Josie's dad, Grady?

2.How did the attitude of Josie's father toward her shape the way Josie felt about herself?

3.What characteristics of Grady appealed to Josie?

4.Josie didn't feel she could live with the guilt of Ian's sacrifice. What are some things she did to assuage the guilt?

5.How was Ian's sacrifice like Christ's? How are Josie's responses to Ian's sacrifice similar to our response to Christ's sacrifice?

6.How did Grady's love for Josie demonstrate self-lessness? How did his love for Josie lead her toward God?

7.Josie reached a point of despair where she felt there was only one way out. What could you say to a friend in desperate straits that would give him or her hope?

8.The gospel seed had been planted in Josie from the time she was young. Why do you think it took her so long to accept it? What was it about her present situation that made her ready?

9. What meaning do you think the title *Sweetwater Gap* has?

Download the recipe for "Aunt Lola's Dutch Apple Pie" at Denise's website: www.DeniseHunterBooks.com

Center Point Publishing
600 Brooks Road ● PO Box 1
Thorndike ME 04986-0001 USA

(207) 568-3717

US & Canada:
1 800 929-9108
www.centerpointlargeprint.com